I0571419

SACRIFICE DREAMS

A NOVEL BY
DAVID CHAPMAN

Copyright © 2018 by David Chapman
Registered with Writers Guild of America West 11 Nov. 2018
All rights reserved.

rightrchap@gmail.com
www.davidchapman.net

ISBN 978-0-578-43216-8 (Print)
ISBN 9780-578-43139-0 (eBook)

This is a work of fiction. Names, characters, places, and incidents either are the product of the author's imagination or are used fictitiously. Any resemblance to actual persons, living or dead, businesses, companies, events, or locales is entirely coincidental.

Cover photograph by eightstock via Adobe

Cover, editing, interior layout by Ruby Lavin

for

<u>The Incomparable 3A's</u>
<u>My FAMILY</u>
ARYN CHAPMAN
ARIEL NACHMANN, ALEX NACHMANN

They found the first one on May 30, 1995, 5:31 AM. A soft, warm, Sunday morning. Fifty four year old Jason Carter's favorite summer night place to sleep off the T-Bird was the sculpture garden at LACMA, The Los Angeles County Museum Of Art.

The garden formed a quiet oasis hidden from the daytime city's throbbing, traffic-choked streets. Cool tree shadows, majestic world-famous sculpture, carefully manicured grass and well tended shrubs made it a place for retreat, contemplation; protected from the outside world by a seven foot high, forest green, steel bar fence.

The night before Carter had climbed over the service gate on Ogden Avenue. The steel padlock hasp and a bolted-on sign provided the two steps he needed to scale the gate. Arthritis and a belly full of cheap wine made it tough, but worth it for the security of a good night's sleep. The gnarled, twisted roots and trunk of the evergreen behind the Zuniga sculpture made a perfect nest for sleeping. No one could steal his shoes or his carefully saved, three inches of wake-up T-Bird.

Carter was a descendent of Confederate Generals, a railroad baron and a banker or two. The Wharton School, a Harvard MBA, and a VP at a prestigious hedge fund assured that Carter would continue the trend. Marriage to a gorgeous debutante, two beautiful young sons and a Greenwich mansion completed the picture.

His life crashed the night a drunken teenager ran a stop sign at a rain-soaked, residential neighborhood intersection and T-boned his wife's classic Jaguar, instantly killing his wife and two sons. Unmourned, the teenager was thrown through his windshield, breaking his neck and eviscerating himself from sternum to pubis on the wiper mechanism.

Carter took a leave of absence from the hedge fund, buried his wife and boys and stayed drunk for six weeks. Finally sober, he quit his job, sold the mansion and contents, the remaining cars and his portfolio. He gave half the proceeds to each of his two schools; holding back five grand for walking around money.

At the Port Authority bus terminal he bought a ticket to Cincinnati. He'd never been there. Between Columbus and Dayton, bored with the bus, he bailed and started hitchhiking west on I-70. Cincinnati could wait. In this fashion he continued west. Buses, hitchhiking and walking till he pitched up in Santa Monica. There is no better place in the US to be alone and homeless than Santa Monica, CA. Tolerant natives, sunshine 250 days year, cheap junk food and lots of parks. He stuck.

Waking in the LACMA garden at dawn, stumbling and shaking toward the exit gate, Carter's heart goddamn near stopped as he started screaming; screaming and running, damn near flying over the locked iron exit gate. His toes poking through his ragged, broken Nikes, and his filth-encrusted fingers flung him over the gate. He landed running, still screaming. His carefully saved T-bird smashed, staining the sidewalk crimson. Glass emeralds glittered in the sun.

A passing black and white heard him, saw him, and chased him down still-sleeping Wilshire Blvd; caught him on the grass under the Monster Boss AM-PM truck at the Automotive Museum and slapped him calm enough to get his story. Carter handcuffed in the backseat, they drove back to the sculpture garden.

Through the green steel bar fence the cops saw, laid out crucifixion-style under Rodin's 'Balzac,' most of a human body. Swarmed by flies, the black-blood-encrusted, coppery-smelling remains of what had once been a human being lay across the marble block that paid homage to Rodin.

The marble block pushed the body's back upward, opening the brutal, deeply carved chest wound. The head was missing. The hands were hacked off and the entire body had been skinned.

The two young LAPD officers threw up in the azaleas, then called it in on a landline.

They found the second one on the entry plaza of Union Station. Three AM, Thursday morning.

A Gen-X couple stumbling home from a hard downtown night found this one. Multiple body piercings hadn't prepared Gen-X Chick for the real thing. The body, a duplicate of the LACMA sculpture garden body; same crucified position, same knife work.

The body lay on the narrow pedestrian walkway that connects Alameda street and sidewalk to the station. The walkway lay between two beds of Birds of Paradise, dominated on either side by forty foot tall royal palm trees, five steps up at the station end. A trickle of plasma ran down the blue tile steps. The body was surrounded by a dried blood corona and millions of buzzing flies.

Flared aluminum torcheres flanked the plaza, uplighting elegant palm trees swaying gently in the warm, soft breeze that set the Birds of Paradise nodding. A hot, sweaty, summer night cloak for horror.

Union Station is a masterpiece of architecture combining Twentieth Century Limited Moderne and Spanish Mission Style; an architect's rhapsody to train travel. Built in 1939 by the Santa Fe Railroad and restored to its former glory in 1995.

Black marble, mahogany inlaid paneling, Spanish tile and huge leather seats, fifty-two foot high ceilings, lobbies inhabited by the ghosts of Clark Gable, Carole Lombard, Randolph Scott and legions of early twentieth century movie stars. Once the gateway to the Nation eastward, today it serves as terminal for the new Metro-Rail system. Not the same.

Alerted by the screams of Gen-X Chick; Metro security called the LAPD.

Detective Lieutenant Mark Brenner caught the call. Brenner was the Whip of the Special Cases Squad. The bizarre nature of the body in the LACMA sculpture garden persuaded LAPD Brass to assign it to Special Cases. LAPD wanted the jump if this proved a serial killer case.

The Special Cases Squad was created and commanded by Brenner's old boss, Jimmy Santos, retired. It was composed of hand-selected detectives with unique abilities. Multiple language skills—English, plus a minimum of two—special forces training, ex-Seals, former FBI people. Skinned, handless, heartless, headless bodies qualified as special, even in L.A.

As Brenner drove, blues and twos to Union Station, he thought about his old boss, his squad and a hostage take down five years ago shortly before Jimmy put in his papers.

It began in a school classroom full of screaming, terrified nine- and ten-year-

old kids. Two guys with AK-47 automatic rifles had burst in and screamed at everybody to "shut up and lie down on the floor." Including the teacher, old Mrs. Santiago. The kids hit the deck, but she hesitated and was clubbed to the floor with a rifle butt.

The school administrators had immediately evacuated the school. The hostages were in an end corner room, facing the street and parking lot on one side and blank wall on the other.

Police sirens howled in from every direction. Then quiet. A bull horn demanded that the men come out alone, unarmed and with their hands on their heads. One of the guys yelled out "Fuck you!" and fired a short burst of the AK's 7.62s, taking out the windows overlooking the parking lot, scattering the cops. Guy One yelled, "Anyone tries to come in here, I'm gonna start killing kids." He was hidden by one of the twin wing walls framing the windows. Guy Two was hidden in the opposite diagonal corner by a door.

The two mutts had fled a bank robbery that went sideways. They killed a cop and two bank employees before fleeing into the school across the street.

Jimmy and Brenner arrived a few minutes later. Jimmy took command. Brenner was Jimmy's number two. Jimmy sent their ex-Special Forces sniper to find a position in one of the three-story houses across the street with a view into the left side hidden corner. Brenner talked to the shot-out windows with the bullhorn, trying to calm the situation and asking the guys what they wanted in exchange for the hostages.

"A van and safe passage out. Two kids are coming with us."

Not going to happen.

Jimmy and Brenner were behind a black-and-white in the parking lot, its ass end backed into a hedge. Over the radio, the sniper reported that he had a clean shot on Guy One in the corner left of the windows. Jimmy told him and the other cops to hold. He and Brenner could see the classroom had two doors from the corridor, corresponding to the wing walls. Guy Two was hidden from them and the sniper by the right wing wall.

Jimmy got on the radio and laid out his plan: Brenner to continue a bullhorn dialogue with the mutts. Jimmy would slide around to the end door of the corridor, crawl inside to the classroom door near Guy Two. Brenner would use the bullhorn to talk about releasing the hostages, about a getaway van. When he asked what color van they wanted, Sniper would take out Guy One and Jimmy would deal with Guy Two. "Color" to be the trigger word.

Sniper, over the radio, "No problem. Nothing between me and him 'cept a hundred yards and an eighth inch of glass."

Brenner, "I should be the one to go around back. You stay here and charm this cocksucker."

Jimmy, "Nah, I'm the better shot. Just turn on your hostage rescue voice and keep his attention right here. And for Christ's sake, gimme time to get there." He backed away from Brenner.

Brenner started a negotiation with Guy One. How do they all get home safely? Did they need food, water, cigarettes? Blah, blah, blah.

Jimmy stayed behind the hedge, entered the exterior hallway door and dropped to his hands and knees. He crawled past the target door, turned, lay on his belly and reached up with his left hand for the door handle, his right held his Beretta. On "Color" and Sniper's rifle crack he flung the door open. Guy Two spun to his right and ripped off a volley of .762s chewing up the doorframe at chest height. He spotted Jimmy lying practically under his feet. He spun back to his left. lowering the rifle at Jimmy.

Jimmy shot him twice from the floor, between his nose and upper lip, blowing brains, blood and bone matter onto the blackboard.

On arrival at Union Station, Brenner coaxed Gen-X Chick out of the art deco, carved and inlaid mahogany information booth where she was hiding and screaming. The cathedral-high ceilings, marble walls and inlaid marble floors knifed her screams into the future nightmares of every watching cop and technician. Medics sedated her and carted her off to the emergency room at County USC Medical Center. Brenner and his team began working the case.

Boyfriend threw up, then passed out in the Birds of Paradise. The following week he left town for a friendlier city.

2

From the outskirts of Orange County's Little Saigon, it's a 2 AM hour and a half on the freeways to the San Gabriel Canyon Road Exit on the 210 Freeway. An hour north, up the twisting mountain switchbacks and steep inclines, San Gabriel Canyon Road just stops, deep in the San Gabriel Mountains.

The Priest checked the time, hid his black van in a dense stand of scrub fir and mountain laurel, then brushed out his tire tracks with a pine branch. He shouldered the heavy bundle of his homemade backpack and walked off into the western darkness. His destination three miles ahead on the Bear River.

An hour later he had hidden the backpack and carefully examined the area around the brush-hidden entrance to a small box canyon high on a narrow rock ledge. It overlooked, two hundred feet below, a large, still pool in the Bear River. Stars and a scimitar moon, reflected in the black water below, provided the only light. Tree frogs twittered, an owl hooted—all else was silence.

The Priest turned and vanished into the cracked rock, a blacker shadow moving in the blackness. Fifty feet into the broken rock he found his canyon as he had left it: empty, undisturbed. The rock walls reached for the ageless stars. He left.

Minutes later he returned with the backpack. He placed its burden gently on a table-sized rock, roughly centered in the canyon. He touched fire to four smoky pitch torches anchored in the canyon walls at cardinal points around the rock altar. The Priest removed his clothes and shoes, painted his body black with sacred symbols on his chest and legs. He pierced his earlobes with a large thorn and blood ran over his shoulders and chest.

The torches revealed a small Asian man lying on the altar, rag-doll-limp, motionless. His head, shoulders and legs sagged off the rock. Sweat oiled his face and dripped onto the cool stone canyon floor. Only his terrified eyes, reflecting the torches, twitched and jumped, staring at the stars.

From the darkness below the altar The Priest removed a volcanic black glass knife. He quickly cut off the Asian man's clothes and ritually washed the now naked body with water from a large clay jar at the foot of the Altar. He painted the sweating skin with the sacred symbols in preparation for the ancient ritual. He perfumed the man's body with ointment from another clay vessel and carefully arranged the helpless limbs.

The Priest raised the sacred obsidian knife in both hands, presented it to the Gods and began chanting his prayers. Nahuatl, the language of the ancient Mexica, echoed from the rock walls. The prayers continued until the sun's first rays hit the top of the canyon's west wall. At that precise moment The Priest sliced open the Asian's chest, cut deep, reached into the still-breathing chest, ripped the organ free and presented the still-beating heart as sacrifice to the sun.

———————

The Priest had found this canyon soon after leaving the Veteran's Hospital. Bumming around, trying to find some sanity, he went on a trip with a fellow released inmate who kept talking about the mountains. The Priest left the safety of his cave in Topanga Canyon and they hitched a ride north as far as Azusa, then walked up into the mountains carrying improvised packs with food and water. After two days of listening to the guy talk, talk, talk, The Priest slipped off during the night, leaving the diarrhea-mouthed fool to find his own way back.

The Priest, entranced by the mountains, pushed deeper on his own. He continued north along the Bear River Valley. Early the next morning he noticed a shelf high above the river. Above that, what looked like walls of rock. He climbed. It took all morning to reach the shelf. He ate the last of his food, drank from his makeshift canteen—a one liter plastic bottle—then explored the isolated shelf, two hundred feet above a large pool in the river.

A sage-scented breeze drew him to a broken section in the high rock face. Examining the rock closely, he noticed a crack, hidden and choked with brush. He fought his way into the crack and kept going. It gradually widened, the scent of sage growing stronger. At a sharp right turn, a startled jackrabbit rocketed away from him, deeper into the passage. He followed. Ten steps further and the walls fell away.

Before him lay a completely enclosed canyon; floor the size of a football field and surrounded by craggy rock walls. Walls three, four, in some places five hundred feet almost straight up. Rock walls cracked, broken, wind- and water-sculpted. The floor was a jumble of broken, upthrust flat rock planes and fallen boulders. Sweet smelling sage grew in the cracks. A small, sweet spring bubbled water. A cloudless cerulean sky capped the walls. The most beautiful place The Priest had ever seen.

He knew he was the first man to ever stand in this canyon. He stood in awe, unable to move; overcome by the beauty, the power of the place. He wept.

He spent a week there. Not since leaving the insanity of Nam had he known such peace. A spiritual calm settled in his soul. Living on plants and water from a spring; he explored in every direction, the canyon walls, the wilderness for miles around. He found the nearest road, San Gabriel Canyon Road, three miles to the east. Except for empty hiking trails, he found no trace of any human being within miles of this place, his Temple.

3

After the second one Brenner invited Jimmy for lunch at Kate Mantilini's. Brenner was seated in the Wilshire-Doheny corner when Jimmy arrived.

Brenner was dark-haired with eyes as black as the bottom of a well. About five foot ten, 185 pounds, shoulders wide as a door from rigorous gym time and a body trimmed by daily three mile runs. Quick in movement but slow to anger. An infectious laugh.

One of his many, multi great grandfathers had been a Jewish immigrant to New York who moved to California with the Gold Rush. He quickly realized that the real, predictable profit came from providing the miners with necessities. He sold his stake and bought groceries and tools. In a year he sent East for his family. Brenners had been in California since.

He and Jimmy went way back, including being Boss and Second on Special Cases. They'd been partners, drinking and handball buddies. Jimmy often joined Brenner on his daily daybreak three mile run. Jimmy was best man at Brenner's wedding. He was godfather to Brenner's teenage daughter, Sally, a job he took seriously.

Jimmy, "You must need help with this Skinner job. Only reason I can think of for the LAPD to splash out for lunch at this joint."

"Skinner...the press dreams up a new handle for every killer that comes down the pike."

"Better headlines."

"Yeah. You got time to do it and the stuff I sent over?"

"Yes to both."

After lunch Jimmy and Brenner paced the conference room of Jimmy's office. Large windows overlooked the leafy streets of Beverly Hills.

He and Brenner were in Jimmy's high tech security firm Techstar, Ltd. Jimmy had started it after his retirement. Owning his own firm allowed him to do what he loved best: hunt, and hire others to do the follow up work. LAPD as backup didn't hurt. The company was now humming along, throwing off money like a $100 slot machine, catering to the A-List Hollywood crowd formed early in Jimmy's LAPD career.

His gal Friday, Millie Langston, ran the day-to-day operations. Millie was drop-dead gorgeous, five six or so, "stacked," as his buddies said in their more polite comments, and, if truth be told, smarter than Jimmy. He'd be the first to admit it. She had been a secretary at LAPD when he met her and he enticed her to join his new firm. She'd blossomed with the added responsibility.

The Skinner files were spread all over the conference table—crime scene photos, witness statements and forensics reports—trying to get a handle on just what the hell it all meant.

Millie brought in a tray with coffee and the fixings. Not an everyday occurrence.

"Hey, Mark, you gonna put our boss to work on something useful? Think of this coffee service as a bribe."

"Thanks, I'm trying. Seems right down his alley".

"Good. It'll keep him out of our hair. He's always happiest when huntin' somebody." She smiled and left.

Brenner, "You and Millie ever...you know, get it on?"

Jimmy, "Nah, we've both thought about it but decided to not risk fucking up a good working relationship. I haven't told her yet but I'm making her a full partner at the end of the month. Now, where are we?"

"You sure you got time to do this thing with us? It's shaping up as a bear."

"What do you want me to do?"

Jimmy was an unusual guy in the police world. Police work had been more than a job; hunting criminals was his calling. He needed the rush of the hunt and believed he was better, quicker and more intuitive, his perseverance greater than any criminal he was pursuing. Paperwork held zero attraction for him. A desk an anchor. Faced with a choice between promotion with a permanent desk job or retirement, Jimmy chose the latter.

Using Jimmy as a consultant had a bonus benefit for the LAPD. In the years after the Rodney King riots, when the press found fault with everything about the department, Jimmy had a positive relationship with them. He always made good copy, seldom fed them bullshit and treated them as people with a job to do. They loved him. It started soon after Jimmy joined the force.

1977: Three AM in West Hollywood, a Saturday. Jimmy, still in uniform, charm talked a .45-carrying would-be convenience store heister with five hostages into calm-city, took him without a shot fired or hostage hurt. One of the freed hostages was a celebrity TV anchor out looking for a pot buy. Jimmy allowed him to skate without publicity and buried him in his reports. The guy repaid the favor by making Jimmy seem like the Henry Kissinger of the LAPD. Jimmy played down the hostage release and the publicity. "All bullshit," was his only comment.

That was the beginning of the Jimmy Stories.

Running his new company and consulting with Special Cases, gave Jimmy the best of all worlds: hunting criminals and financial independence.

Brenner brought Jimmy up to speed on The Skinner case as Jimmy leafed through crime scene photos from both homicides.

"Okay, here's what we got. Two bodies, male, both Asian, we think. Doc's running more sophisticated DNA tests on that. Doc thinks there is a plant-based poison involved. Again, more lab tests being run on the blood work. We'll get all the lab reports in about a week. Hearts were cut out while these guys were alive. Traces from the knife indicate it was stone, maybe glass, razor sharp. Weird. Some hair and fibre evidence; but thats no good without a suspect. Both MO's exactly the same. No ID's, no missing person reports. Nada.

"I got the Chief calling me every day for progress reports. The Commissioner's calling the Chief everyday 'cause the Mayor's calling the Commissioner. The media got on this one quick. They're blowing it up into another Manson thing. The public's going nuts and Hizzoner's taking the heat. All the media's got going this summer is a serial killer and politics, so Skinner's getting the coverage."

Jimmy, "You holding back the detail about the hearts?"

"So far. Again, I don't know how long we can keep it close. The tabloids are willing to spread the bucks around on this one. All they have to do is find some hungry technician or EMS worker. Cop for that matter. Ready to leak.

"I've got Callahan and Gomez canvassing the drop spots and Mandy and Carlotta running missing persons files. Zilch on both so far. Susie Chan, our resident computer whizkid, is running everything we got through VICAP and NCIC, anywhere else we can think of. I sent all our info down to the FBI. We should get some feedback from the Behavioral Lab in a week or so."

"How's Nolan gonna handle this?"

"I've got the job and pressure direct from the Chief. It'll give me the clout to handle Nolan; if we show the Chief we're making progress. Cut Nolan a little slack, life'll be easier for all of us. He's got problems of his own. Don't worry about it; I can take the heat. Tell me about this Aztec idea of yours."

Brenner indicated the book Jimmy was holding on top of the crime scene photos.

"Your description reminded me of something I'd read or seen years ago. This book was buried on a shelf at home. A couple of its pictures and descriptions sound like the victims you described. Take a look."

Jimmy put the book on top of the mess on conference table and opened it to a post-it tagged page.

Brenner, "Jesus. So where do you go with that?"

"I've got an appointment with a history professor up at UCLA this afternoon. Specialist in Mexican history. Maybe he can point me in the right direction."

"This is a copy of the file with everything we've got so far, take it with you." Indicating the piles of paper on the table. "See if the professor's got any ideas on the missing body parts."

"Yeah. I'll touch base after I've talked to the guy. I'm on cell if you want me."

"You got it turned on?"

"Yeah, yeah, I got it turned on. Hello to Sally for me."

Brenner was almost out the door. "We gonna drop this fuck, Jimmy?"

"Sure, Mark. It just might take a while."

4

Brenner had gone back downtown. Jimmy left his conference room whistling. Goddamn, he liked this. Maybe he should've stayed on the job, but what the hell. He could pick when and what he wanted to work on, minimal brass bullshit, his own hours. Life was pretty damn good.

The only fly in the ointment was Captain Dan Nolan, LAPD. He and Jimmy had been classmates at the Academy and competitors for twenty-three years. Nolan had taken the political route up through the ranks, tests and desk work. He had an obsessive eye on the chief's job. Jimmy moved up on his street work. At the time of Jimmy's retirement, they were both being looked at for promotion to Captain—assistant to the Chief. A desk job. Nolan got it when Jimmy said to hell with the desk and packed it in.

While not Brenner's direct superior, Nolan used any opportunity to make Brenner's department life miserable. He could and did constantly lobby the Chief, publicly second-guessing Brenner and undermining him at every opportunity. Nolan was intensely jealous of Jimmy's popularity with the press and the LAPD rank and file. He would do all he could to see that LAPD shut Jimmy out of the Skinner case.

In the parking garage Jimmy chirped the alarm off of his British racing green, '82, Jag XJ6 and headed up to UCLA. The Jag had just been returned, tuned up by his garage. He silenced the racist talk show host beloved by his mechanics and selected Merle Haggard on the Bose CD system. Merle sang about misery and gin as Jimmy tooled up to see the Professor.

The car was deceptive. An L.A. chop shop that owed him a big one had done the work at cost minus. They had pulled out the miserable Lucas electrical system replacing it with one from a new Camry. Jaguar might recognize the engine, but barely; even with the auto transmission it would do zero to sixty in about seven seconds flat. The notorious cooling system was also gone, replaced with one from a Ford 150 pickup and some mechanical wizardry that Jimmy didn't understand. He did know he could maintain a tail, sitting on the Ventura Freeway for hours, and not worry about the damn thing exploding.

Jimmy took Wilshire west. He loved watching people; improvising, creating routes, zigging and zagging his way across the city. From Wilshire he turned right on Westwood and immediately spotted a Tower Records store.

Sally Brenner's birthday next week. Shit, I almost forgot. What was that new group she was swooning over last week? Twenty minutes later, he had generous gift certificate, a card and a comic note. Perfect.

He found his way back to Lindbrook. It turned into Hilgard and he enjoyed watching the coeds all the way up the hill to the UCLA information booth. He parked as directed in a metered slot, buried four quarters and headed off to find Bunche Hall.

Jimmy's sunglasses, faded blue jeans and lanky six-two frame almost blended in with the casual, cool campus look. He blew the look with the black silk hopsacking blazer that concealed his shoulder-holstered 9mm Beretta. College students didn't wear jackets in a heat wave. Most of them didn't carry guns, either.

As usual, he was fifteen minutes early. His Dad's obsession with punctuality ingrained. He decided to walk a bit. This campus always made him vaguely jealous. Money evident in abundance, the climate, the lazy grace of the students, palm trees for Christ's sake. Hell, he could have gone to school here, had the grades, but what difference would it have made in his life? Probably not married that blonde cheerleader-heiress, that's what. It seemed to him that you were aware of the many possible choices in life only long after you had acted on what seemed so limited at the time.

───────────────

These musings almost made him late. He stepped into Bunche Hall, out of the afternoon's heat, at five to four. His shirt was clinging to his back after the short walk. A gal directed him to Fulo's office.

Fulo was skinny and short. Five-three on a tall day, stringy black hair over his collar, Charlie Manson eyes. He wore the professor's uniform of wrinkled chinos, loafers, a blue work shirt and, even in his office, a baggy linen jacket.

Jimmy quickly discovered that Fulo knew his Mexican history. He was bright, articulate and totally unimpressed by the gruesome murders that Jimmy outlined for him. He listened with scary intensity. His questions were to the point, blunt, and uncluttered with jargon.

His office was like a well-appointed home study, spacious and quiet. Late afternoon sunlight poured through the high, dark wood framed windows illuminating the dust mote's dance. Central air conditioning hissed softly from the overhead ducts making the office a cool oasis. Two mission oak tables now held copies of the crime scene and autopsy photos. Accepting another of Jimmy's unfiltered Camels with an I'm-trying-to-quit grin, Fulo said, "And you've found none of the missing parts?"

"None. We're certain the victims are killed, carved up and skinned in one location, then dropped—no, placed—where they're found. Public spaces. So far, very public spaces. The only evidence at the find site is the body. No blood, no ground disturbance, nothing."

"What about a link through the drop sites? Both public spaces, both with strong public, cultural resonance. Anything in that?"

Jimmy lit another Camel, "Probably. But I haven't figured it out, yet. This killer inhabits brainscapes only he sees."

Fulo took a large folio from the shelves and opened it on top of the crime scene photos. He said, "The Aztec book you brought is based, in part, on this. This is a sixteenth century drawing by Father Bernardino de Sahagun of an Aztec sacrifice. He assembled this book based on the memories of old men who had lived the Aztec culture.

"The similarities to your photos are—well, just look. While these books are not restricted in any way, they are also not well known. Your killer might be using them as reference. Incidentally, Aztec was not their name for themselves. Thats a nineteenth century name for the Mexica. That's what they called themselves."

Looking from the drawing to the photos, Jimmy said, "This drawing was done four hundred and eighty years ago but it could be a drawing of our John Does. What's going on in the background—these other figures?"

"To give you a quick overview: the Mexica's religion revolved around human sacrifice. Depending on the result desired from the Gods, the sacrificial victim could be a virgin female or a young, presumably virgin male. It could be a Mexica Warrior, a prominent volunteer or sometimes a slave, but the one most highly prized, the one that found most favor with their Gods was a captured enemy warrior.

"The more valiant, the more favor. Many Mexica wars were staged solely for the capturing of warriors for sacrifice. The victim was placed, back down, across the Altar, high on the stepped temple pyramid. While still alive his or her heart was cut out with a sacred obsidian knife and offered to the Sun. The victim, if a warrior, was skinned. The priest would put on his skin and dance to the Gods to inherit his power. Usually the priests ate his heart, again to transfer power to the priest. Other body parts were cut up and shared with the people for a festive meal."

Jimmy said pointing to the book, "So the dancers, those guys in the floppy Dr. Denton's, are dancing in the skins of human beings? Jesus."

"Yes, not a pretty idea to the modern mind. But not that uncommon to the mind of the sixteenth century. The motivations were some variation on this same theme. Appease your Gods, steal and gain your enemies power. The question here is, how does your guy—and it is almost certainly a guy—how does he so closely duplicate a practice eradicated, along with most of the Mexica, almost 500 years ago?"

"A scholar, a student, maybe a librarian—I doubt that—a used-to-be one of the above," Jimmy was trying them on out loud, "I don't know. It seems an unlikely group to be into human sacrifice. You got any other candidates?"

"Not off the top of my head—give me a few days, I'll mull it over. Leave me your card, I'll call you if I think of any other likely—wait a minute, there's a couple of paperback books by a guy named Gary Jennings. I've got copies here you can take with you."

5

Driving to his office after talking to Fulo, Jimmy called Brenner. Snarky Mike Foccachio picked up the phone. "Nah, he ain't here. Went over to the Doc's office to take a look at something Butter Butt spotted in one of the Skinner photos. Want him to call ya?"

Jimmy, phone static-ing under a heavy power line, "Her names Ginger. The one with brains enough to run the advanced DNA. Yeah, ask Brenner to give me a ring. I'll be in the office in about ten minutes."

He punched off more of Mike's bullshit, no goodbye. Sexist, sour bastard, to this day pissed off about a five year old Chinese immigrant bust. If he hadn't acted like such a dipshit—ah, the hell with it.

Traffic snarled up in Beverly Hills, again. Jimmy watched as sparkling clean four-wheel-drive SUVs, built for off-road work, slogged up Rodeo Drive across Wilshire Blvd. Traffic was the price he paid, along with sky high rent, to be where the rich folks felt comfortable.

Not that any of his clients came to him, Jimmy thought. For all that it mattered, he could be in Burbank, cheap Burbank. But it didn't work that way, on either score. They called, or to be very precise, their assistants called, and you went to them. Wherever They were, Mulholland or Aspen or New York. There was one harebrained trip to Cairo, yeah, the Egyptian one, about a kidnapped Shar Pei. A very wrinkled dog, for those not in the know.

His rich TV-star client, on location in Cairo, wanted Jimmy to get her pet back from the dognappers in L.A. The two day trip cost ten grand, plus Jimmy's fee—five grand—and the ransom another hundred Gs. The client was willing to pay it; think of the tabloids, SUPERSTAR SPENDS $115,000 FOR RETURN OF BELOVED PET.

Jimmy blew that headline when, back in L.A., he found three bored teenagers holding—read: playing with—the Dog. He scared the shit out of them; threatening Life and parental revocation of their American Express cards. He returned the Dog to it's estate that day.

Jesus, Jimmy, you're working up a lather over getting rich. Be glad they're sending some of that cash your way. Too much money fucks up a lotta heads, and stop talking to your dumbass self.

He pulled into the parking garage, wondering what his ole Irish mom would have thought of all this foolishness. Probably laugh and tell him to relax and enjoy it. He locked the Jag and whistled himself through the stifling heat of the garage to the elevator.

―――――――――

Jimmy's office, on North Maple Drive, was in one of the new, almost handsome, dark brick and glass structures that dominated the neighborhood. It was a pretty, tree shaded neighborhood, humming smoothly with the commerce of show folks.

Jimmy's building, five stories of offices surrounding a large, lushly landscaped courtyard was equipped with the latest in high tech security. Discreet video cameras and motion sensors fed the guard's desk, a donut-shaped marvel of waist-high, bulletproof glass with visible monitors and complex electronics. It was like looking into the guts of a computer tower. Jimmy, acting on the owner's requirements, had designed the system to take maximum advantage of its PR aspect. Jimmy often thought every decision in Hollywood was governed by PR.

The guards—uniforms, badges and walkie-talkies aside—did what doormen have done since the high rise building was invented; kept up with the coming and going of tenants, watched the girls, gossiped and napped. Mike was no different.

"Como esta, Jimmy?"

Jimmy, "Muy bien. Mike, que dice el boletín meteorológico?"

"Whoa, whoa, Jimmy. My Spanish can't handle that, yet."

Jimmy, "Keep practicing; you're getting there. I asked you what's the weather forecast. Your answer: caliente, hot.

He saluted Mike so-long and headed for the elevator and his fifth floor office.

The interiors of Jimmy's office, thanks to Millie Langston, looked more like a small, prosperous law firm than the private eye's office of fiction; no Philip Marlowe, Lew Archer, Elvis Cole or Spencer here. Millie, office manager, confidant, advisor and soon-to-be partner, insisted that the office be a refuge from the sometimes tawdry, often dangerous and always loony world in which they worked.

Millie was in reception, talking to their long time receptionist Susan.

"Put Bobby and Liz on hold for the next couple of weeks. Jimmy is going to be up to his butt in LAPD Serial Killer land."

Everywhere, Millie's quiet, elegant taste was evident; the warm Berber wall to wall carpeting overlaid in places with good orientals, rich walnut veneers, controlled lighting, and art from living regional artists. As usual, Jimmy felt a sigh of relaxation on entering.

Jimmy's office was a more personal version of the reception area. He had two Remington bronzes; 'Coming Through The Rye' and 'The Mountaineer.' Bought at auction years ago when paying for them was a stretch. The western motif was relieved by a huge, modern Persian rug over the Berber, and several paintings in brilliant colors, by California artists. His desktop was a thick slab of walnut, the chairs and sofa covered in soft leather. At the end of the day, office empty, phones dead or dying, Jimmy and Millie usually kicked back in his office for a wrap-up of the day's happenings.

"White or red?" Jimmy looked into the bar fridge as he selected a Tecate for himself.

"Red, I think, tonight—that's not the best white we've had." Millie, taking a sip of the Mouton Cadet, smiled, "Jerry Martin called today. He's got a problem that he wants to discuss with you. Long as we've known each other, he still plays it close. Wouldn't give me a hint about what it is. I set up an appointment for you at nine tomorrow morning."

"Something important?"

"He sounded stressed. I thought maybe you should see him before you get too involved with this Skinner business. You have a tendency to disappear into that kind of case. He's been too good this office to put him off."

"True, darlin'. I'll see him first thing."

Jimmy's Hollywood connections, Martin included, arose from a single, life-changing event. Taking a horse to Chasen's. He hadn't thought of that for years.

1974, Jimmy, just out of the Police Academy, had a shot at impressing the current Playboy Playmate. He thought the then-hot Hollywood restaurant, Chasen's, might just do the trick. The joint was known for its full house of Hollywood celebrities. Though Jimmy'd felt as out-of-place as a red-dressed hooker at a Baptist picnic, the stunning chick found it all 'just marvy.'

Jimmy and Playmate had had dinner, dessert and brandy and were contemplating yours or mine when all hell broke loose at the front entrance.

Jack and Warren, pissed to Christmas, were trying to bring Warren's horse to Jack's table. Horse was buying into this idea with even less enthusiasm than the stuffed-shirted Maître d'.

Horse was big enough to protest, violently. By now, he'd kicked out all the foyer glass, destroyed the Maître d's stand, and would have reared if the low ceiling had permitted it, further pissing him off. Tuxedoed and gowned patrons were scattering, fearful for their lives. Jack and Warren were ducking flailing hooves and huge bared teeth as Maître d' beat a hasty retreat to the kitchen.

Jimmy stood up, left the girl at their table and walked calmly toward the enraged horse, his right hand out and open, palm up. Talking to the horse.

Jack told a reporter later that it was the damnedest thing he'd ever seen. That three-quarter-ton terrified, pissed-off horse stood still and listened. Jimmy, still talking, took the horse's halter, stroked him softly on the neck murmuring in his ear, then backed him gently out of the restaurant and put him back in Warren's horse trailer. He returned to the restaurant to a standing ovation.

Jimmy didn't make it with the Playmate that night. Warren and Jack bought the drinks till dawn when Jimmy had to be back on the Job. The three guys became asshole buddies. Chasen's didn't press charges and Jack never did figure out what Jimmy was saying to that horse.

That was the beginning of Jimmy's Hollywood client list. Everybody in town seemed to know Jimmy. Early on, because of Jack and Warren, he was invited to the A-List parties, at first as a curiosity, later as a regular when it was found he could hold his own. No bad thing to have a friend in the LAPD, either. The new crowd of hot young stars and the old, established Hollywood bunch all called Jimmy if they had a little problem. He handled it and kept his mouth shut—valuable commodities in a town like L.A.

6

Cinco de Mayo, 1995. A month before they found the first one. The celebration of Mexico's Independence Day in Olvera Street was spinning through the late afternoon, rushing toward a late night. An air of celebration permeated the entire city. The afternoon sun splashed golden light and warmth over Olvera Street's Plaza and adjacent market. The day's dying breeze rustled the trees and swirled tourist litter against the low brick walls and across the inlaid brick walks. The sound of mariachi music throbbed from a band deep in the souvenir stalls that displayed brilliantly colored clothes and paper flowers. Smells of Mexican food filled the air.

In spite of the afternoon heat, exuberant Cinco de Mayo celebrants swirled around the group. There were ten or fifteen boys and men and a half-dozen women in a loose half-circle around the base of the huge fig tree in the Plaza. The tree marks the place where the City of Los Angeles was founded by Mexican citizens in the summer of 1781. The founding group of forty-one included Mulatto, Negro, Indio, Mestizo and Español pioneers, a multi-racial effort whose lesson was lost on later generations.

The Priest was at the center of the quiet group, telling the story of the time when the Mexica People saw the Sign, foretold for centuries of an Eagle holding a snake, sitting on top of a Saguaro Cactus. The sign that they should settle in that place and build a powerful and magnificent city. The city that would become the center of the Aztec Empire. The City of the Sun.

The listening people gathered under the tree that hot afternoon ranged in age from fifteen to seventy. The oldest, a woman, had been blind for decades. She looked up at The Priest with clouded, unseeing eyes and the ghost of a smile, remembering Mexico and hearing this story as a young girl. The youngest, a pimple-faced boy half listening, flirted with a beautiful girl across the circle. She ignored him, intensely. They were all Mexican, Mexican-Americans, legal and illegal immigrants, visitors. The spectrum of L.A.'s Mexican population. All but one.

He was a man in his forties—Asian, out of place. Quiet and attentive, he understood the rapid Spanish. He and his wife owned and ran a souvenir cart on the corner

Screaming tires shredded the quiet afternoon. A red '65 Mustang convertible ripped around the corner, top down, four Asian gangsters aboard. It bounced up onto the sidewalk and down the steps into the plaza, flying across the inlaid brickwork with one AK-47 and two modified Tec-Nines firing on full automatic, spraying 7.62mm and 9mm rounds into the listening group.

People scrambled for cover behind trash cans, each other, any illusion of protection from the hail of bullets, the noise and terror. The Priest's old instincts, dived toward the car, pulling the teenage boy with him. A bullet tugged at The Priest's foot. They pancaked into the brick paving and lay still while the fire storm flew over them, too close to the car for the shooters to see or hit. As The Priest hit the brick, he saw the Asian man sprint for the Plaza wall. The man jumped onto the upper Plaza and rolled behind the three-foot diameter Bay tree. Bullets blew huge chunks from the tree but missed the man. The Priest admired the instincts of a soldier. No hesitation. See the closest cover and dive for it.

Total silence, then ringing ears, then screaming chaos. The car gone, people wailing in anguish, pain and pandemonium. The Priest checked his foot. A bullet gouge across the bottom of his rubber heel, no problem. He checked the boy. Okay. Face and elbow scraped bloody from hitting the bricks.

Then, stunned, unbelieving, he turned to help his people. The story group was a ballet of horror.

The old blind lady, an old man, the beautiful girl—all dead. Arms, torsos, legs—chopped up by automatic fire. Bits of skull fragments, brain matter, torn flesh on the dusty, dry, eucalyptus leaf-strewn Plaza. Empty brass cartridge cases twinkling in the dying sunlight. The stink of burned gunpowder drifting over everything.

Adding to the chaos, the street quickly filled with screeching sirens; cops and ambulances and fire department rescue vehicles. The Priest did what he could to help but the professionals quickly took command and pushed The Priest and other samaritans to the sidelines. Just another drive-by shooting in L.A. to the pros.

The Priest slipped away, head pounding, vision blurred with rage. The void, the old Vietnam blackness gripped him. Rock & Roll; full auto fire. The jungle. Torturer, bamboo cages, jungle death; he had to protect his people, he must. His camp, he had to get to his camp.

He was flying through the air. Thrown, tumbling, propelled by a huge explosion. He hit hard, his back on a stone altar. He was high above the jungle on top of a stone pyramid. In the clouds, an eagle circled, flew down, and pecked at his name tag: THE PRIEST. Barely able to open his eyes he recognized the Asian man from Olvera Street. The man stood, grinning on the back of a Jaguar, his body writhing with hundreds of encircling snakes, holding a glistening obsidian knife. The knife rose high over The Priest and, screaming, he realized he was the intended victim, the blood offering to the gods. This Asian motherfucker. This non-Aztec Priest, killing him, killing his people. The glittering knife slashed down!

The Priest bolted upright in his sleeping bag, drenched in sweat stinking of terror. Night sounds. The ocean boomed, an owl hooted, swooped on a screeching night creature. His heart slowed. The Asian man, what did he have to do with this? He had moved so fast. An ex-soldier, no question about it. The target? A hit? A contract on him? The shooters, Asian. Connection? Too many questions, too hard.

The snake brain state beckoned, trying to push back reason. Sacrifice haunted him. The answer? The low clouds parted. A full moon; an eagle gliding to his nest across the moon. A sign, surely a sign. Sacrifice was the answer, the key to restoring his people's future. Blood on the stones, sacrifice to the sun, hearts and blood to feed our demanding gods.

He, The Priest must do it. He must be The Priest for the Mexica, his People. His mind slid onto another plane, another dimension. He felt it happening, welcomed it. Not since Nam had he felt so at home. Peace, true peace, lay here in total madness.

Topanga Canyon intersects the Pacific Coast Highway about a third of the way from Santa Monica to Malibu. Here, California's coastline runs east-west along the northern coast of Santa Monica Bay, a surprise to many long-term residents who envision this ocean coast running north-south. It is an hour west from Santa Monica to the bus stop at the corner of the Pacific Coast Highway and Topanga Canyon Road. At that corner, The Priest had two choices. He could walk a mile up Topanga Canyon Road and then head west into the canyon or walk west on the PCH, drop off the road where Topanga Canyon Creek went under the highway and go north up the creek bed.

Either route eventually brought him to his camp. It was hidden from the world; a mile in from the beach and half a mile from the road; an area plagued with mud slides, rock falls, scrub vegetation, voracious insects, fires and blistering sun. Few ventured there.

In the early homeless days, avoiding people and wandering farther and farther up the beach, he noticed the sand cut where Topanga Canyon Creek trickled across the beach. Curious, he traced the creek back into the hills. It wandered up the canyon; crossing back and forth under the road. About a mile in, a hundred year flash flood had piled tree trunks, brush and boulders forty feet above the creek at the top of a rock fall. The scree from the original fall cascaded down to the creek. It looked like there was a space behind the flood debris.

He climbed the shattered rock pile to explore. Working cautiously through the logs and brush, he discovered a cave. The fierce water flow had scooped out the soft material of the hill and then plugged the opening with logs and debris.

Refuge. He remembered his grandfather telling him stories about Tlalli Yiollo, Earth Heart, and Tepe Yiollo, Mountain Heart, the earth deities of his people. Stories of the genesis of his people in the womb of the earth; their ritual use of caves as places of communion with these deities. The earth: giver and eventual receiver of life. He had found a home.

He camped in the existing cave. Over the next months he made it bigger, digging back into the hillside. He scattered the excess sand and gravel in and along the creek banks; spreading it thin, blending it into the natural landscape. Calling on memories of Vietnamese tunnels, he shored up the roof. He lugged in the basic comforts: a sleeping bag, black plastic to light-proof the interior at night, Coleman lanterns, water, canned food, a small cook stove. Invisibility was an obsession. He never entered the canyon observed.

In summer, when possible, he moved up and down the creek on rocks. Winter, when water was flowing, he'd wade in the creek or take varying paths on its banks. He approached the cave over the rock scree to avoid footprints. At night he used the plastic sheets to contain light from his lanterns. He trapped the surrounding area with noisemakers. He could see the Pacific through the log wall. Stormy days and nights he could hear it.

The ocean rhythms spoke to him. He spent his days walking the beach, exploring the canyons. He found plants, made teas. They calmed him, eased anxiety. Not a cure; he knew that was not possible. The cave worked its magic. In the womb of earth mother he felt safe for the first time in years.

———————

Haunted every night after Cinco de Mayo, by dreams of sacrifice, he spent a feverish week never leaving camp, consuming only water, sleeping in hour-long bites, hateful dreaming. Visions of blood on everything. Mexica-Indian slaves beaten, burned, brutalized. Huge blood-filled eyes pleaded with him for help, salvation. Non-class citizens, bodies lying in sun scorched arroyos, children's bodies found suffocated in sealed trucks, farm workers dead in hundreds in airtight shipping containers.

They waited for Him. Him the Savior, the only Priest to His People. He must act, now. The Gods, the World must notice. Sacrifice, a drumbeat in his blood, over, over and over. The Asian man, the guy from Olvera Street. He was a soldier, a warrior. Worthy sacrifice. Find, capture him. Sacrifice him.

The Priest's brain cooled, the thinnest veil of reason sliding forward. He began to function. He spent almost a month learning his target on Olvera Street. The massacre had formed a strange bridge. A few quiet conversations; the man and his wife were boat people, disgraced VC, terrified of the Immigration and Naturalization Service, discovery, deportation. The Priest continued to tell his stories.

At night he watched Ngh Do. He followed him home to Little Saigon, waited, watched. One or two nights a week Ngh Do visited an illegal whore-house-gaming parlor, emerging in the morning, and staggering home. Other denizens of this place had the look of ex-VC. Eyes, or arms missing or damaged, the look of ex-soldiers of any army, but these spoke the musical dialect of North Vietnam. A shudder ran through The Priest each time he heard it.

He spent hours in the hills around his cave in Topanga Canyon searching for Grandma plants. An Apache specialty; cooked and distilled, mixed properly and administered in the proper dosage, they induced instant paralysis of the voluntary nervous system, all involuntary systems functioned normally. Breathing, heart beat, sweating, blinking—all remained normal, but the victim's muscles would not respond to brain commands. A drop on the end of a pin was enough.

He continued to watch Ngh Do at night. Ngh and four or five friends would pack into a banged up '75 Chevy Camaro and disappear. A week later The Priest bought a black van. In it he followed Ngh and buddies to a bar in Costa Mesa. The Priest stored VC faces in his memory, amazed at how many had made their way to L.A.

7

Jimmy Santos was from Monroe, Georgia, a small Southern town about 25 miles Southwest of Athens. He grew up in the late '50s and early 60s. Open spaces, hunting, guns, dogs, horses; he had a special affinity with horses. His dad, Mexican-American, was a Sergeant-Major in the Marines, working out his thirty with the Navy ROTC Unit at the University Of Georgia. Dad was a hard man who liked his bourbon straight and discipline tough. He seemed incapable of separating his Marine's life from that of his rapidly growing family's. Jimmy was the third of five sons. His dad said he had wanted a baseball team but settled for a basketball squad. Jimmy's mom failed to see this as funny.

Attempting to instill responsibility, discipline, and the care and feeding of animals in his boys, his dad bought their first horse: a gentle black mare, a nondescript Heinz 57 of horse. Jimmy was five. Too little to climb on in any normal way by himself, he sat on the horse's ears as she ate grass. Annoyed, she lifted her head to get rid of the weight and Jimmy slid down her neck onto her back. At age twelve he gentled and was the first to ride the two-year-old quarter horse, a stallion colt given to the boys by an indulgent uncle. His Dad saw it as a challenge.

Jimmy loved horses. He was a horse whisperer before the term was invented. He and a brother or two would leave the house with their horses early morning and not return till dark. In that part of Georgia the world was simple enough that this was possible. Crime, superhighways and fences everywhere were thing of the future.

His other early passion was hunting. He got his first BB gun at six. At ten or eleven, after tough, thorough lessons on safety, cleaning and use, his dad allowed him to go into the woods alone with a 22 rifle. He hunted rabbits and squirrels. At thirteen he taught himself to flip a penny in the air and hit it with his single shot 22.

Jimmy's brothers loved the athletic sports fields. Jimmy preferred the woods, the hunt, the solitude. The woods became a sanctuary from his iron-eyed, domineering, weekend alcoholic father. In the silence of the woods he could erase the sounds of Dad taking a belt to his youngest brother in the adjoining room and his own impotent rage. Occasionally, Jimmy or one of the other brothers would be thumped on the head from his Dad's big middle finger. Like flicking something off his finger, never a beating. The little one got the worst of it.

Another refuge was time spent with a secondary Dad; John Ivey, the crusty, old—to Jimmy—redneck doctor who lived across the road and taught him to shoot a shotgun and loaned him a 20 gauge when they hunted together. Doves, quail and other game birds were added to his list of targets.

When he eventually got his driver's license, he became Doc's driver on their hunting trips into the North Carolina Mountains. Doc Ivey also took him on late night coon hunting trips. A bunch of older guys sitting out in the dark woods listening to the hounds chase raccoons and sipping bourbon through the night. The smell of cigar smoke and quiet conversation in the night woods, a favorite memory.

Jimmy grew into a southern gentleman. Tall, six feet and a bit, a swimmers physique, coal-black hair and eyes from dad and milk-white skin from Irish mom.lite, introverted, shy and witty, he also inherited his Mom's Irish way with people. Monroe's little old ladies loved him as did crusty old Doc Ivey.

The exception was a predilection on the part of some of his redneck classmates to challenge his Mexican heritage. Jimmy's older brothers had taught their classmates that this was an unhealthy line to pursue; but there always seemed to be younger ones coming up who didn't get the word. They all had to try it on.

"What kinda name is Santos?"

"You Mexican, what you doin' with a white girlfriend?"

"Yo Pa a bean picker?"

"Hey Santos, where's your sombrero?"

In his younger years, Jimmy would flush red and swing at the cracker for all he was worth. He brought home many black eyes and bloody noses. As he got older, he learned to grin and ignore it. Wit and sarcasm became his weapons.

In high school, one slow witted cracker was unaffected by words. He and Jimmy were scrambling for a loose basketball in a Phys Ed game. The ball got booted into the low stands. Jimmy was slightly ahead in the race for it when Cracker gave him a violent shove from behind and screamed, "Git it, Beaner!"

Jimmy stumbled up into the stands, grabbed the ball, turned and threw it as hard as he could at the back of Cracker's head, then followed it, running.

As Cracker turned to face him, Jimmy hit him in the face with a flurry of fists so fast that Cracker never got his hands up. He just sat down on the polished wood gym floor, blood pouring from his nose and split lips, streaming down his chest. The coach pulled Cracker up by the arm and led him off down the hall to the nurse's office. He never said a word to Jimmy.

The sheer number of Hispanic students at the University of Georgia kept the overt racial slurs to a minimum. Occasionally, from a passing car, some drunken frat boy would shout racial epithets at groups of Hispanics but face-to-face incidents were rare. Jimmy ignored them.

Jimmy was in the car lane at the visitor's gate to Sony Studios in Culver City. Jerry Martin's assistant had set up a drive-on for Jimmy. He couldn't resist his cynical thoughts prompted by lining up at the gate. Assistant—no secretaries in the film business anymore, and no Columbia Studios lot anymore. Christ, the Studio that produced "You Can't Take It With You," "All The King's Men," "On The Waterfront", and "Lawrence Of Arabia," now a Japanese sub-holding.

He parked in the VIP lot as instructed by the young Latino security guard. Drive-ons were the studio's way of keeping tabs on the flow of traffic on and off the lot. Also, a not-so-subtle reminder that you were entering special turf and you should be suitably impressed.

Martin's office was in the Thalberg Building, the holy of holies on the lot. Offices of all the top studio people were strung down its historic corridors. This had been home to Frank Capra, John Huston and Arthur Penn. Their movies haunted the hushed carpeted halls in original poster form, constant reminders to the current occupants of how great movies could be. Martin's assistant, Mary—a tall, handsome, efficient woman in her mid-thirties—gave Jimmy a cup of black coffee and ushered him into Martin's office precisely at nine.

Martin reminded Jimmy of a bear. Medium height but wide, decisive in movement, with inquisitive eyes and well-trimmed black beard. He met Jimmy at the door to his office and guided them to the sofa area of his enormous office. In an industry where revolving doors best described most movie executive's career trajectory, Martin's huge office testified to his 20-year longevity in one of the hot-spot jobs in the movie industry. He and Jimmy had been friends for thirteen of those years.

In late '82 Jimmy had found, cleaned up, and returned to the set one of

Columbia's teenage stars who seemed hell-bent on early and total self destruction. Jimmy pulled him, cursing and crying, out of a Hollywood Boulevard by-the-hour motel room an hour before the tabloid paparazzi descended, alerted by his junkie hooker and a cash-hungry desk clerk.

Martin made sure the kid, his agent and studio brass understood the PR catastrophe that Jimmy had averted and the bucks the studio saved by shooting on schedule.

That the kid later OD'd in a similar motel room came as no surprise to anyone. But it wasn't on Jimmy or Martin's watch.

"You're looking good, Jerry. Susan got you on a diet?"

"Yeah, bought me that damned bike over there for Christmas, insists I do twenty minutes a day. She told Mary out front nothing but commissary salads for lunch. I've dropped twenty pounds in eight months, cut back to three cigars a day, I guess the martinis are next. How about you, life treating you okay?"

"Never better. Millie said you've got a problem you want contained. You can trust her, you know. Whats up?"

"I know, old habits. We're distributing a picture for Torchlight, Freddy Ruben's company. A thing called Seascape, Alison Reed directing, Julia Williams starring. It has some period locations, shooting down in San Pedro. The line producer, guy named Don Singleton, was approached by a local gang lad, calls himself, Mustafa Mohamed Ben-David, probably born Johnny Jones.

"Anyway, he wants to cut himself and his buddies in on the action to the tune of fifty grand, just for openers. Wants it under the guise of minority hiring, security guards, craft service, location consultants, usual kinda shit. If we don't play ball, pickets, boom boxes at max volume near the set, drive-bys, you know the drill.

"If we go along he'll feed it to the media and make himself a hero to the locals. The industry will find every one of its pictures held hostage by some yo-yo with the same idea. I want you to try and talk some sense into Mustafa. I don't want the cops and our legal department blowing it up into something serious; In New York, years ago, Republic ran into a similar situation. They paid the guy off. Before it was over the NYPD and the FBI were all over it. Turned into a fucking nightmare for everyone and especially the studio and the producers."

"I'll check with the Sheriff's department, see if Mustafa's got a sheet, then go have a chat with him. You want to give him anything, besides a crack upside the head, that is?"

"Nada. Not a damn thing Jimmy. Bastard'll never go away if you do. Blow this jerk outta his socks, convince him what a bad idea it is to fuck with Sony."

"You got it. Mary's got phone numbers for everybody? I'll need to talk to

Singleton."

"He's expecting a call. I told him you'd probably come on board. Get what you need from Mary, leave Ruben's outfit out of it for now. Singleton came straight to me—we'll bring Reed and Ruben into the loop once you get a handle on it. They're new, not used to this kinda shit, at least not the Hollyweird kind."

"I'll check in in a day or two. Don't let Susan cut the martinis, a man's gotta keep one vice. Ciao."

Jimmy was on Overland headed for the office when the never-ending street construction brought traffic to a halt. He cracked open the window, lit a Camel. Same as my old man, thought Jimmy, not for the first time. Hated the bastard.

After the shootout at the school, Department policy dictated that he see a counselor to deal with the killing of Guy Two. It was declared a good shooting by LAPD but policy was policy. Jimmy thought of it now because all the counselor wanted to talk about was Jimmy's rage at his father.

It had come up early in their first meeting when she asked him about his parents and siblings. Jimmy gave her a skimming over view. She asked him for details. He gave her an outline of the family, father, mother, four brothers, him the middle one. She asked him what each was like and he gave her more detail starting with his mother and descriptions of his four brothers followed by a sketch of his father.

She zeroed in on his father being last and having the skimpiest bio and asked him why and to expand. He told her about his thirty years of Marine service and his job at the University of Georgia, mentioned that he was Mexican-American, and that he was dead and then sat in silence. The silence went on for minutes. She just looked at him, waiting for more.

Jimmy said, "I don't like to talk about him."

"Why not?"

More silence from Jimmy. She was equally silent, looking at him.

This stalemate went on for a couple of weeks. She would bring up Jimmy's father and he would go silent. Eventually he told her about the boating accident years ago on Lake Lanier that killed both parents when a power boat cut their sailboat in half. He talked at length about where the lake was in relation to the home place and how his mother loved to sail. He gave vivid descriptions of his mother, long, loving and detailed but would again grow silent. She waited for minutes and finally asked,

"What did you feel about your father?"

31

Jimmy, "I hated him."

The dam broke. He told her at length in detail about his father's mistreatment of his youngest brother, the rage he felt but had no way to express and his developing desire to get out of the house and away from that situation. College, the Marines, his impulsive marriage and move to California, the LAPD.

Mercifully for Jimmy, his sessions ended shortly afterwards. She never made clear to Jimmy what his rage had to do with killing a bad guy about to shoot him with an automatic rifle. It seemed a straightforward proposition to Jimmy.

Years later his oldest brother explained his father's treatment of the youngest. The youngest had the misfortune to be the spitting image of his maternal grandmother whom his father hated. For Jimmy it was too little, too late.

He cracked open the window. Smoke curled out to join the construction dust. Heat shimmered up from the asphalt. Skinner beginning to pile up the bodies. Just beginning. Still not much to go on. What's he trying to say? Who's he saying it to? Brenner seems to be holding up okay. Press relentless. Mayor and Commissioner going nuts. Nolan doing everything he can to fuck over Brenner and embarrass me. Someday I oughta to shoot that prick.

The next morning Jimmy was on his way south on the 405 headed for the 110 to San Pedro to see his old buddy, Cunningham. Normally he avoided freeways—no telling when some damn fool was going to pile drive the car ahead into eternity. Trapped on a freeway, or anywhere else, was Jimmy's vision of Hell; claustrophobia dating back to getting stuck in a laundry basket in a childhood game of hide and seek. Surface streets worked just fine for him. But to get to San Pedro, the 110 Freeway was it.

His phone call with the Line Producer, Singleton, gave him the particulars on Mustafa's demands. Singleton was a little miffed that Martin wanted Jimmy to handle it, but gave Jimmy everything he had. Jimmy was sure that after thinking about it, Singleton would be happy to be out of the line of fire, particularly if things went south.

Jimmy had then called the San Pedro Harbor Division of the LAPD and had a chat with Lieutenant Jack Cunningham. Cunningham was an academy classmate and had worked with Jimmy out of Hollywood North for a couple of years. In 1988 he had married a woman from San Pedro and transferred to

Harbor Division. He was expecting Jimmy in San Pedro in time for lunch.

Jimmy clicked his CD player over to Mozart's piano concertos, moved into the faster middle lane and headed down to I-110, the Harbor Freeway, which would drop him right into San Pedro.

9

The Priest was born Francisco Villa on November 11, 1952, on a parched West Texas-Mexico Border farm. He was born at home, midwife only, in a sun-baked, tin roofed, sandblasted wooden shack to Maria and Hernando Villa at 2:35 AM after fourteen hours of labor. Nothing in Francisco's life would ever get much easier.

At age two his dad split. His daddy's Mother and Father moved in. When he was four years old, three redneck Texans, shitfaced on mescal and machismo, raped his mother as Francisco watched. When she managed to get loose enough to fight back, fingernails clawing bone deep, the soberest one shot her. They left her to die. It took a week. No lawmen ever investigated.

He continued to live in this hard-scrabble place with his grandparents. The old man, Paco, was Mexican, Indian and only God knew what else. Grandma, also a Maria— a source of confusion for the boy—was Apache and Spanish. His were not peaceful bloodlines.

Paco seemed ancient to the boy. Actually he was a fit, white-haired fifty three. Paco was a Shaman. His father before him and the fathers before that were Shaman. Fathers, grandfathers and great grandfathers back into unwritten time. A time when Paco's and Francisco's ancestors walked southeastward from Atzlan, an island off the northwest coast of Mexico, to a place ordained by their god, Blue Hummingbird.

At this place, as predicted long before, they found the promised sign, an eagle holding a rattlesnake sitting on a cactus. Here they founded the great city of Tenochtitlan on Lake Texcoco in the year 1325, near the center of present-day Mexico City.

It was a walk measured in generations, recorded in the memory of each succeeding Shaman and passed on to Paco together with all the preceding centuries. Paco honored and remembered them all. Paco couldn't read a lick, but he told Francisco of the day in the Mexica year of 1 Reed when the first white men appeared out of the southeastern sunrise astride strange beasts and terrified the entire city.

How the great Moctezuma greeted these strange creatures in the middle of the wide causeway that connected the island city to the mainland. Moctezuma was carried in his magnificent litter covered in hammered gold and silver and shaded by fabulous green quetzal feathers. The strangers were bearded white men in shining metal coats, mounted on tall deer. The white strangers from the east seemed to fulfill ancient prophecies of the Mexica people; that their Plumed Serpent God would return to them from the east in the year of 1 Reed. These white men were accompanied by thousands of Indio-Mexican enemies of the Mexica. Whites and Indians were dressed for battle.

Paco told this as if seen by him as a young, precocious boy. He was telling the memory of a distant multi great grandfather who died in battle with Cortez's men, four hundred and seventy seven years ago.

Paco brought stories to life. Told them so that Francisco would remember them. Again and again he reminded the boy of his inherited duty to remember and retell the ancient stories of his people. His duty to tell them accurately to the Mexican people of today. To remember time in discrete pieces, years, months, days. He insisted that Francisco accept this ancestral legacy of important work; his duty to the Mexica people.

He filled the boy's head with stories. The stories never stopped. Mexico's battles with the feared and fervently hated United States. He returned over and over to the greatness of the Mexica. The glorious days of their advanced civilization, their religious rituals, Jaguar worship, slavery, conquest, blood sacrifice, huge temples carved from the jungles. Their advanced calendars, mathematics, medicine, agriculture. It was a heady brew, washing over the boy in tidal waves of images. He was drowned in magic, mysticism and savagery.

Grandma taught healing. She knew every plant in her world and its uses. For an hour or so each day she taught Francisco. He followed her into the desert to gather plants. He helped her find the clay deposits that were the material for her pots and plasters. He learned the uses for animal and bird parts as healing agents. She taught him the ways to prepare and administer the potions. Francisco absorbed Grandma's teachings.

He preferred Paco's stories, but Paco insisted that he learn it all. A Shaman is also a healer of his people, he reminded Francisco over and over. Look after the mind and the body and you will have a well people. A culture was created in him, sacrifice, ancient references, totemic rituals, mystical points, planets, plants, structures connected to the desert and the stars, formed on a base of terror and primal loss.

10

Jimmy parked under the eucalyptus trees in the San Pedro Harbor Division's parking lot. The harsh sunlight threw black shadows across the parking lot where it wasn't baking the official cars. There was a well-marked visitors parking lot where Jimmy left the Jag. The difference between this station and his old home station was stunning. None of the chaos, civilians flowing in and out or cops with hookers or teenage gangbangers in handcuffs. Small town USA.

Jimmy checked in with the blonde civilian dispatcher holding down the front desk with a female officer and asked for Cunningham. The blonde gal had three-inch-long fuchsia fingernails. On the ring finger of each hand the nail had a gold bangle attached. The nails matched the color of her lipstick and her shiny pedal pushers. He just stood and watched, fascinated, as she manipulated the intercom, notified Cunningham of his visitor then scooped up an officer's call from a radio car, all while protecting the nails. He couldn't take his eyes off of them.

Cunningham was out in five minutes.

"Jimmy, how you doin' man? You hear that racist jackass Donahue this mornin' raggin' on our latest serial killer? All over AM radio. Heard you were in tall clover up in Beverly Hills, what you want to come down to San Pedro for?"

As they shook hands, Jimmy tried to conceal the shock of seeing his old squadmate for the first time in ten years. Cunningham had gotten hugely fat.

His neck was bulging over his loosened collar, tie pulled down and sweat beading on his forehead. His plaid polyester sport coat was a foot from closing. Even the calves of his grey, shiny pants were stretched tight. Obviously Jimmy was not hiding his surprise.

"Yeah, I know, Eleanor is feeding me too good, gets her feelings hurt if I don't eat everything in sight." Cunningham said all this turning redder and redder. Looked like he was having a heart attack.

"Hell Jack, could be worse, she could not feed you at all. I'm doin' okay. You want to eat first, or—Jesus, have you seen that women's fingernails?"

"Yeah she's some piece-a-work, that one. Sweet, but out there, man. Let's go get a bite, I'll give you the general picture on this dirtbag over a burger."

"Mustafa's always been a fuck-up. Born and raised right here in San Pedro, got into trouble first time when he was ten. Tried to steal a car. Course he didn't have a fucking clue what he was doing, managed to get it into reverse, tromped the gas, rammed the hell out of a car across the street. Jammed his doors closed. Little bastard couldn't get out. Set off the alarms on both cars. The uniforms pried him out after about an hour.

Probation. The usual bullshit. Then in and outta juvie. Mother a crack-smoking hooker, father unknown. Finally, when he was eighteen popped for possession, drugs and weapons. He did his first hitch with the big boys up at Quentin. Managed to get his GED and worked in the prison library, kept his nose clean, read a lot. Got out on his first shot at parole."

Jimmy and Cunningham were at a corner table in Cunningham's favorite lunch hang out, Pete's Place, a sports bar and grill on Pacific Avenue. The joint's air conditioning unit was losing the battle against the heat wave and the heavy lunch crowd. Everyone in the place seemed to know Cunningham but he still chose a chair in the corner facing the door. He noticed Jimmy noticing his choice and shot him a brief grin. Old cops.

They ordered from Milly, the fortyish, efficient waitress after she made nice over Cunningham's new buddy and asked about the wife. They made small talk about the old days and mutual friends. Milly brought the food and left.

Jimmy, slathering his burger with catsup, "He stay outta trouble when he came back here?"

Cunningham, with a gesture to his waistline, had ordered the Individual Sardine Platter, with potato salad and coleslaw.

"For a while. Then he started his own gang, too much reading, wanted to start a revolution. Called his gang The Che Coalition, bullshit, attracted a bunch of half-assed educated kids, gonna change the world. Other local gangs thought this a crock, big turf battle over in the McDonald's parking lot. Mustafa shot a guy, killed him. Busted, sent back to Quentin for twenty five. Released a year later on appeal, some technical fuckup. But not before he'd hooked up with one of those old Black Panther types they still got up there from the sixties. He came out really revved on this revolution shit."

"Anybody up there in particular a strong influence?"

"Hell, Jimmy, I don't know. This is all grapevine horse pucky, street talk. What's your beef with the guy? Seems a long way from Beverly Hills. This have anything to do with the fundraisers that TV stars been giving for this asshole and his so called movement?"

"I got a client wants me to talk to the guy, you mind leaving it at that? Whats the name he was born with and where can I find him?"

"You don't give much back, do you? What the hell, you're buying. It's Mousie Dawson, he has a flop down on Third, right next to the bodega, the Northwest corner of Elm. You can't miss it, got a poster of Che glued on the door."

"Cute. With this background help I think I can avoid some grief for you and my client. The kinda' grief that brings out the worst kinda press. Tell me about the fundraisers."

"I don't know much. Again, street talk. This broad up in Brentwood invites a buncha her TV and movie buddies to a pool party, they get to meet real Black Revolutionaries, donate some bucks to help the Black community prevent another riot, feed kids, that sorta thing. Kinda like the New York Black Panther parties of the Sixties. Hell, thats probably where the idea came from, one of those guys at Quentin."

"They raise any real bucks?" Jimmy finished his coffee and signaled Milly for the check.

"Word on the street is thirty five to forty grand—not huge but not exactly chicken feed. Enough to make Mousie a local hero."

"Who is this actress? I haven't heard anything about her parties. Usually big PR. Lotsa media hype."

"Rosie Dempsey, you know the broad. Roseanne without the trash mouth. Well, I gotta get back to the shop. C'mon, You can take a look at Mousie's sheet."

Jimmy was sitting in an interview room at a battered table in Harbor Division, thinking, twenty years; I've spent my most of my life in this place or one just like it, nothing seems to change, dealing with another lowlife trying to run a scam. Same colors, smells, one table, three chairs and tension. Swapping favors and information, cop work. Part of the glamour of hunting dirtbags. Like this Skinner case. I wonder how Brenner is coping with Nolan? Any new bodies falling since I last talked to him? Nah, he would have called. Wonder if

Fulo has any new thoughts? Oughta call him.

Cunningham dropped Mousie's inch-thick file on the desk.

Jimmy opened it to the latest mug shot and sat there staring.

"What the hell is this, I thought the guy was black?"

"Oh, yeah—weird, huh? Everybody does the same double take. Mousie's mother was very light skinned, father white, Hispanic. Mousie says American Indian, anyway he came out white. What raisin' he got was from his black Hispanic grandmother, chooses to live black. Makes a big deal of it. Strange dude."

Jimmy had no problem following Cunningham's directions to Mousie's neighborhood. He parked the Jag a half a block from the bodega corner. He could see the Che poster on the front door of a small post-war house, right where Cunningham described it.

To Jimmy's surprise, the house was freshly painted, the tiny yard was clean, grass trimmed, flowers growing in carefully tended beds and flower boxes under the front windows.

Sitting in the front porch shade, catching the fitful breeze, were three men and a young woman, all in their early twenties. Body piercings, tattoos, too-big jeans, tank tops and shorts made the obligatory homie statements. As Jimmy started up the front walk, one of the guys, a tall, well-built black man stood up.

"What'chu want, man? We ain't buyin' nothin' today—you a cop?"

His muscles bulged the tank top. Probably used to frightening whitey by just being on the same side of the street.

Jimmy smiled his best Southern smile at the guy.

"Not recently. I want to see Mustafa, he around?"

Jimmy put his foot up on the first step, crowding their territory. Tall Man didn't like that.

"What'cha doin' man—what'chu mean 'not recently,' you either a cop o' you ain't, which is it?"

Jimmy drug it out; lighting a cigarette before answering. "What I mean is, not recently. I was a cop for twenty years, retired. Now is Mustafa around?"

"Not for you, Mr. Not Recently, now get the fuck outta here, you spoilin' our afternoon."

"You always this hostile before you know what somebody wants? Okay, you tell Mustafa, when he's tired of hiding behind you and that window blind over there, that Rosie Dempsey wanted me to talk to him. Tell him to find me. Ciao, big man."

Jimmy turned and headed for his car. He heard the screen door squeak open behind him.

"Hold up man, hey, mister." It was the young woman, rising from the porch steps, obviously smarter than her big friend. "We get hassled all the time by the cops, all you white guys. Kikkoa here, he ain't a bad dude."

Jimmy could tell she wasn't going to let it go, so he turned. As he did a tall, rake-thin man was coming through the screen door. He was shirtless with prison-developed muscles and tattoos. A red and white cowboy bandana held his long black hair back over his gold ear ringed ears. He had the most piercing black eyes Jimmy had ever seen; hawk-like, fierce.

"Kikkoa, he just—" the girl squawked to a stop as Mustafa gently touched her shoulder,

"Uh, Mustafa, this guy—"

"I heard, Mshobe, its okay, I'll talk to him. Leave us alone out here, y'all go on in the house."

"But—" Tall Man started.

"Its okay, Kikkoa, I'll be safe as long as he knows you're close, right mister?"

"Yeah," Jimmy drawled, "He scares the shit outta me, can't you tell? I think I'd worry more about Mshobe there, at least she's got a brain behind that steel ring in her eyebrow."

"Cut the shit Mister, who are you and what do you have to do with Rosie?"

The four gang members loped off into the house letting the rickety screen door slam closed.

"C'mon into my office over there, let's keep this private."

Jimmy strolled to the curb, leaned against the rusted-out fender on a pick-up truck and waited. Off balance, Mustafa took a beat then tried to nonchalantly join him.

"Now, what'chu' want man, you wastin' my time?"

"I don't think talking about fifty grand is a waste of time, do you Mousie? That is your real name isn't it?" Keeping this creep off balance.

"Hey man, how you know that? You said you weren't no cop. Who the hell are you—who you been talking to and whats this got to do with fifty grand or Rosie?" He hooked his thumbs into his belt doing his best to look defiant.

"How did you get the handle Mousie, not much of a tag for a hot shot revolutionary—little and grey, were you, when you were younger? The schoolyard mouse? Those folks in the house know about that? Probably not."

"Hey, fuck you man, get to the point. My name has nothing to do with anything."

"Watch it, Mousie, your accent slips when you're not careful. You didn't sound black just now. Gotta watch that."

Jimmy flipped his Camel butt onto Mousie's carefully trimmed yard. Mousie watched, started to say something, then thought better of it. His face blazing, he growled at Jimmy.

"Talk sense or take a hike, motherfucker. Get outta my face."

Jimmy knew that only a message from Mousie's money, Rosie Dempsey, was keeping Mousie from swinging on him. He was almost ready to do it anyway or more likely call out his troops and let them pound Jimmy into the sidewalk. Jimmy switched tactics. "Sony Pictures."

Mousie's mouth fell open, "What, what you talking about man? What the hell is with you?"

"I heard you want to be a studio executive, Mousie, help Sony Studios make movies. Did I hear wrong?"

"Man, I don't have to talk to you 'bout that, get the fuck outta here 'fore I get Kikkoa and Buddy to stomp you into a dog's breakfast. Get outta my 'hood, outta my face."

Jimmy just grinned.

"Oh, you'll talk to me, 'cause nobody else at Sony will talk to you. And you think you got a scam worth some big bucks. Wrong. You're gonna back off and not hassle those nice folks. You are gonna forget all about the movie business. Closest to the movies you're gonna get is the news at six and eleven when they bring your ass in for extortion."

"Extortion, hey, you got it all wrong, man. I met the director 'a this movie at Rosie Dempsey's party. She said I oughta' talk to that dude, Singleton, gave me his phone number, 'bout hirin' some'a the local people, help the unemployed in the community. We got big time unemployment down here. Sony should be willin' to help out. They gonna make big bucks outta shootin' here, man, should share the wealth. 'Sides I don't think they gonna want a PR stink, pickets or a lotta noisy kids slowin' up the shoot."

"You know, Mousie, you're breaking my heart. If I hadn't spent the morning doing my homework and gotten your proposition straight from Sony, you'd have me going. I'd want to jump on your band wagon, maybe even wave a picket sign with you. But you're just a cheap hood on the make, trying to get one over on Sony. You don't give a flying fuck about anything except Mustafa Ben-David, a.k.a. Mousie Dawson. We'll be talking, see you on the news at six."

Jimmy turned and left, giving Mousie no time for a reply. He got in the Jag and drove off. In his rearview mirror Mousie was slouching back to his revolution.

Jimmy punched his office number into the cell phone, asked Millie to find out all she could about Rosie Dempsey and her fundraising for Mustafa Ben-David and friends. His next call was to Jerry Martin.

Jimmy, "Hey buddy, we may have a problem. You didn't tell me that your director sicced Mustafa onto Singleton. By the way, you were in the right ball-park about his real name. It's Mousie Dawson."

"What do you mean, my director sicced Mousie onto Singleton?"

"Mousie met her at a party. He pitched her his line about the unemployed in San Pedro and she bought it. Gave Mousie Singleton's name and phone number. Told him he should call about work on the movie she was shooting."

"Shit."

"Yeah, makes it messy. You want me to talk to her?'

"Where are you? Sounds like you're on cell."

"On the way back into town from San Pedro."

"Swing by the lot. Alison and Singleton are here for a meeting. When that breaks up you can help me explain the facts of life to her."

"You got it. See ya."

Jimmy snapped off the cell phone, thinking. The new director flavor of the week. Alison Reed. Wonder woman who, out of nowhere, had made forty million bucks for Sony opening weekend of "Cut Artist." An action flick with two unknowns and special effects that had the town talking. Topped out at a hundred and seventy five million, domestic. Martin was gonna be handling her with kid gloves. This should prove interesting.

11

Alison Reed stood up, and up. She must have been damn near six feet tall in her polished Luchese cowboy boots, slim faded jeans and a denim work shirt, sleeves rolled to the elbow. Long, dark brown hair, the greenest eyes Jimmy had ever seen, a wide sensuous mouth with the barest trace of lipstick, no jewelry and a tan that comes from being outdoors for a reason. She reminded Jimmy of Kathryn Bigelow.

She smiled and Jimmy realized that he was staring like an idiot. Jerry Martin and Don Singleton, also smiling, watched Jimmy. They were used to this reaction from guys meeting Alison for the first time. Movie star beauty in a director was a shock.

They were gathered around the coffee table in the sofa area of Martin's office. The room was wired with tension, time pressure and close deadlines.

Martin made the introductions, "Alison Reed, Jimmy Santos. Jimmy, Don, I think you guys talked on the phone. Alison, Jimmy is Ex-LAPD, a private detective who's helping us with a problem on Seascape."

Alison's smile at Jimmy slid away in reaction to the threat of yet another problem on her project. She turned to Martin, "What problem?"

Jimmy noticed the room's atmosphere chill as he answered, "Mustafa Ben-David, real name Mousie Dawson, is trying to pry some bucks out of Sony using your picture as a lever. Don, you want to fill in the details?"

Martin and Singleton settled onto the leather sofa. Jimmy and Alison took the facing armchairs. Alison sat forward on the edge of her chair and rested her elbows on her knees, chin in her hands she listened intently.

Reluctant to seem part of the problem, Singleton quickly sketched in the situation for her.

"Acting on what he said was your advice, Mousie called me and demanded, in effect, that we pay his people to work on Seascape or they disrupt your shooting."

Martin to Alison, "Did you tell him to call Don?"

"Sure, I met him at a party at Rosie Dempsey's. He pitched the idea that he was working to improve the depressed community of San Pedro. We're shooting there for two weeks and I thought maybe we could help him. Hire a few of his people for security, PA's, whatever. What's the big deal? Don, are you sure he was threatening us? Maybe you misunderstood him?"

"Oh, I understood him okay. We'll be there with boom boxes blasting is not a complicated concept."

Jimmy, "He was that blatant about it?"

Alison, "Surely he didn't say that?"

"No, what he said was that his people loved to watch movies being made and that a lot of the younger ones never went anywhere without their music. Further that a lot of them liked to watch from up close while listening to real loud music in their cars. Heard any of those car stereos lately? He says he can prevent all that."

Alison sat back in the chair, arms and legs crossed, her foot bounced impatiently.

"Oh, come on Don. You are taking this in the worst possible light. Besides, what could it cost the picture to throw a few dollars to the local people?"

Jimmy jumped in, realizing that Martin could use his help. Making a picture is a high pressure situation involving long hours and intense, months-long professional relationships. A smooth, supportive, working partnership with the director is critical to a successful project. Neither Martin nor Singleton could afford to be the bad guy. "Alison, the real problem here is Mousie. He's trying to extort jobs from Sony. You may be budgeted for the kinda jobs he's asking for, but Don should have a free hand in choosing the people. You give in to Mousie on this picture and he hits up every Sony project with the same deal. Blackmailers don't stop at one score."

Jimmy relaxed back into his chair and continued.

"He's got a rap sheet going back to age ten for auto theft. He'd be in Quentin now for murder if his lawyer hadn't beat the rap on a technicality. He's not the kinda guy you want in charge of your security."

Alison sat forward and pinned Jimmy with her stare,

"Hold on a minute. A criminal record doesn't mean he's not trying to help his community."

Jimmy shrugged. Then on a hunch, "How much money was raised at those parties for Mousie's good works?"

Alison waved this away. What difference did it make? "I don't know. Rosie did it two or three times for the people down there. Two hundred, two hundred fifty thousand all in, maybe."

Singleton, "Jesus!"

Martin, "Are you serious?"

Jimmy waited out the astonishment, lit a Camel and said, "The cop I talked to in San Pedro said the word on the street is that Mousie raised thirty-five, forty thousand. I wonder where the other two hundred K wound up? Are you sure of that figure?"

"Rosie's assistant told me. She was real proud of Rosie for her good work. There was no reason for her to lie."

Jimmy rose, looking for an ashtray. Finding none, he stubbed out his smoke in Martin's trash can. He sat on the arm of his chair and turned back to Alison, "You'd think that if Mousie was on the up and up, he'd want credit for all the money he'd raised. Not just a fifth of it. Forty grand is making him a hero. Wonder what two hundred and forty K would do for him?"

"Aren't you jumping to pretty cynical conclusions?"

"I don't think so. I met a lot of Mousies during my twenty years on the job." Jimmy realized he was coming on too strong. Time to ease off a bit. "Look, I've only talked to him once. I'll check it out further, maybe I'm wrong." To Martin, "I'll call you in a day or two, let you know what I've learned."

Alison felt a slow flush of anger beginning to rise in her cheeks. Damn them, she thought, here we go again. Damned patronizing, redneck cop.

"You guys wouldn't be ganging up on me, would you?"

Jimmy, "No way, no reason. Normally you'd never hear about this. It's our job. Not a director's problem. Till Mousie brought your name into it. I'd planned—Jerry, Don and I had planned—to deal with it, not let it out of this office." Jimmy realized it did sound like they were ganging up on her. He grinned. "Well, maybe we are, just a little bit. But it's for—"

"Don't you dare say it's for my own good." Alison blazed. Then sitting back and collecting herself, "I've got it. What's important here is the film. If Mousie checks out to be the sleaze you think he is, bust his ass and keep him away from my picture. Okay?"

"Yes ma'am." Jimmy's face split into a wider grin. "You got it. I'll call ya'll with an update."

Alison tried to keep from smiling but after a beat she gave it up. What the hell, she thought. Goodbyes and nice-to-meet-you's said, Jimmy left.

Alison, "Jerry, can this hurt Seascape?"

"Sure it can. You and your actors can't work with rap music blasting through the set. The picture's budget can't stand to lose shooting days or lousy soundtracks that have to be dubbed later."

"Is there anything else we should do?"

"I don't think so. My bet is Jimmy will back this guy off, make him leave your picture alone. That's the best solution."

"He can do that?"

"Careful—now who's jumping to conclusions? Don't let that drawl fool you. Yeah, Jimmy can do it. Bet on it."

During her high school senior year Alison had developed an interest in becoming a film director. Long talks with Dad, Mom and her school counselors convinced her that a liberal arts education then film school was the path to take. Money was not a problem thanks to Dad's income and Grandpa's trust. Dad and Mom encouraged a part-time job to foster her independence.

She and Mom visited a half dozen, pre-scouted campuses; Sarah Lawrence, Vassar and Radcliffe but one look at Bennington in Vermont sealed the deal. Her Mom never tired of telling the tale. She said Alison got out of the car, looked around, took a deep breath and said, "This is it!"

Catalogues had described the option of her being allowed to build her own major and Bennington had everything that interested her. Another plus was its small size and idyllic campus in the hills of Vermont. She could work part-time weekends at the only art supply store in Bennington. It was also a 'fur' piece from home in Minnesota.

She was taking the first steps to Hollyweird.

12

He took Ngh Do, his first victim, at three AM on a Friday night. He walked up behind him as Ngh staggered home from the whorehouse. Ngh turned in fright at the sound of footsteps behind him and saw The Priest—recognition, puzzlement, surprise. He started to say something. The Priest brought the blow gun up and sent the dart into his throat. Ngh slapped at the insect sting and collapsed soundlessly to the overgrown sidewalk, his eyes twitching in terror. The Priest scooped him up like a child, carried him to the black van, dumped him in the back, got in and drove off, slowly. It took ninety seconds. He picked up the 57 North near Anaheim Stadium and, at just over the speed limit, headed north to the San Gabriel Mountains. To his Temple, to his first Sacrifice.

The Priest had made a tiny, six inch blow gun from a reed and painted it black. The darts he fashioned from bamboo. Hard, porous; the perfect needle to carry the poison. Crow's feathers found on the forest floor for guidance. The dart barely one-half inch long. He practiced for hours. At distances to four feet, he could hit a bottle cap every time after a week. He continued to practice for thirty minutes every night.

School, when he turned six, was a misery for Francisco. It was a hot, dusty one hour walk to the sun-scorched, treeless Texas lot that held the small brick school building. In a poor land he was among the poorest.

He was embarrassed by his tattered clothes, that he had no mother or father. He was pathologically shy and always talking this strange shit. At six, classmates didn't want know about milkweed root, cactus juices, gecko lizard guts or Aztec history. He embarrassed the Mexican kids and pissed off the Texans. Every day he went home for more weirdness.

When he was twelve years old, Grandma walked out into the desert. That Saturday morning sunrise, the desert was still. Nothing—creature, plant nor sand grain —moved. Only a hawk hunting in the white sky and Grandma walking. She became a tiny figure among the Saguaro cactus then disappeared. She did not return.

Paco said she had gone to join her Apache ancestors.

The old woman, as a young girl, became the center of that night's story of warfare between Mestizos and Apaches. Francisco learned how Grandma had become Paco's wife.

Francisco's life changed little after Grandma's leaving. Paco picked up the medicine teaching, insisted that Francisco attend the local school and constantly continued his story telling. Francisco was growing tall for a Mexican boy. Paco said it must be the old Grandma's Spanish blood. The Apache line also began show in Francisco's sinewy muscles. Paco had an ancestor reason for everything.

When he was thirteen years, Francisco first began to suspect that he was crazy. Paco's welfare check was late again and he was acting more batshit than usual. The blonde Texas classmate he'd been staring at, too shy to speak, was smiling at him and the white, spinster teacher was making his classroom life miserable. Out on the playing field senior Paul Buchanan picked the wrong time to make a loud, wiseass crack about Francisco's handmade moccasins. Francisco felt his mind leave his skull in a flash of light.

What seemed hours later, he found himself walking the dusty road toward home, hands scraped, hurting and bleeding.

That night Paco gave him hell about being suspended from school for two weeks. When Francisco just looked at him blankly, understanding nothing. Paco had the good sense to ask Francisco if he remembered the day. Francisco did not. Paco started over, where the story began for him.

The white school principal had driven up to the shack in his battered Ford mini-van and sat on his horn until Paco ambled out to see what he wanted. What he wanted was to give Paco hell about his grandson's behavior.

Culling out the racism, Paco learned that Francisco had attacked and almost killed a fellow student. The white boy, Buchanan, had made some remark and Francisco exploded. He'd hit him three or four times. When he was down, Francisco tried to choke him to death.

It took four students to pull Francisco off the unconscious Buchanan. Francisco's eyes were berserk. He spit into Buchanan's face, kicked him in the nuts again and walked off into the desert.

Only Buchanan's own sorry record kept the school from calling the sheriff. Francisco stared at Paco as if for the first time the old man were lying. But Paco did not lie. If Paco did not lie, Francisco was crazy; his reasoning was as simple as that. Too simple, but not totally wrong. The pressures on his good mind had increased for years. He'd finally snapped.

From that day, Francisco became even more withdrawn. Not knowing how he had gone there, he became afraid, particularly of anything involving other people. The Buchanan boy seemed somehow to blame for the blackout where Francisco's actions had shamed Paco. The blackout became a place, a piece of geography, as real as a cave, filled with dark mysteries; a violent, threatening void.

Paco continued his teachings. Francisco's terror resisted. Unconsciously, a chasm began to open between them. Paco rummaged the centuries, searching for a cure. He found none, and cursed his failure. He was ashamed, and the boy felt it and was more terrorized, assuming himself the cause. Neither man could find material to build a bridge. Downward almost three years they spiraled.

———————————

Warrior! Paco's magic! The word conjured power, strength. It knifed into them on the same night. They sat smoking, high on a butte, watching the night sky whirl. Warrior! A sign? A cure? In short, charged sentences they talked. The way of the warrior was action, killing of fear, the ancient Mexica way. Fury. Blood. No more inner searching for them. In their common exhilaration they mistook sickness for cure. Their Mexica heritage brought them together.

The outside world conspired to give them an enemy: The Vietnam War. For weeks they talked. The breach was healed as they planned Francisco's initiation into the warrior world. He quit school. Paco poured Mexica war stories into his newly receptive brain. The glories of Mexica warriors past. The joys of battle. The camaraderie of fighting men. The honor. The power. In late summer, lying about his age, Francisco boarded a bus bound for Paris Island, South Carolina, home of the US Marine Corp basic training base. The Priest was about to emerge.

13

Paris Island was a hellhole. Lying in the low country of South Carolina, it sat on a coastal, marshy peninsula between two tidal rivers that emptied into the Atlantic. It was sand and salt marsh and brackish streams and saber-tipped plants and vicious bugs and blistering heat. A place where almost once a year a few of those teenagers died from drowning or heat stroke or accidental shooting or helicopter crash. There were hundreds of accidental ways to die on Paris Island. It was the place where the Marine Corp hammered teenagers into its idea of men.

Francisco exulted. Paris Island embraced violence—taught, drilled, demanded it. Never walk, run. Don't talk, shout, or better, scream. Never avoid, hit—harder.

In this place the geography of his blackout was communal terrain, fought over to command. Rage a weapon, honed. Boyhood's King of the Mountain played with guns. Years of hiding his every violent impulse fell away. He was Home.

Brutal physical training. Temperature and humidity in the high nineties. Obstacle courses. Climb, jump, crawl. Run 5, 8, 10 miles with a full 60 pound pack. Blisters on shoulders from the pack and on feet from the unforgiving boots. Sunburn and dehydration. Hand to hand combat. Instructors hell-bent on making it real.

Many recruits wound up in the infirmary. Not The Priest. He sent two of his hand-to-hand combat instructors off to the medics on stretchers. Weapons training— knives, grenades, handguns, rifles, M90's, RPGs, machine guns—he mastered them all. On the rifle range—a twenty inch diameter target, five hundred yards away—expert, best in company. Live fire exercises—belly crawling under the shriek of fifty caliber machine gun bullets, the thump of grenades, the whistle of shrapnel. Paco's stories of Mexica warrior training were his guide. Nothing the Marine Corp could dish out could compare with Mexica boot camp.

Classroom work was attacked with equal enthusiasm. US rank structure, enemy unit identification, weapons maintenance, a special fascination with map and terrain reading—he absorbed it all. When ordered, he led his platoon on night terrain marches. night swamp crossings with a topographical map and compass his only guidance. Performance flawless.

A few took it all as a joke, a gung-ho bore. One big, athletic motormouth tried to stick Francisco with a nickname, "Cisco". He thought this funny as hell, probably even original. Francisco did not. A nickname was not for a warrior. In his newfound confidence he calmly explained this to the guy and told him to stop. Motormouth found him hilarious, "Sure, Cisco, how 'bout 'Little Warrior Cisco' since you 'bout a whole head shorter'n me?"

Francisco hit him in the solar plexus, expelling a blast of foul breath, took a half step back and kicked him under the chin, pulling it just enough to avoid neck breaking. Motor-mouth falling, Francisco kicked him in the nuts, hard, and, deadly calm, walked away. No blackout this time, no guilt, no shame. An enemy defeated.

The Drill Instructor who saw this told a buddy that he'd never seen anything like it. The "Mex" was standing calm and relaxed, talking to this big asshole troublemaker—in an eye-blink, a blur of movement and "asshole" was lying on the parade ground holding his nuts. The "Mex" moves quick like an animal, no warning; one heartbeat he's dead calm, the next, he's knocked you on your ass.

On his final night at Paris Island he got his new name, one he accepted. That night, in a Paris Island bar, his barrack mate, skunk drunk, had made a beer-fueled stew of Francisco and St. Francis and Monks and Priests. "The Priest." It stuck. When he hit the beach in Nam he was The Priest—he no longer thought "I", he thought, "The Priest." He was barely seventeen.

14

After the Cinco de Mayo massacre, The Priest's life reverted to his old pattern. He regressed to the man who was discharged from the VA hospital years before. No more books, no more learning. Visits to the VA shrink, Annucci, were a return to masked nothingness. He went only for Uncle Sam's checks. He pulled up the old wall of grim bullshit that baffled the Doctor. He was unreachable, deeper in psychosis than in 1986. Annucci pored over his notes searching for a clue, a turning point, a trigger. He found nothing but a vague time frame.

A week, sometimes two weeks of the dreams would send him into the night on the hunt. VC prey. Pick off the weakest, the most vulnerable, those alone, away from the herd. He dressed to fade into the landscape—scruffy jeans, faded chambray work shirt, beat-up work boots. He assumed the posture and demeanor of a poor working Mexican and vanished into the L.A. cityscape, invisible to all.

The second victim was a man named Phu Bah. He owned the Vietnamese food stand in the Vietnamese Cultural Court on Westminster Avenue. On the sweltering night of June 8, 1995, Phu Bah sent the cook home after cleanup was finished, opened a beer and sat down with his books to see if another dime's profit could be squeezed from the food stand. He wiped the sweat from his face and neck as he pored over his books. Phu Bah's wife had discovered the joys of American consumerism and she gave him no peace about their low status in life. Phu Bah hated going home.

By midnight he gave up in disgust, waved goodnight to the security guard and walked out to the parking lot. Lit only by widely-spaced yellow street lights, and brutally hot even at this late hour, the parking lot was divided into halves by a hundred yard long pedestrian strip of stalls running north-south.

Flanking these stalls in two rows on the east and west were a line of life-sized marble statues of Asian wise men and heroes. They glowed gold in the sulfurous light. The Priest was concealed, blending into the darkness behind the statue of Confucius. Phu Bah, deeply distracted, trudged toward The Priest. He never heard the whifft of the dart that hit him in the right carotid artery. One moment he was walking to his car, the next, he was sinking to his knees in bewilderment as the concrete sidewalk rose to meet him. The Priest scooped him into the van and thirty seconds later was driving out of the Cultural Court. In two and a half hours he was at his Temple.

The Priest had watched him for two weeks.

Phu Bah had been a bouncer in a cathouse in Saigon. He was also an informer for the VC. He passed them scraps of information the hookers picked up from American GI's. In return, money flowed, and he had all the women and liquor a man could want. When real intelligence was meager, he made it up. The last of his fabricated reports was his undoing. Based on a half-truth, it had caused the deaths of seven VC who stumbled into a Military Police action. Phu Bah spent the remainder of the war in hiding, coming out to the US with a boatload people.

Prey number three was a former ex-VC Lieutenant, Tran Danh, who hung out in a dark, cheap and very popular Vietnamese restaurant in Little Saigon's Vietnamese Mall. After a meal, he and two of his cronies drank too much and bragged about their war days. Seated in a back corner booth that gave the illusion of privacy, they regaled each other with heroic exploits against 'the running dogs.' On four consecutive hunting nights, The Priest ate a small meal in the adjoining booth.

Danh had been a VC cell leader in Saigon. Working undercover, he had directed a company of scooter bike assassins that prowled the streets of Saigon. A squad of two men or a man and woman on a small motorbike cruised the streets. The driver picked the target and the person on the back provided the fire power. They raked outdoor cafes with machine gun fire or tossed grenades into crowded bus shelters. The the fast, agile bike darted away into the narrow twisting streets, impossible to capture.

Danh's favorite story involved the coordinated attack by four scooters on a US Marine scouting party. Two M113 Personnel Carriers and two jeeps with fifty caliber machine guns, carrying about twenty grunts in all, made it a habit of stopping at a roadside beer and pot joint every time they came in from the bush. A cool one and a toke before reporting into the fire base became a ritual.

Danh watched this happen one afternoon, squatting in the dust outside the joint. He watched for days to see if it was a pattern. It was.

One week later the patrol stopped again. After a couple of beers and a toke or two, the grunts, relaxed and off guard, began to regroup at their vehicles. The rear doors on the hated APCs were open, men were getting in, milling around the jeeps, laughing, joking, playing grab-ass. The swarm of motor bikes hit them.

Two center bikes threw satchel bombs into each of the APC's open rear doors. The wing bikes and then the center two opened fire with stolen Uzi machine guns. It was chaos. Guys who dived into the cover of the APCs died instantly when the satchel bombs exploded simultaneously. The other grunts were caught in the open, unable to reach the heavy machine guns because of the withering fire from the Uzis.

Befuddled from the suddenness of the attack, seventeen died. Three guys managed to return fire. They wounded one VC in the calf, another in the hand.

Two huge palm trees burst into flame from the exploding APCs. White frond smoke spiraled upwards joining the black fumes from burning fuel and tires. Danh received a medal for planning and executing the attack. In the air-conditioned California restaurant, Danh always drank a toast to this victory.

———————

Taking this man was going to be difficult. Danh always stuck close to his comrades. They left the restaurant, climbed into a battered Jeep Cherokee and sped off. The Priest followed in his van. They always went into the Locust Valley Mobile Home Estates, parked the jeep and disappeared into one of permanently grounded mobile homes. They lived there together. Mornings they left together and reported for work at the construction site of a new strip mall. They were inseparable. The Priest, always unseen, their shadow.

The Priest reconnoitered the restaurant; no hope there. The only other possibility was the construction site. The Priest watched it for four days, parked in the adjoining lot, slouched down in his van. He spotted a slim possibility. Every morning after the crew's break, Danh extended his by ten minutes, vanishing into one of the portable toilets at the edge of the site. The foreman yelling at him called this to The Priest's attention.

The next day The Priest parked close to the portable toilets. Danh ducked into one of them after his break. The Priest walked to the toilets and entered the one next to Danh. He waited. The stench in the summer sun was awful, the air still, stinking and stifling. He heard the other man stand up, zip his pants; the jingle of his belt buckle. The Priest stepped out of his toilet. The latch on the Danh's toilet door snapped open. All in one motion The Priest snatched the door open and slammed into Danh and stabbed a dart into the startled man's neck. Danh sat down, trying to glare up at his attacker as the control of his muscles vanished.

The Priest cracked the door open and checked to see if he'd attracted attention. No. The Priest counted on the construction noise as cover. It worked. He picked up Danh, carried him to his van and drove off. The war stories of the loudmouthed fool, now sprawled helpless in the back of the van, brought The Priest's Nam memories to the surface.

Fording a shallow river—Firefight—Instant, deafening, blanketing small arms fire. Whoosh of incoming .87mm rockets—EXPLOSIONS—bouncing, slow motion sky—raining jungle—50 caliber machine gun tracers splitting the sky—EXPLOSIONS—Deep Slow Blackness. River running Red. The blood of seventeen soldiers chewed up by the 50 caliber VC machine gun.

Stillness following the blasts seeping into conscious, painful silence—ears ringing a song of cicadas. Bodies rafted, twisting in the current. A macabre reel in the mud slow river. Animal life along the river waited—stillness a defense—silence safety. Five Marines and The Priest captured.

The Priest came to, naked, sit-crouching in a shit encrusted, urine-mud-floored bamboo cage. No room to extend any muscle. Through a wall of steaming rain he could barely see five other cages, Marines in four. AK-47-armed VC swarmed the area. He passed out. A monkey-faced bastard hammering his cage with a bayonet handle almost brought him back. A poke with the bayonet did. The rain had stopped. Naked, tied to a stake centered between the cages was his platoon leader, Recon Sergeant Mike Reynolds.

Razor-edged combat knife in hand, a VC Captain was interrogating Reynolds in pidgin English. The Sergeant was too far gone to answer. For each unanswered question the VC made a quick practiced incision high on the Sergeant's chest, grabbed the skin tab created and ripped downward. Blood-rain ribboned down, puddled with bits of flesh at their feet. A liquid, red and white vest. Question—no answer—cut—pull. Again—again.

The VC Captain didn't care—quivering with the pleasure of cutting. Every time The Priest looked away a bayonet poke brought him back. The Ser-

geant twitched twice, slumped into the reddened ropes, and died. The VC captain—disappointed, disgusted—spat on the corpse and walked away.

This became the pattern. Day after day, a grunt tortured. Always a new technique. The Torturer was a walking, working encyclopedia of torture; the man loved his work. The Torturer could take a man right to the brink, back off, return him to his cage, then, temporarily sated, walk away.

Occasionally new soldiers joined the party. Guys died often. The Torturer and Monkeyface enjoyed making The Priest watch. His own special torture. Soon it wouldn't matter—his mind was sliding away. He felt reason slide rearward on his brain, leaving the frontal lobes, crossing the cerebellum, burying itself in the primordial stem. He didn't want to bring it back. It felt so good to hide there in a snake state.

He was held by an isolated VC unit, interrogation of prisoners their presumed mission. Torturer had no interest in information; his questions were unintelligible. His genius, his interest, was torture. He was the boss and his cadre didn't care.

The camp was at the closed end of a jungle canyon, protected on three sides by high cliffs and dense vegetation, accessed by a narrow foot path winding downhill. On the rare no-rain, no-overcast days The Priest figured out that sun, south and Marines lay in the direction of the path. Food was meager. Water was rain. He had to get out. Monkeyface gave him the chance.

Night, pouring rain, a waterfall of blackness. Monkeyface, bored with sentry duty, came poking with his bayonet. The Priest avoided the first jab. The second, he grabbed the blade and yanked down viciously, pulling the startled VC's hand into the cage. He grabbed Monkeyface's wrist, yanked down again. Monkeyface's nose cartilage, smashing into a bamboo bar, knifed up into his brain. He was instantly dead. The Priest had a badly cut hand and the razor sharp bayonet.

He quickly, silently sliced his way out of the cage, dragged the corpse into deeper darkness and stripped it. He cut a deep slash between the upper ribs, dug his hand into the chest and ripped out the heart. He held it aloft in delicious victory then took a huge bite from it. He threw the remains into the jungle. He forced himself into Monkeyface's too-tight pants and shirt, picked up the AK-47 and went hunting.

He moved silently through the rain-misted darkness. He left thirteen Vietcong throats cut in silence as they slept in bloody vengeance. He kept Torturer for last. No sleeping death for him.

The Priest smashed him in the temple with the AK-47, dragged him outside his tent, sat him against a tree trunk, tied his arms behind him around the tree, gagged him then sat down to wait. Torturer's first sight on opening *his eyes: The Priest honing the bayonet.*

The Priest knifed Torturer's pants and shirt off. When he resisted, The Priest smashed the butt of the bayonet into his temple. Kneeling, he made a careful, six inch, horizontal cut in Torturer's lower belly, reached in and pulled out a rope of intestines. He draped them over the screaming man's thigh. If Paco's Apache stories were accurate, it should take four or five agony filled days for this motherfucker to die.

He made one last turn around the camp. He cut the hearts from all the dead and piled them at the foot of the torture stake. He cut one souvenir ear from each dead VC and both from Torturer. The cages were empty. Torturer had killed his last GI yesterday. The Priest slipped off into the heavy, wet darkness and Vietcong legend.

The Priest knew that his mind had gone. The damage begun long ago was complete. The black cave that had haunted him since thirteen had swallowed his mind. He was operating in magic, mystery, in the long-avoided cave, in the snake state. Nothing painful, nothing denied, he was a soul apart— avenger.

It took seventeen days to make it back to the American fire base at Pleiku. When he could move, he glided through the hot, wet jungle. He dodged pa- trols, ate bugs, plants, roots. The AK-47 worked, but one shot and every VC within hearing would swarm him. He wouldn't chance it—if cornered, may- be, but not to eat. Grandma medicine healed his hand, streams gave him wa- ter. A night raid on a village gave up better clothes, sandals, a little food.

Night five—late, the glimmer of a campfire through tangled growth. On his belly he slithered to within nine feet of the temporary camp. Ten VC were packing it in for the night. They posted a sentry, rolled up in their thin blan- kets, slept. The Priest lay log-still for two hours watching. Only eyes moving. The Sentry fought sleep. Bug sounds and night animal cries kept them com- pany.

The Priest slid up behind the sentry fast, silently. Left hand over his mouth and nose and slipped the bayonet in under the right ear, three and a half inches into the brain. Death instant, silent. He killed his way around the camp, cut throats the trail.

He used a machete to hack out a large stake, made a cross, drove it in the ground then arranged the corpses, heads against the cross into a macabre flower pattern. He harvested hearts and put them as gags in dead mouths. Several trips into the bush moved all useful gear, except what he needed, into a pile. He rigged a workable timer fuse with a candle and gunpowder to hand grenades and slipped away. Just before dawn a satisfying explosion told him that the VC would soon find the destroyed cache and his message. His legend would grow.

Day eight—making his way cautiously from tree to tree along an un-named riverbank. The jungle was dense, vines, bushes and trees growing right out of the waters edge. A rifle shot from nowhere whanged off his hip-carried canteen and knocked him ass over tea kettle into the river.

He hit the water and let his equipment pull him down, swam thirty or forty yards downstream underwater and slowly surfaced just his eyes and nostrils, under an overhanging root cluster.

A VC patrol was spread out on both sides of the stream, poking long sticks into every crevice they could see along the bank. Those they couldn't reach with sticks they fired into with rifles. They blasted a floating log mid river. They were moving downstream toward The Priest. The slow moving, mud filled brown water had became a dangerous hiding place.

Salvation floated down the middle of the river. The Priest eased under-water and slowly, carefully, avoiding any splash or movement of his new hiding place, he surfaced inside the hollowed-out rotting carcass of a water buffalo. The air, if you could call it that inside the carcass, was putrid, thick, eye-burning. Floating just under the surface, nose and eyes only above wa-ter, he drifted with the carcass downstream away from the VC.

He knew he'd made it when in frustration one of the VC loosed a volley of automatic fire into the buffalo's carcass. The only reaction they got was the slow turning of the carcass in the brown water; the Priest too low in the water to be hit by the fire. He continued to drift in the disgusting stink until the carcass ran aground two hundred yards downstream, well away from the patrol. He stayed inside the decaying haven till dark.

Clothed in assorted scraps of captured uniform, carrying a VC backpack, the AK-47 and the bayonet, dark skin jungle burned, hair wild under a black rag, eyes feral-cat-intense, he walked up to the sand-bagged, barbed wire protected gate to the base at Pleiku. American accented profanity served as password.

He'd been missing for forty-seven days—six on patrol, twenty-four in captivity, seventeen returning to base. In a place where insanity was the norm and acid-induced behavior typical, his return caused little comment. He spent a couple of days lying to an intelligence officer, the only kernel of truth the capture, death and dying of his Recon Team.

He explained his escape on the stupidity of VC guards and his unharmed walk through the jungle on his Marine Survival training. Nothing about his contribution to the war's body count. The string of dried ears on his belt told the story. This deep in the war, ears were common souvenirs. There were no hard questions.

The Priest made sure the paper pushers notified Paco that he was among the living—he'd have bet a year's pay Paco never doubted it for a second—got himself assigned to a new Recon Team and began deep incursion patrols into VC land. He had juked his service number and the spelling of his name enough so that the Marine Corp computers and their stoned operators lost him. He spent some of the happiest months of his life. Killing.

The Priest thought of it as his Hearts and Flowers Campaign. He went out with his unit and after the first patrol firefight—all okay, quiet. The Priest vanished, alone, into the jungle. He stayed out twenty three days spreading VC death in ever more macabre ways.

A scouting unit found. Seven of them, hanged. Cause of death: severed spinal cords, hearts cut out and stacked on a crude stone altar. Bodies swayed in a circle, looking down, mourning their hearts.

Another jungle clearing, birds singing, rain dripping, sunlight shafts through the high canopy. Twenty eight VC corpses naked in a circle, arranged head to toe, eyes heavenward, a pebble on each, arms outstretched and twenty eight hearts stacked central in a maggot-eaten pyramid.

When the VC unit commander who found this camp got his bowels under control, he ordered autopsies. Cause of death: ingestion of a deadly snake poison, probably in the water ration—death agonizing, hearts removed post-mortem.

VC terror increased. Something was in the fucking jungle. Silent, invisible, killing with a savage depravity till now reserved to themselves. The Priest was intoxicated with death—victorious, sacred creative death.

Every twenty to thirty days The Priest would come in, always at a firebase where he was unknown. Report, bullshit the record keepers, get reassigned, resupplied, hang out with his new unit until they went out, then vanish into the jungle alone. Had the Brass known his body count they'd have asked the CIA to clone him.

15

In spite of the upstairs maneuvering by Nolan, Brenner continued to carry the ball on the Skinner Case. Pressures to wrap it up were enormous and growing and Brenner was calling on Jimmy with increasing frequency. Jimmy loved it. Jimmy, Brenner and Doc were meeting in Doc Jensen's office.

The office was a flawless reflection of the quiet, precise man who was conducting the meeting. It was painted a stark white, the furniture the best of fifties and sixties Scandinavian design, the sparse art on the walls, good prints of Mondrian and Albers. His desk was a large slab of birch balanced on two thick glass panels.

Each item on its uncluttered top was laid out as if for an imminent operation. None of it county issue. Doc, rumor had it, was worth a lotta dough. Him or his wife of twenty-seven years.

Doctor John Jensen had come to the US with his family when he was twelve years old. They had settled in northern Minnesota where his father became a successful lumberman. Young Jensen grew up in that hard, cold climate.

It came as no surprise to his family when he decided to follow his grandfather into medicine. From the many universities that accepted his application, he had chosen Stanford in Southern California. As he put it, "I want to go somewhere with more than one day of summer."

He was the number two man in the L.A. County Medical Examiner's Office and essentially ran the operation. Dr. Johnathan Myer, the head of the department, and Jensen had long ago worked out an arrangement that suited both men. Jensen would run the place, brilliantly, and Myer would be the public face.

Brenner, "Doc, you got anything new for us on The Skinner?"

"The DNA results from Washington came in. They tell us the three victims are from Southeast Asia. Possibly Vietnamese and from the aggregate previous wounds to the bodies, it's probable that they were in combat. Our side or VC, no way of telling. It's possible that they aren't veterans. A lot of civilians got shot up in that war.

"All three killed the same time of day, about sunrise. Oh, there is one thing—the plant poison. I won't go into the technical details but what it does is immobilize the victim's voluntary muscle control. Beyond the immobilization, which could last for many hours, it is basically harmless. What did you get from the FBI Profiling Lab?"

Brenner, "Mostly the same old, same old. Dysfunctional family, twenty-five to forty-five years old, a loner, might still live with or near his parents, you know the drill. The thing that hit them is there seems to be no sexual component to any of this."

Doc, "Tough to tell, but I think I agree with that. Working with partial, very clean bodies makes it iffy, but they don't feel like sexual killings and we have absolutely no evidence to suggest otherwise."

Brenner, "They did pick up on Jimmy's idea of the similarity to Aztec ritual slaughter. They point out that our perp is sending a message, to whom or what they don't guess."

Jimmy, "They have any idea how this guy mimics Aztec ritual so closely?"

Brenner, "No, though they do point out that there is enough research material available that if you wanted to study it, you could do what this creep is doing."

Doc, "This Vietnamese angle; no missing persons reports from Little Saigon?"

Brenner, "None, I've checked with the Sheriff's department, local jurisdictions, put in one of our Vietnamese people undercover, so far, nothing. If they're illegal or ex-VC, their community won't report missing people to law enforcement. They look after their problems themselves. Keep a very, very low profile."

Jimmy, "What about that? Thousands and thousands of boat people made their way here. Maybe some ex-GI has decided to get some revenge and shooting them isn't dramatic enough."

Doc, "This bird has got a more complex agenda, something deeper at work here."

Brenner, "Could be, Doc, but if it is a Vet doing VC, his agenda don't matter a whole hell of a lot."

"It does if it leads you to a way of understanding and finding him."

Doc leaned back in his chair and proceeded to light his pipe.

Jimmy, following his lead, lit up a Camel, "Doc, you got any clout out at the VA hospital? Anybody you'd trust enough to keep their mouth shut and to run this Vet idea by them, at least get a little feedback?"

"Maybe. I'll check with a couple of guys I know over there. We'll run into all kinds of confidentiality issues, and besides, there is nothing to say that our guy isn't totally healthy and laying brick in Pomona. Hell, he could be any one of the tens of thousands of guys who came home and appear perfectly normal."

As Jimmy and Brenner walked to their cars, Jimmy brought up Nolan. "How you holding up under Nolan's bullshit?"

"Ah, what'cha gonna do? He's a prick and everybody in the department knows it except the Chief. The good thing is he ain't good enough to take over this case and politically he's too savvy to try. He'll stay on the sidelines and try to bitch it up, if he can do that and not get caught. He can't afford to lose his place on the ladder. If the Chief leaves it in my lap, he's gotta back me."

"Anything I can do?"

"Nah, let's just catch this fuck. We can all go home laughing. Oh, Sally sends love and thanks for the birthday present. You gonna send me ear plugs to go with it?"

16

Millie had done the research on Rosa Dempsey, the San Quentin connection and Mustafa. When Jimmy got in the office that afternoon, she had a preliminary report on his desk. She gave Jimmy a rundown.

"I talked to one of her assistants, Rosa's that is. She told me that Rosa got interested in Mustafa through an old-time liberal lawyer friend, name withheld, who keeps in touch with an aging client up at Quentin.

"Seems Mustafa got close to this guy in Quentin, sucked up good and convinced him of his revolutionary fervor, wants to help his community, do good for the poor, you know the spiel. Anyway, Rosa got talked into a few big-time money raising parties. She kept the publicity low key because, according to the assistant, she didn't really quite trust Mustafa. What the hell, raise a couple of hundred thousand, two hundred fifty thou, maybe it'll go where its supposed to and do some good or it doesn't, what harm's done? None of the donors will miss it. Rosa is phasing it out, still doesn't trust the guy."

Jimmy, "Word on the street is that Mousie raised thirty five or forty K. Your figure confirms what Alison Reed told me. That Panther in the joint might not like that much. Using his lawyer buddy to set up a scam—benefitting Mr. Mousie to the tune of two hundred K plus. Well, well, the plot thickens, or did somebody already say that? Mousie, your dick is in the wringer and I'm ready to turn the crank. Millie, you are the best!"

"Yes, I am, and your redneck roots are showing, Mr. Jimmy Santos."

"Yep, they sure are, did you get the names of that ex-Panther and his lawyer? Silly question, of course you did."

"Rufus Clackum." It was three days later; Jimmy was back in San Pedro. Ki-kkoa had gone through his guard dog routine. Mshobe again had prevailed. Common sense told her that if Jimmy had access to their money, Mustafa had to listen.

Mustafa now leaned against the rusty truck. Jimmy wondered if it ever moved, or was even capable of moving on its own. Probably not. The sun was cooking the street, empty except for Jimmy and Mousie. Not a breath of breeze stirred the limp palm fronds. The name Rufus Clackum had hit Mustafa like a fist.

"I went up to Quentin yesterday, had a long talk with old Rufus, he doesn't get many visitors up there these days. I brought him greetings from Ron Green-leaf and you, of course. He seemed surprised at so much attention. Mentioned that you never wrote to him, mystified him a bit, I think. He said—"

"Man, what you tryin' to do to me? I don't give a fuck what that old man—"

"You don't get it do you, Mousie? I'm not trying to do you, I've done you. Now shut up and listen for once in your miserable life. I talked to Greenleaf, Clackum's lawyer and longtime friend, the man you used to get next to Rosa Dempsey. I told him Rosa wanted a report on where the donated money was going. He had no problem with that because you'd done such a fine con on these people, they believed you were on the up and up. He—"

"Hey, man I am, I'm—"

"You want to keep talking, or do you want to hear how deep in the shit you really are?"

Jimmy's lightweight khaki poplin suit, pale blue shirt and foulard tie seemed to defy the sun's heat. His sunglasses reflected Mousie's growing agitation.

"Okay, okay, I'm listening." Sweat was forming two darkening circles on the tank top under Mousie's arms. His neck, chest and forehead were glistening with beads of sweat.

"So, I had this chat with Greenleaf, told him pretty much what he wanted to hear, he called and set up a meet between Clackum and me. I spent a day on it, up to Quentin and back. Clackum was real pleased to hear how good you were doing, how you're helping the community and all. He talked about you as the son he will never have, seemed real proud of you, Mousie."

"That old guy believes what he wants. I don't owe him nothin'."

Mousie looked like his skin was crawling with spiders, eyes darting, sweat running from under his headband.

"The money's going to the kids, man, right where it's supposed to. You—"

"Cut the shit, Mousie, I talked to Rosa's assistant, that group has given you two-hundred, forty-seven thousand dollars and change. Your pals are bragging all over San Pedro how you've spent over forty K on your programs here. That makes me wonder where the other two hundred K are. What'ya think, Mousie, under your mattress, maybe?"

"Ah, you got it all wrong man, that assistant, she's lyin', I ain't got no two hundred forty grand from them people, nothin' like that."

"Mousie, Mousie, we could stand here all day and argue, but I don't find your company that interesting. You ever hear that advertising slogan, 'Reach out and touch someone,' well, I'm going to tell Clackum the truth. How you've used him. Made him look like a senile, soft, old fool. Used his name and his thirty year friendship with Greenleaf to con two-hundred forty K out of Greenleaf's friends.

"I think Clackum will then reach out and when he touches you, it's gonna sting. What do you think? Remember that dude from Watts last year, the one they pulled outta the Catalina Channel, been used as shark bait. Rumor had it he'd tried to screw one of the brothers safely locked up in Quentin, name was Mohammed, wasn't it?"

"Shit man, I ain't done—"

Mousie pulled off his headband and used it to wipe the sweat out of his eyes. His hair hung greasy and damp over his ears.

"Sure, Mousie, sure. Can't have you winding up in the Channel, can we? Now here's what we are gonna do. You and I are going to your bank, safety deposit box, mattress, wherever the fuck you've got that two hundred K stashed. Then you and I are going to pay a visit to the pastor of that African AME Church down the block. You're gonna become the biggest single donor in Church history.

"You are then going to sit down and write a very courteous letter to Mr. Don Singleton at Sony Studios, expressing your regrets that you will be unable to assist him with his scheduled shoot in San Pedro. Press of community work, etc. And, lastly you are going to forget the name Rosa Dempsey. I think she can bear your abandonment. Is this all clear, anything I need to repeat?"

"How I know you keep yo' mouth shut—still shop me to Clackum, the cops?"

"You don't. Life's a bitch, but then you know that. Let's hit it Mousie, you got a busy day. Look at the bright side, two hundred grand to that Church and you become a bigger hero."

Jerry Martin returned Jimmy's call at five-thirty the next day. No hello, no how are you, just, "Jimmy, what the hell did you do to that guy? Singleton got a hand delivered letter this morning; Mustafa wishing us well with the shoot, saying his time was taken up with church work, would be happy to help in any way we requested, emphasis on requested."

"We had a 'come to Jesus' chat, he realized he was in over his head." Jimmy gave Martin an abbreviated rundown on what had happened. "I convinced Mousie that I had talked to Clackum and Greenleaf, from there on it was all downhill."

"You didn't talk to them?"

"Why spend your money on a trip to Quentin?"

"He didn't question that?"

Jimmy leaned back in his office chair and put his feet up on the desk.

"Nah, he's such a bullshit artist, it never occurred to him that I would run a scam by him, too much ego in the way."

"Can't he check?"

"What's he gonna do, call up Clackum and ask him if I've been up there talking about what a fool Mousie'd been making of him? I don't think so. He'll just write this one off. He's probably running some other scam already."

"You got that right. Send us a bill and have an extra martini for me tonight. Susan finally got around to those. Call me, come over next week for lunch."

"You got it. See ya."

17

Jimmy walked over to the office window. A pretty lady crossed the street below. Jimmy thought of Alison Reed. Wonder if I should call her and let her know that Mousie is history. Call her 'cause I'd like to talk to her. Nah, shit! Just a case of 'look ma, no hands.' Want to brag a bit. See how good I am. Well, what's wrong with that? Good job. Saved Sony a bundle and her picture one huge pain in the ass. Not a bad day's work. What the hell, fool, you've been thinking about her everyday. Enough with the loner bit. Pick up the phone and call her. He did.

Jimmy thought they all looked about fourteen, the kids running around Alison's office. The one on the reception desk, the self-important one scurrying past, arms loaded with scripts. The copy machine operator, seen through an open door behind the reception area. The short, dark, terrier of a guy who eventually appeared and said, "Hi, Mr. Santos, I'm Eric, Alison's assistant. Alison said come on back, can I get you coffee, water?"

Jimmy thought, Mr. Santos, that's my father. He said, "No thanks, we're on the way to lunch—you have a big apprentice program here?"

"Not at the moment, later in the year we have some from AFI or USC, but right now it's just the staff. Oh, you mean everybody looks young. Most of us are twenty-three to twenty-five, around there. Mary at the front desk is older—twenty seven."

Jesus, thought Jimmy, 'older', well maybe on the kid's side of thirty, twenty-seven didn't look so young. To Eric, "All film school graduates?"

"Most, but not all, a little bit of everything—Mary's a biology grad. I've got an MBA from Harvard. Here's Alison's office."

Alison dropped a hair brush into an open drawer, closed it and came around the desk, hand outstretched in welcome; she seemed wired. "Jimmy, come in, did Eric offer coffee, water—do you want anything?"

Nerves were zinging all over the place. His and hers. Quick little glances back and forth. Probing appraisals. Insecurities and confidence ricocheting between them. Jimmy thought, my god, she's even better looking than I remembered and I remember beautiful. She must have guys lined up for her.

"No thanks."

In an effort to relax the tension, he gestured to the office; then ran three sentences together and realized he was making no sense.

"You want to show me around before or after lunch—this place is jumping. That marquee is something." Jimmy pointed to the stucco structure covered with lights that filled her window. "Did you pick this office because of it?"

Alison's office was in the brick office building at the corner of Broadway and Third Street in Santa Monica. Her windows overlooked the Third Street Promenade and the Thirties Cineplex Odeon movie marquee. She stood at the window and looked down at the sun blazing on the handsome stuccoed structure, then turned and smiled at Jimmy.

"No, it was the empty one when we started. I fell in love with it. It reminds me of what this business used to be...I made reservations for lunch, Italian. Is that okay?"

"Sure. It looks like the office is busy as hell."

"Yeah, my picture has been green lit and there's three others in various stages of pre-production right now. Another two or three in development. This company is hot. At least for now—we'll see after the next release. Come on, I'll show you around."

Jimmy thought there was a disconcerting air of impermanence about the place. It was as if the whole operation could fold tomorrow; everybody could pack their personal stuff in a small suitcase or an empty liquor box and move down the hall or across town to another production company, do the same job without missing a beat.

All the equipment was brand new, rented, of course. Maybe that was it—the sameness about everything, no history, no personality; it hadn't been around long enough. The formica furniture, beige file cabinets, black Merlin phone system, lots of stunted plants.

Jimmy thought, I'll bet there's a place in L.A. where you can call up and say, bring me a movie office. All they'd ask is how big and next day they'd pull up in a big truck and unload your office, right down to the bottled water, droopy plants and coffee machine—take it away just as quick.

Alison, "Freddy Ruben, producer and owner of this company, made a fortune in oil leases or something, sold out, collected his billions and decided he wanted to make movies. Hired a couple of guys who presumably knew how, managed to out-bid the studios on a good script or two, hired more people, and now he's a player. His first release, Bobtail, with the then-unknown comedian, George Shadrak, made a hundred twenty million, domestic. Now he's hot and totally addicted, its like gambling to these guys."

"How do you fit in here?"

"I was offered a terrific script, worked with the writer to polish it, convinced Julia Williams' agent that it was for her and brought the package to Ruben. He'll spend almost enough to do it right and mostly leave me alone. They set me up with an office here and an office for my assistant; they can look over my shoulder, we share all the production facilities, everything gets charged to the picture."

"What's it about?"

"A love story set on the Oregon coast during Prohibition. The people are involved with rum running—bringing illegal booze down the coast from Canada. Vancouver to the rocky coves of the Oregon coast and the harbor in San Pedro. Come on, enough about movies, let's eat. I'm dying to hear what you did about that Mousie person."

"What you'd call a wrap, I think."

They were in I Cugini's, an Italian place on Ocean, seated at an outdoor cafe table that overlooked the Pacific and swam in carbon monoxide from traffic. Outside so Jimmy could smoke, not missing the irony of adding to the pollution. While they waited for their order to arrive, Jimmy apologized for sounding like the stereotype of the LAPD cop at their first meeting. Assured her that Mousie was history. Jimmy smiled at her look of mild astonishment.

"Just like that? He just went away? There has to be more to it than that. C'mon, spell it out for me." Alison leaned into Jimmy; smiling, her body language reinforcing the request.

"Okay, but this stays between us. Jerry's the only other person who knows the details."

"Promise; now what happened?" The waiter served their food—rare tuna steak for him, large Caesar salad for Alison, and a shared bottle of Pinot Grigio.

The smile of anticipation on her face reminded Jimmy of birthday parties. Jimmy relaxed back into his chair and between, bites of the tuna and sips of the excellent Pinot Grigio, laid it all out for her. He was blushing when he finished explaining the con he had run on Mousie. He lit a Camel as Alison burst into laughter.

"You conned a con man. I can stop worrying about Seascape?"

Her relief was apparent in the smile that illuminated her eyes. She gestured a toast to Jimmy with her glass of Pellegrino.

"Lunch is on me."

"Thanks. I don't know if you can stop worrying, but you can worry about things that matter."

The tension between them had relaxed as Jimmy told her about Mousie and the Skinner case, and they drifted into comfortable small talk, common to all in that wacky world, about the 'biz'. New projects, recent openings they'd seen, who was directing what, the newest green-lighted projects, which studio exec was moving to what job and when. Last week's grosses and predictions about Friday's openings.

Alison told Jimmy in greater detail about Seascape and her hopes for the picture. The comfort level between them became that of friends, heightened by a newly met, attractive, man-woman, electrical fizz. Two hours zipped by unnoticed until Alison glanced at Jimmy's watch. She started.

"Jesus." She checked her stainless steel man's Rolex and jumped up, bumping the table.

"I'm late for a casting session. Sorry, you get this tab and dinner is on me when it's convenient for you. Thank you, you've made my day. Call me. No, I'll call you."

The last said over her shoulder as her long stride carried her through the opening to the sidewalk. She had dashed out before Jimmy could say a word. He just sat there staring at her very pleasant, disappearing back. Damn, he thought, that is the most exciting woman I've met in years. Beautiful, independent, talented, what in hell does she see in me? Wonder if she'll really call? Hope so. He stubbed out his smoke and signaled to the waiter for the check.

18

A Sunday afternoon on Cabrillo Beach in San Pedro, the site of the first white man's landing on the West Coast of California. 1542, a Spaniard, Juan Cabrillo. Picnics were ending, children and dogs yelping and running around, a few barbecue grilles still scenting the air with hot dog and hamburger smells. On the water, colorful sail boards flew in the stiff breeze. The setting sun was creating a pink light show in the western storm clouds. The day's heat was easing. Across the harbor, far enough to not intrude on the festive afternoon, the sulking grey bulk of industrial San Pedro.

The Priest sat with a mixed group of Mexican-Americans. He was well-fed from their grills and picnic baskets, their beer coolers. Three old women, one's older husband, a couple late middle-aged, a few in their late twenties, one woman with a baby on her lap and her tired older children. These Sunday afternoons were their way of putting away the week, enjoying the company of their families and friends. This public beach was theirs on this day. No Anglos, no bosses, no cops, no one calling them Spic; a recharging before the coming week, doing it all over again.

The Priest telling a story of the early days in the life of the Mexica. Obeying the orders of their god, Huitzilopochtli, Blue Hummingbird, they asked Achitometl, one of their current allies, for his beautiful daughter as a wife for Blue Hummingbird in a ceremony to worship Coatlique. Not understanding what this meant, he agreed.

His daughter went to Tizaapan, then-current home to the Mexica, where she was beautifully dressed, feasted and then sacrificed to Coatlicue, Serpent Skirt. A goddess of the underground, traditionally described as black, dirty, disheveled and of shocking ugliness, graphically represented with rattlesnake motifs. Following ancient custom, the daughter was flayed and her skin was worn by a priest in an agricultural rite symbolizing the renewal of life. Invited to participate in the ceremony, Achitometl recognized the skin of his daughter and—

As his voice continued the story for his people his mind wandered. He remembered the very early days with a shrink at the VA hospital.

"The small arms fire and the rain—bullets and rain drops. I felt maself fallin' back'ard in'tah the wet dark. GI next to me fell, covered mah face with his body, I couldn't breathe—GI's kept pilin' on us—buried in wounded, screamin' Americans. The VC came in when none'a us moved, slippin' in, in the rain, up close and puhsonal—AK-47s, full automatic, rock 'n roll loosed into the body pile. I didn', couldn' move. A round—"

A suet pudding of grey-haired woman dozed in the chair behind her desk; reading glasses slipped far down on her nose, mouth open and drooling.

Stupid bitch doesn't hear or believe a word I'm saying, thought The Priest. Making up all these hot war stories just for her, and she nods off. Probably into the smack locker now and then. I'm out of here.

He banged the front legs of his steel chair down onto the dirty tile floor and stood sharply. The old bag behind the desk started violently.

"Mr. Villa, I've asked you repeatedly not to do that, you know it startles me." She always acted as if The Priest's main concern in life was her peace of mind. "Is our hour over already? We were making such good progress."

"With your nappin', you mean?"

He always put on this phony black accent with her, made it easier for him to get away with bullshitting her, made it easier for her to treat him like shit. That seemed her joy in life, tormenting Vets who had to talk to her.

"Time for me to go sweet thang, gotta go make a livin' out there in th' real world, got my eye on a Seven-Eleven for tonight. You got any idea how much money's in them safes? Nothin' tween you an' a hunnert dollars 'cept a skinny guy or a fat girl with bad skin and teeth. Tha's how they want ads run—s'truth, I seen 'em."

"Good bye Mr. Villa see you in two weeks, Don't forget to sign out at the desk."

Olebitch, his name for her, was dozing again before he softly closed the door—couldn't give her too many shocks in one day, they might assign him a real shrink. Forget to sign out, not likely, only reason he came to this shithole twice a month was to sign out. That's what kept Uncle Sam's pension checks flowing his way, money that paid for his freedom, his camp up in the hills, his ability to avoid the human race. No, he wouldn't forget. But, it was a huge fucking drag—talking to some ugly, dried up, tight-assed Anglo bitch for an hour.

19

The fourth one—a woman, Nguyen Tranh. Leaving after a reading of Vietnamese poetry at the Vietnamese Community Center and heading for her car. The Priest had spotted her weeks before in Phu Bah's food court, talking with a group of VC men. She had been a VC captain, in charge of a tunnel supply dump. At night she wrote poetry or sang Vietnamese folk songs in the tunnels. She'd been wounded in the arm during the Tet offensive when a US unit stumbled into her tunnel. Fourteen grunts were killed by claymore mines boo-by-trapped in American bodies.

She was walking across a half lit parking lot towards her car when The Priest stood up from behind a parked car and sent his dart singing toward her left carotid artery. A slight movement of her head and the dart deflected off her brass bangle earring. She startled The Priest when, instead of running or screaming, she attacked.

All the men had been so easy he'd never considered defense. Now, here was this tiny tiger slashing at him. She kicked his right knee with such force that he almost went down. He slammed back into a parked car but managed to stay on his feet. She kept pressing the attack, raining martial arts strikes on his neck, chest and abdomen. Grim, totally silent, she was intent on killing him.

Coming out of his surprised stupor with increasing pain, The Priest forgot all his Marine training and brought a roundhouse punch up from the ground. He hit her square on the chin with everything he had. She dropped like a stone and lay still. Shaken, his hand probably broken, he fished another dart out of his belt pouch and pushed it into her neck. She relaxed, a rag doll at his feet. He gathered her up into his arms and stashed her in his van.

That she was female: immaterial. She was a warrior. Worthy, desired sacrifice. He had no hatred for the ex-VC. They were warriors, warriors that he knew. They were worthy of the Gods.

The days that followed were calmed by the knowledge that he was helping his people, he was making a world where their Gods would smile on them, give them a just, rightful place in the Anglo-dominated universe. Blood and harvested hearts would prepare the way.

2.0

Very late in the war, rumors trickled back to the Americans through captured VC; ghost stories of a phantom warrior, descendant of Genghis Kahn, riding the night mists, wafting through the jungle spreading terrorizing death. The typical GI's reaction: Right On, Brother.

A bored young Army Intelligence Lieutenant, Michael Graham, began tracking the rumors. The common threads were hearts and increasingly, brief fleeting sightings by the VC. This man, maybe a Marine, wanted credit, however subconsciously, for his war effort. Young Graham checked out bizarre happenings, mass killings, massacres of VC, where no known US forces were operating, anything however vague about hearts. As his file grew, so did his knowledge and description of the phantom warrior. The pins in his map clustered along the Ho Chi Min trail, north to Khe Sanh, south to the area of Pleiku.

He postulated a remarkably accurate scenario; radioed every firebase between Khe Sanh and Pleiku requesting info on any GI wandering in from the jungle with no dog tags, no recorded unit, fit for and requesting a new LURP or Recon assignment. Possible physical description: medium height, dark skin, black hair, green eyes. He signed the message with his firebase commander's name and sat back to wait.

Replies, half hearted and mostly bullshit trickled in; the tech sergeants who dealt with his request figured out what was going down and backed the mystery man.

As with many of life's efforts, this one was rewarded by pure luck. Graham saw the guy he was looking for in the chow line at his own base west of Dakto. The man standing quietly in the chow line was shirtless. Ropey muscles corded his arms and torso.

Even in this group of soldiers, his physical condition was outstanding. His alertness missed nothing, including Graham's attention. Of all the soldiers in line, he alone carried his captured AK-47, his trophy ears long abandoned as childish. One look into the guy's deranged green eyes and an hour's quiet interrogation convinced Graham that he was talking to the phantom warrior.

As they talked, Graham's cool, composed confidence relaxed The Priest. Too many crazed months alone in the jungle played their part. The Priest cracked open his mind a slit, allowing Graham the tiniest shard of his soul.

He told the Lieutenant how he got his nickname, The Priest. Other soul shards: VC deaths, a warrior's duty to his Gods, his nation, family, comrades. The style of death a warning to his enemies of his rage, his skill.

Graham thought, I'm fucked. I've caught this guy, a raving, fucking lunatic. A homicidal maniac and also a criminal embarrassment to the Marines and the US Government. A Solid Gold Hero to every Dog-face in Nam. Well, fuck, Francisco Villa, if that was really his name, your war was over.

Staying easy, calm, betraying nothing of his racing thoughts and revolted mind, Graham left the office for "two coffees" and summoned a medic, with sedative and four base MPs.

It almost didn't work. Overconfident of the four-to-one odds, the MPs crowded into the office in a group. The Priest took out the first two with an office chair and, when the other two rushed him, flying-kicked the one on his right with a crunching blow to the sternum, landed wrong and rolled against the wall.

MP Four thinking The Priest was hurt, pulled his forty-five and jammed it into The Priest's neck, screaming, "Freeze motherfucker, freeze!" The Priest uncoiled rattlesnake-quick, coming to his feet with MP Four's gun hand in his and The Priest's thumb between the gun's hammer and firing pin. MP Four couldn't fire. He was sent flying through the air to land in an unconscious heap at the Lieutenant's feet. The Priest back-fisted Graham sideways over the desk and made for the door, guarded only by the frightened medic.

The medic jumped aside as The Priest dashed through the door and, in a last-ditch attempt to salvage something, jabbed The Priest in the ass with the hypodermic needle. The Priest ran fifty feet into the compound and collapsed. Unconscious.

The Priest vanished from Vietnam as quietly as he had appeared.

The Priest came out of the drugs, head splitting, vomiting, terrified, strapped in a straight jacket on a gurney, locked in the mental ward on the palm-lined campus of the Veteran's Administration Hospital on Wilshire Boulevard in Los Angeles, California. A place that looked like a prosperous college campus in the tropics. A place where those who were allowed to walk the campus did so in a fog of cigarette smoke and drug-induced catatonia.

Graham had been purposefully vague filling out the commitment papers. He wanted to avoid anyone knowing what this crazy motherfucker had been up to on his unauthorized multi-year reign of terror. Graham wanted him out of the war, out of Nam, and mostly out of his goddamned life. Let some other asshole deal with him, keep him locked up for-fucking-ever.

But the VA didn't work that way. Overcrowded wards, filled with serious full-time wackos, allowed the marginal, the con men, those who could and did work the system, to hit the streets before their beds got warm. With orders to report twice a month for psychiatric counseling, The Priest joined the great disenfranchised on the streets of L.A.

The Priest hung out. The beach, sleeping under the stars. Freedom. He had a medical disability discharge and the lifetime pension that goes with it. The year was 1975, early September. The last thing he remembered in Nam was that cocksucker, Military Intelligence Lieutenant leaning over his stretcher calling him a homicidal maniac. He knew his mind was in bad shape. Now was a time to heal, a time to think.

The Priest's stories to his people, now a constant in his life, continued. "Tizoc was the King who followed Axayacatl. He was not a Warrior-King. He won no glory for his people, no captives for sacrifice. He was poisoned by his brother, Ahuizotl, in 1486. Ahuizotl was then the Tlaccatecatl, head of the military council. Four days after Tizoc's death the elective council met and appointed Ahuizotl as Tlatoani, King.

He became our people's greatest, most feared military leader, a truly heroic warrior. In his first campaign along the Gulf Coast, he brought home eighty thousand captives for sacrifice. At the rededication of the Great Pyramid of Tenochtitlan these captives were sacrificed.

It took four days. The great pyramid ran red. The plaza was ankle-deep in blood. The skull racks were full. Leaders from every neighboring state were invited to watch this demonstration of Ahuizotl's power, the power of his Mexica Nation. Ahuizotl used this sacrifice to terrorize the hearts of his enemies. He raised the level of violence to new heights—"

This story was being told by The Priest, in Spanish, to one hundred of his people. They were gathered in the shade on the grass just above the sand at Cabrillo Beach. Another sweltering Sunday afternoon.

A grey-haired old man, sitting close to The Priest, allowed his mind to wander. The old man's skin was the color of an old saddle. His eyes an almost-black brown, hair turning white. He'd been to each of the story sessions over the summer. Every weekend. At first there were only three or four of us, now a hundred. This young man before us is special. He brings together the young and the old. A Shaman, a strong link to our almost-forgotten past. We must remember. It must not be allowed to die.

The old man smiled and squeezed the hand of the ancient, bent old woman who sat with him. The rest of the people sat in rapt attention, most hearing these stories for the first time. The Priest continued the story, "During his reign, Ahuizotl, more and more became Huitzilopochtli, the deified, mythical warrior-king. He continued to build his empire. He conquered cities and claimed much land and riches. He..."

———————

On his next visit to the VA, they'd switched shrinks on The Priest. The new one was a small, sixty-five-plus prune-faced Italian guy, Dr. Bart Annucci. The Priest fed him the same shit he'd given the Anglo bitch for years. At the end of the hour, Annucci, with no hint of anger or reproach suggested that next time, perhaps, The Priest might like to talk about something real.

For the first time, The Priest left the hospital with something to think about. Annucci reminded him of Paco, his grandfather—small, skinny, white hair—but it was more than the physical, something about the penetrating eyes, the intensity of his gaze. The Priest would think on it.

Time flowed. The Priest felt his mind healing. The sessions with Annucci; perhaps he was ready to talk to someone. A deeper calm—Annucci a Shaman?—who the hell knew? The Priest began to talk to Annucci. Nothing much, at first, or so The Priest thought—disconnected bits of boyhood—Mexica story fragments—early feelings about Nam—high school—his Nam capture, cages, torture—not the killings, never the killings—thoughts in shell burst fragments—shrapnel of the mind.

Slowly The Priest's trust began to grow. His evasions and lies were still there, they always would be, but he touched on Shamanism; Annucci recommended a book, told him how to get a library card—use Annucci's address, he knew The Priest was living rough. Told him of the Westwood Library nearby to the east. Annucci didn't mention it again. The Priest told him of reading—returning the book. Annucci mentioned one on Mexican history. The Priest read it.

His book education had begun, books to flesh out Paco's stories. Voraciously he attacked the library. Book after book, English and Spanish, the history of his people. Devoured by lantern light in the Topanga Canyon camp, by day on the beach, in the woods.

In recent years, the librarians had taught him to use the computer. Bad weather days he holed up for hours researching His People. Paco would laugh his ass off. The Priest on the Internet. Maps, atlases; they gave form, structure to his world. Here on a silent screen he could explore the spatial relationships between his cave, his Temple, the Hospital, his city.

He began to seek out his Mexican community: the blue collar, the unemployed, the forgotten not-seen Mexican, the illegal immigrant always in fear of the Feds, the working people sending their money back to Mexico. He looked a little odd—too tall, an oddness in the green eyes—but his people accepted him. His Mexican Spanish was excellent.

He began to tell stories—the marketplace, a bench on the street, the bus, in a small bar where he had a beer. Anywhere his people gathered they loved his stories. Largely raised in an oral tradition, swift in imagination, they took flight on The Priest's stories.

They recognized, before he did, his role as Shaman. He was living his ancestral job of centuries. It felt good. The people encouraged him, gave him small gifts, fed him, bought the cervezas. He allowed his hair to grow longer, no more Marine Corp whitewalls. For the first time in years he paid some attention to his appearance, keeping his clothes clean: faded jeans, work shirts, boots and always a large Buck knife sheathed on his belt. A remnant weapon, legal but lethal.

After one of his stories over a beer in a smoky cantina, one of the guys asked if he'd want work the next day, cash off the books, cleaning up an Anglo's yard. Without much thought, The Priest agreed and joined the casual, pickup labor force that maintains the landscape of L.A.

When physical needs demanded he visited Angelina, a Latina hooker in East L.A. She had picked him up after one of his story sessions in a bar.

The years passed. Slowly, with no plan or direction The Priest began to join the world. He still lived in his cave up in Topanga Canyon and when he felt the need visited his Temple in the San Gabriel Mountains.

With money from the pickup jobs he occasionally rented a cheap motel room for the night and stood in the shower for hours. He rented a post office box and wrote to Paco for the first time since his discharge from Nam. Weeks later he got a letter from Paco, dictated to his new disciple, an orphaned Mexican kid Paco had found in his little border town. The letter, of course, also told a story—Aztec messengers running to Cortez.

22

A C above high C pierced the summer Saturday night with the pure intensity of an acetylene flame. The scruffy trumpet player was rocketing hot brass licks high over all the other entertainers and noisy crowds on Santa Monica's Third Street Promenade; the place was swarming with people. The trumpet player's long black hair flopped in his face, his scrawny frame seemed incapable of such energy. His wrinkled white shirt, sleeves rolled up over the forearms, hung loose on him. A large crowd had stopped to listen to the astonishing virtuosity pouring from his instrument. With total nonchalance the slight, unshaven man held them, rhythmically swaying to old show tunes in the soft summer evening.

"What on earth is a man with that talent doing, playing here?" Alison stood close and spoke into Jimmy's ear.

"He's got a serious jones. Smack. Been here off and on for about three years. Disappears from time to time. Gets a real gig, tours with a band, then gets hooked again and comes back here."

Jimmy moved to the front of the crowd and dropped a ten in the open trumpet case. The trumpet player bobbed his head in thanks, recognition. Jimmy rejoined Alison and they listened to the last notes of the set then continued wandering.

"How do you know things like that?"

She took his arm as they looked in the architectural bookstore window. Jimmy smiled at her in the glass reflection, "I talked to him one slow night, between sets. Lonely guy, originally from Saint Louis. Been playing since he was a kid. I like talking to interesting-looking strangers. People who excel at what they do, love. Learn all sorts of things that way."

Jimmy had on a black silk hopsacking blazer over a blue chambray work shirt, jeans and loafers. Alison wore tan linen slacks and jacket over a white silk blouse, brown flats. Her Kathryn Hepburn look, she called it, laughing. Jimmy thought she looked better than Kathryn ever did. The looks from many guys on the Promenade seemed to agree.

Alison had called two days before just as Jimmy was leaving the office; almost seven PM. She reminded him of her dinner promise, inquired about his schedule and suggested Petruchio's in Santa Monica. They made the date. The conversation drifted to her work, the status of Seascape. This and that, easy and relaxed. He smiled as he hung up the phone. A strictly no-BS lady. Magical.

It had been an evening filled with sexual frisson between two attractive, confident people. Drawn to each other but cautious, willing to take time, explore. Little or no first date tension. Petruchio's had been busy but not frantically so. Oso Bucco for Jimmy; Pasta Primavera for Alison. A martini each before and a bottle of excellent red with dinner. Cappuccinos and Sambuca.

Good conversation; the hilarious goings-on in the narrow world of Hollywood, local political races, a book Alison had recently read. Jimmy lightly touched on the Skinner case, outlining his unique function vis-a-vis the LAPD and his first impressions of Rod Fulo. Both were feeling mellow and enjoying each other. They'd decided a walk on the Promenade would be good. The trumpet player was an unexpected bonus.

Alison glanced at her watch, "Well, I'm going to have to call it a night. Seascape's writer is in town for weekend script work and we're starting again at eight tomorrow. She wants to play golf in the afternoon. Life is going to get very busy for me over the next few months. We start shooting in three weeks."

"I'll walk you to your car. Time for another drink?"

"I'd better not; notes to go over before bedtime. You go ahead. I'll be okay."

"I'm sure you'd be fine. But, if it's okay with you, I'll make sure you're safely in your car."

"Is this a detective's bodyguard thing?"

"No, more an I-want-the-extra-few-minutes-with-you thing."

"I like that." Alison smiled and took Jimmy's hand.

They walked down Arizona and turned into the alley access to the parking garage. At her car, Alison turned and kissed Jimmy lightly on the lips.

"Thanks for the best evening in a long time. I'm giving an at-home kick-off party for Seascape next Saturday. There'll be a bunch of people you know, including Jerry. Will you come?"

Jimmy grinned, "I'd like to see you before that. Is that possible?"

"I don't think so. Much as I'd like to, I've got meetings, casting, script preparation, a hundred things. I seldom get out of the office before ten, eleven at night. There's just not enough time right now."

"Then Saturday it is. I'll call you mid-week for the details. It'll give me an excuse to talk to you. Good night, safe drive."

"Ciao!"

Jimmy watched as she drove out of the garage. As he walked to the elevator and his car he thought, maybe, just maybe, this is can be something really good; a lady to spend a lot of time with. No more nights sitting alone, classical music on the radio, drinking Tecate, smoking and looking for something to read.

23

She was lying on the plaza of the Los Angeles Children's Museum. Practically in the shadow of the Los Angeles and Federal law enforcement establishment. Like the others, her body formed a headless, handless crucifix. Beyond her head, spelled out in colorful childlike lettering, the name of the museum. Ridiculous contrast to her terribly mutilated body.

Crime scene techs had put up a screen around the body to confound the few TV crews down on the street. Uniformed cops were busy keeping them and the other press behind the crime scene tapes.

Tiny in death, she was diminished further by the same barbarity worked on the three men before her. The same MO as the Skinner killings, except this one was a woman. An anonymous caller had phoned it in to 911. Brenner had called Jimmy at five forty-five AM. It was now about six thirty. The sun was well up on what promised to be another scorcher of a day. It already felt like eighty-five degrees.

Jimmy to Brenner, "I don't fucking get this. Serial killers don't change sex of victims. It just ain't done—make sense to you?"

"Nope. Copycat seems out unless it's one of ours. I don't for a minute believe that. None of it makes sense to me at all."

Jimmy moved in for a closer look, "Those look like old bullet wounds in the upper arm—there. She's consistent in that at least."

"Yeah. Bullet wounds, stab wounds, one with shrapnel in his ass. This buncha' victims already had a hard life before they ran into this guy."

"Well we got one continuing thread—wounds? Soldiers, guerrillas—what the hell, whose?"

"Excuse me, Lieutenant Brenner," one of the Uniforms interrupted, "We got a guy over here. Think you might want to talk to."

"Sure Sarah, what's up?" Brenner seemed to know every person on the Job. "What'cha got?"

"Street guy, says he saw a van. He was sleeping over there in that cardboard box, sleeping bag and all, he woke up, the place is swarming with cops, ambulances. He stumbled out into Dan's arms. Scared the shit outta both of them. We got him over at a black and white if you want to have a chat with him."

"You bet, let's do it. C'mon Jimmy."

The guy spoke with a stingy voice, squeaking it out of his frail frame. "Fucker woke me up, man," taking it as a personal affront, "Pulled in here, headlights shining right into my place, you know? Got out, opened the back, messed around there, got back in, drove off, you know? Didn't turn the headlights on. Dangerous, could'a hit somebody in the dark, you know, man?"

Brenner, "I don't think he'd give a shit. What'd he look like—what's your name?"

"Name's Paul, Paul Sayer."

For a street guy this one didn't seem too bad, thought Jimmy; smell not too ripe, halfway clean, eyes clear, not strung out on shit. Maybe, just maybe we're going to catch a break. The man was about twenty five, five ten, skinny with scraggly blond hair, slightly mad but not round the bend. He leaned back against the police car somewhere between insolence and fear. He was scoping out Brenner's gold badge hanging from his jacket pocket.

"An, an' I don't know what he looked like, man, he was always on the other side'a the van from me in th' fuckin dark, man, you know? Might as well been a fuckin' ghost, you know, all I know, he woke me up. The headlights flashed right over my place, man. I rolled over, there was this van pulling up, stopped, door opened, feet under, he closed the door, messed around the back, drove off. What'd he do, man? Woke me up, you know?"

Jimmy, "Yeah Paul, we know, interrupted your beauty sleep, out here communing with the stars in your box—but tell me about his feet. It was a half moon out here last night, clear, you musta seen something. Street light on the corner. You mentioned his feet. Tell me about them."

"What, c'mon man." Whining, "What'd he do?"

"Tell me about his feet, Paul, he barefoot, sandals, what?

"Boots, he had on boots, man, you know the kind you buy at the Army-Navy—what difference does that make?"

"Good, Paul, now what color?"

"Black man, shiny, real shiny black, man, all those boots are black, you know that."

Brenner, "What about his license plate, you see a number?"

"Nah, man, he turned all his lights off, its dark out here, plus I'm blinded from havin 'em in my eyes—all happened quick, man, in, out, mess around and out an' I—"

Jimmy, "Yeah, he woke you up, you were still half asleep. What about his height, you see his head over the van, through the windshield when he opened the door?"

"Man, what's wrong with you, you think I'm lying out here waiting for some dude come along, so I can describe him to you? I was out here—"

"Trying to sleep," supplied Brenner, "But think a minute, from under that hedge over there, through the windshield, you might have seen his head— think a minute—?"

Paul scratched his head, indicating thinking.

"Maybe, man, it seems like his head was inside the van—you know, lower than the back door top—I think."

Jimmy and Brenner kept at it but that's all Paul had to offer: dark van, black, shiny combat boots, medium height. They got the name of the shelter where Paul stayed occasionally so that they could find him again. Then ran some sight line checks, using a couple different emergency vans, guessed the guy at about 5-8 to 5-10.

Sometime earlier that week the City Department of Public works had dug up the street along the stretch where The Skinner parked. The asphalt patch was in place but a thin layer of clay residue stayed in the gutter. In it were two good tire tracks and three or four footprints. Brenner asked forensics to make casts. Their look said, "Duh."

Jimmy memorized both sets of tracks. Brenner was encouraged that, at last, somebody had finally seen the perp. They had the foot and tire tracks. Maybe Skinner was getting careless.

Tracks. When he was seventeen Doctor Ivey took him bear hunting in the North Carolina mountains. They spent a glorious fall week tracking a huge black bear that was killing local livestock. The rogue bear had decimated a sheep herd, terrorized local homeowners and was killing cattle when he could catch them.

Fall in the North Carolina mountains is one of nature's purest gifts to man. The air is invisible diamonds. The trees blaze with color. Reds, browns and yellows so deep rich and beautiful they make the heart ache; a riot of color against the cerulean blue of the sky, the blackness of the wet rock.

Jimmy and Doctor Ivey tracked the bear over the rugged mountains by day and camped where night found them. They spent the night hours in quiet conversation mostly about nothing. Some long-ago accident had marked the bear's right front foot. It made a distinctive footprint. On the fifth day they found him.

Jimmy shot the beast with a one hundred yard shot from his open iron sight, lever action 30-30. The shot killed him instantly. They skinned him, dressed out the meat and lugged hide and meat back to base camp on an improvised travois.

24

"I got a call from Dr. Jensen, Mr. Santos, but I still don't understand your exact position in this matter. Are you with the police?" Jimmy shifted in the hard chair, resisting the urge to light a smoke. They were in the office of Dr. Horace Tilley, head of the VA hospital.

Dr. Tilley's VA office reminded Jimmy of of his old Marine colonel's office; perfect for the head of the VA hospital. Grey steel, quartermaster issue desk, chairs and filing cabinets. All strictly military issue down to the Stars and Bars standing in the corner. Not a personal item in sight. A picture of Bill Clinton and the current head of the Veterans Administration centered on the wall behind his desk. The reek of Tilley's lunchtime bourbon hung on the air. Jimmy sat in one of the straight-backed, unpadded visitor's chairs; a hint not to waste Dr. Tilley's valuable time.

"Not exactly, I'm consulting with Lieutenant Brenner, LAPD Homicide. We've worked together in the past. We figured maybe you'd like it better if things weren't official, at least at first. Let me tell you what we think we've got and then you can tell me if you can help."

Jimmy ran it down for Tilley, outlining what they knew of the case and emphasizing the possible Vet's angle.

"It seems to me, Mr. Santos, that you are jumping to conclusions, clutching at straws—" Jimmy was wondering if he would string another cliche on that sentence when Tilley caught himself and tailed off with a shrug.

"Doctor Tilley, we need a place to start. I know this sounds like a fishing expedition, but if you're willing to go with my basic premise, this hospital is a good place to start. A Doctor here might have some knowledge of a man who fits my hypothesis. I realize you can't turn over files on my say-so, but maybe I could talk to your doctors. This hypothetical description might ring a bell with one of them."

"I'm going to have to give this some thought. I'll bring it up at our staff meeting tomorrow, see if any of our people are willing to talk to you. We're here to serve, but as I'm sure you understand, there are difficult ethical issues here. Our first duty is to our patients."

Awash in more cliches and realizing he had gotten all he was going to get, Jimmy rose, offered his hand. "Thank you, Doctor, I'll call you in a couple of days. We'll be most grateful for any help you and the hospital can give us on this."

He gave Tilley his card and left. Seething. Authority figures and alcohol. Bad memories.

———

All the adult men in his early life were hard drinkers. His Dad, Doc Ivey and the sculptor who lived down the road and tolerated his hundreds of hungry questions about art. The sculptor indulged in alcohol-driven rages. Doc got sloppy and maudlin. His Dad never drank during the week but the weekends could be rough. His dad always needed an extra couple stiff hits of Jim Beam before tackling a difficult job.

A Saturday morning. Jimmy about thirteen. It was his favorite time of the year. Fall, the crisp Georgia air, the deep haunting smell of pine trees preparing for winter. Someone nearby with an early morning wood fire burning, the smoke smell a deep bass note in the air.

Dad had decided it was time to slaughter and dress out the calf they'd raised for beef. He had started that Saturday morning early on with several serious hits of Jim Beam. The boys could smell the bourbon.

He'd sent Jimmy and his brother to catch the calf and lead it to the clearing back behind the barn. The boys had no trouble catching the calf. They'd fed and watered it since the day it was born a year ago. Dan had bottle-fed it when there was a problem with the cow's milk. Jimmy had taught it to eat solid food by hand-feeding it a mixture of warm milk and crushed grain.

Each boy held the calf between them with a lead rope tied to the side of its halter. They were on opposite sides of the animal, about three feet away from it. Dad took up station over the calf's right shoulder holding an axe.

The black and white calf stood there. Still. With a warning to hold tight, Dad swung the axe, blunt side down, in a complete whistling arc over his head and hit the calf on the head between the ears. For a heartbeat the calf was still, then it lunged forward, ripping the ropes from the boy's hands.

Wobbly-kneed, head bobbling, it lurched down the hill toward the creek. Dad and the boys ran after it.

Just before it got into the creekside brush it collapsed, head downhill. It lifted its head once, flopped back down and died. Dad cut its throat with his pocket knife and it bled out. They tied a rope around its back legs and the car bumper and dragged it up the hill to the barn where they hung it up by its hind legs, skinned and butchered it.

Jimmy still had nightmares about that morning.

25

Thunder rumbled down the canyon. The Priest woke, looking toward the sea. A thick, swirling ground mist filled the canyon. Raindrops the size of quarters thudded into the log wall, popping loudly on the black plastic. The wind whipped up the canyon, lashing the chaparral and scenting the air heavily with damp sage. He rolled out of his sleeping bag and began to make coffee on the camp stove. Today he planned to go down to Cabrillo Beach at San Pedro. It was the day of Ochpaniztli, the beginning of the major harvest ceremonies honoring the earth goddesses, a day for celebration, family gatherings, storytelling. Shit, the weather. He punched on his small radio, searching for a weather forecast.

He found AM, CAL-K-LUV's Mike Donahue, "—All Mexican immigrants?"

"Yeah, I'm tellin' yah, they're all a bunch a thievin' wetbacks."

"C'mon Jerry, tell us what you really think. You're really on a rip this morning. It's true, many of our Mexican compadres are here illegally and that the great State of California spends billions of dollars a year to support them, keep them on welfare. And further—"

The Priest hammered the radio silent. His rage was massive and instant. The air in the cave vibrated with it. Donahue. Enemy. Racist. Race-baiting voice of Anglo arrogance that The Priest hated. Enemy. The word scorched his brain, flooded his thoughts, pulsed through his blood. White, Anglo, Enemy. All thoughts of Ochpaniztli vanished. Sacrificial images flooded his brain. Donahue's disembodied voice threatened, criminalized his people, diminished the Mexica in the eyes of their Gods and the world. Destroy the enemy. Destroy Donahue. Silence his filthy words. Sacrifice him on the stone altar. Carve out his poisoned heart. Offer it in triumph to the all powerful Huitzilopochtli!

Donahue would not be easy. Research, planning, a trip to the library. The branch in Westwood was always helpful. The little old ladies there were thrilled that a Mexican Boy, as they thought of him, spent so much time reading.

26

Donahue was a minor celebrity in Los Angeles. A long article in The L.A. Times on right-wing talk radio and a brief profile in People gave him a start. Donahue was from Little Rock, Arkansas. Graduate of a small, unknown liberal arts college, he had moved to L.A. soon after serving in the US Army in Germany; no Vietnam tour for him. Donahue got his first job in radio in 1979, with a small station playing country music. He was a DJ for three or four years until talk radio began to find an audience.

Donahue had found his medium. His personal inclinations were outrageous, racist and ultraconservative. He soon found that right-wing nuts were desperate for a voice. He gave it to them.

Nothing was sacred; the most outrageous speculation, innuendoes and accusations were welcomed as comments from his listeners. Within a year, Donahue's CAL-K-LUV was the second or third highest-rated talk radio show on the west coast and syndication nationwide was imminent. Advertising revenues quickly made CAL-K-LUV the prime profit source for its parent conglomerate. Donahue was challenging Rush Limbaugh as king of right-wing radio and winning.

Donahue's private life was not as successful. Married five times and divorced five, he had seven children that he never saw. Alimony and child support payments kept him in constant terror of a ratings drop. He had a strong penchant for younger women. "Twenty-one, tops, for marriage, and four years together, then goodbye," Donahue was quoted in People.

This from a guy who would be fifty-seven on his next birthday. The same article referred to his small Santa Monica mountain ranch as Donahue's home.

He had held onto that through all the marital turmoil. Donahue made several references to it as if he and Ronnie Reagan shared the same lifestyle. Horses, wood chopping, good-old-boy type activities that endeared him to his redneck audience.

In fact, the photo spread revealed the ranch to be eight acres of scrub desert brush and scorched pasture that couldn't support the two sway-backed saddle horses that dozed in the dilapidated, pole-fenced corral. There were a couple of falling down outbuildings that he called barns. The ranch house was a postwar, two-bedroom shack, baking on its treeless plot. To a casually perceptive viewer, it called to mind Tobacco Road, L.A style. No ex-wife wanted it.

Other photos in the articles showed Donahue to be a skinny, six foot three guy with thick lensed, black horned rim glasses, and pronounced ears that stuck defiantly out from his balding head. He always wore jeans, plaid western shirts with pearl snaps, expensive cowboy boots and Stetson hats. He drove a 1969 black Cadillac convertible with chromed steer horns as a hood ornament.

On the Tuesday after hearing Donahue's broadcast, The Priest parked his van in a side street that allowed him to see the CAL-K-LUV parking lot on Santa Monica Boulevard. He had some of his gardening tools thrown in the back as a thin excuse in case a cop got nosy. Just another spic gardener waiting on his buddies to quit work up the street and go home.

At four thirty-five Donahue left the station, got in his distinctive Cadillac, put the top down and headed west to pick up the 405 north going home. That assumption, that he was headed home, was The Priest's mistake. He was hanging back five cars behind when, without signaling, Donahue peeled off at the Sunset exit and disappeared. The Priest was trapped by traffic and couldn't follow.

The next day, The Priest stayed in lane behind Donahue. Again, he used the Sunset exit, turned left and drove west toward Brentwood, the Priest four cars behind. Donahue took a quick right on Church, now headed north parallel to the 405. A half block down, he pulled over and parked in front of a new apartment building. He climbed out, went to the door, was buzzed in and disappeared. The Priest U-turned and parked facing north so that he could watch the entrance to the building.

During the two hours waiting for Donahue, there was a constant in-and-out of uniformed airlines personnel. The Priest guessed that Donahue was upstairs screwing a stewardess. Confirmed thirty-five minutes later when Donahue and a beautiful young uniformed woman appeared in front of the building and kissed goodbye. She headed for the parking garage while Donahue got in his Cadillac and headed back to the northbound 405.

Forty five minutes later, hanging back as far as he dared, The Priest topped a small rise and saw, a mile ahead, Donahue pull into the unpaved driveway of his sun-parched spread. He parked, went in and, minutes later, lights outlined the windows in the evening dusk.

The Priest pulled his van off on the shoulder, got out and jacked up the rear pavement side of the van. He pretended to fix a tire as he kept an eye on Donahue's house. He took the wheel off and let the air out. Leaving the spare buried in its compartment, he leaned the flat against the van and sat down to wait for help. None came. Low brush partly hid him from Donahue's house. When it got full dark, he threw the flat tire into the back, locked up and slipped off down the hill toward Donahue's house. Any passerby would see the van up on the jack and figure that the owner had gone off to find or fix a tire.

The Priest was just making the turn around the house side of the corral when the exterior light over the back door snapped on. The Priest threw himself behind the big metal watering tank. Tumbleweed had piled up against the tank and fence. The horses ambled over to sniff this stranger in their corral.

Donahue opened the back door and a border collie dashed through the puddle of light and into the darkness, yelping at the chance to finally empty his bladder. Donahue never came outside. The collie raced around the dusty yard, marking his territory at the corner of the barn and the tool shed. He was headed for the corral and trouble for The Priest when he picked up a rabbit's scent and raced away.

The Priest closed his buck knife and slipped it back into its sheath. He was lying practically under the horses, in six inches of old horse shit, dust and mud where water spilled over the sides of the tank. These odors masked The Priest's scent from the dog.

Irritated by the dog's barking, Donahue opened the back door and called him in. Minutes later, Donahue reappeared, stumbling on the back steps and tossing an empty beer can away before heading for the barn. The Priest, stifling a sneeze from the dust, crawled around the tank, keeping it between him and Donahue, the four-inch buck knife again open in his hand. Donahue vanished into the dark barn, turned on a light, and came out a few minutes later with two three-gallon buckets of horse feed. He headed straight for the corral.

The horses left The Priest and ambled toward Donahue's side of the corral and the food trough. Donahue dumped the grain into the wooden trough, scratched one of the horse's ears and, whistling, returned the buckets to the barn, doused the lights and went back into the house. He never realized that he was yards from his death.

On the PCH, driving to his cave, The Priest realized he had enjoyed the stalk. He got a high from getting close enough to take Donahue. It was an adrenalin rush identical to the jungle ambushes. The hunt in the urban environment of Little Saigon was not the same. Melding into a dark city street was a different, less challenging skill. There was something primal about crawling on the ground, in and among other animals to get close to the prey. He still had the edge, the skill. It excited him.

The next night The Priest was waiting for Donahue at the corral. Donahue didn't weave home till three-thirty AM. He had a woman with him. The collie hit the back yard in agony, pissed a blue streak and was immediately called back into the house. The lights went off and Donahue went to bed. He didn't feed the horses. The Priest used the opportunity to wedge some tumbleweed under the feed trough and slightly rearranged two burlap bags that were hanging on the fence.

The next night Donahue's Cadillac turned into the dusty driveway just after sunset. The Priest watched and waited. Donahue made his way into the house alone, opened a beer and turned the dog into the yard. As the dog started his nightly routine, a jackrabbit streaked away to the east. The collie took off in joyous, full-throated pursuit.

Donahue called the collie a time or two, gave up and walked out to feed the horses. Donahue had dumped the grain into the wooden box trough and bounced the second plastic bucket to dislodge the last grains when, two feet away, The Priest materialized out of the tumbleweed and burlap bags on the other side of the trough, close enough to touch. A dust-covered, black-clad apparition in a black headband with the most frightening green eyes Donahue had ever seen. The apparition had its fist to its mouth. Donahue heard a soft whifft.

Donahue reeled back. Eyes bulging, skin white, mouth working, he looked like a fish on a gaff. His hands were up in front of him warding off—what? He was trying to scream when the tiny dart hit him under the jaw. A bee sting deep into the soft flesh of the neck. The drug hit. His hands came up to the sting. He continued to stagger back under the momentum of his initial terror. His boot heel snagged in the mesquite. His legs and then his entire body collapsed. He went down like a dropped rag. His Stetson, lost in the fall, tumbled across the dry sand. His eyes danced in terror. He hadn't made a sound.

The Priest left him lying in the darkness and pulled on a pair of soft leather gloves. He looked for the dog. Gone. He went into the kitchen, found the dog food, dumped a fifty pound bag of dry Gaines onto the floor and flipped open the toilet lid. He wedged the back door and screen open. He opened the corral gate and jammed it into the brush to keep it open; the horses could forage. No reason the animals should starve until somebody came looking for Donahue. He picked Donahue up in a rough fireman's carry and walked off to the van. The bastard was heavier than he looked.

The Priest was on the Ventura freeway headed east, running just slightly over the speed limit. Fifty-five or under, the CHP became suspicious. Thought you were running drugs. It was two AM and the traffic was light. A Mexican border station played quietly on the radio, the open windows blowing warm air through his sweating hair. He was beginning to come down from taking Donahue.

Donahue was flat on his back on the floor of the van. A broad web belt held him in place, not that he was going anywhere; the drug would incapacitate him for hours. The Priest didn't want him flopping around back there on the turns.

The Priest was thinking about the perfect site to present Donahue. This one needed something special, a place that would command attention, send the message that his People were special, not to be fucked with. They sailed through Glendale, Pasadena, then Monrovia. Just off the northbound exit at Azusa was a highway patrol road block. Three cars were ahead of The Priest giving him just enough time to flip a dark blanket over Donahue's still form. In this town of car break-ins everybody hid the contents of their vehicles. He pulled up to the roadblock manned by two CHP officers.

He produced his driver's license, registration and insurance papers. They wanted to chat. At two AM they had nothing else to do. Unfortunately, he was the last vehicle in line. On the surface, he remained cool, making jokes about the late hour, guys who worked graveyard shifts, the lucky stiffs who pulled the day jobs. His hand, out of sight on the steering wheel, was cracked-knuckle-white. After an almost comical sniff of his breath and a cursory glance into the back of the van, they waved him on. The Priest continued up into the mountains. His heart gradually slowed. His grip on the steering wheel loosened. He couldn't be caught or stopped. He had too much work to do. Dumb fucking cops should leave him alone.

He realized that he needed a gun. Maybe several. A gun would have cleared that road block if he'd needed to use it. Those cops back there were relaxed, tired. They'd never have known what hit them. A hand gun for sure, a Browning like in Nam would be ideal. Fifteen 9mm rounds that could stop a bus, accurate to fifty yards. A rifle. Maybe the AK-47. One of his Mexican buddies had hinted about a source. Soon. He returned to the problem of where to present Donahue.

27

Approximately twenty-four hours after his chat with the CHP, The Priest pulled the van into the valet parking lane at the Dorothy Chandler Pavilion in the Los Angeles Music Center. He'd decided this was the perfect spot. The Music Center was built in the sixties and seventies boom of building 'cultural centers.' The Music Center consisted of the Chandler Pavilion, the Mark Taper Forum and the Ahmanson Theatre.

It was three thirty-seven AM. Even at this late hour the breeze through the van's open windows was hot. He sat for a half an hour watching for any signs of life. When he saw nothing that troubled him he got out, quietly closed the door and went around to the back of the van. Again, he waited. Fifteen minutes this time. Still nothing moved. A faint hiss of traffic in the distance, the white noise of L.A.

He opened the rear doors of the van and looked in on Donahue's remains. He put on a black cotton cover-all, latex gloves and a black cap taken from a cardboard box. He slid Donahue to the back of the van on an old canvas tarp. Tenderly, but with effort, he picked him up in a fireman's carry and headed for the fountain in the center of the plaza. Dead center, pun intended, of the oppressor's cultural pretensions. The L.A. Anglo's hundred and forty year old culture. Get real. The Priest's chest filled with disgust. The Mexica's culture goes back three thousand years. I spit on your Anglo culture.

The central fountain in the plaza was a three foot high concrete platform. Centered on this platform was a towering bronze Jacque Lipchitz sculpture, 'Peace on Earth.' The water jets in the plaza were off but the concrete was still wet. Somewhere in the distance a car alarm began to blare.

He placed Donahue, headless, neck to the foot of the sculpture and feet to the east. He checked to make sure that Donahue's arms pointed north and south, then left. In the green mercury vapor lights, the gangly corpse mirrored in the water-dampened concrete.

Traffic sighed. The van rolled away in total silence.

A chill on the back of his neck woke Jo Jo Sparks. A car alarm gave its last few bleats as he snapped his head up. He was pulling the midnight to eight AM security shift in the Mark Taper Forum, the small theatre in the Music Center complex. His post was down three or four steps, in the lobby of the Taper. Thompson had a hard-on for him and had kept him on this miserable shift all month.

He yawned, shook his head and stretched, trying to come to full wakefulness. What the hell had woken him? Then he noticed the fading bleating of the car alarm. Probably a good thing. If old Thompson had found him dozing, he'd be looking for another job tomorrow. SOB was tough, man. Thompson had a habit of coming around in the wee hours to make sure his people were awake, doing their job.

Jo Jo looked out to the plaza just as The Priest rose from arranging Donahue, took his last look around and left. Jo Jo's impression was of a tough, confident man. A man who knew what he was doing and would not appreciate being interrupted. Cautious, Jo Jo sat and watched until he was sure the man was leaving. Only then did he get up and go to check out what was going on.

To his right, out the door, he caught a glimpse of a dark van rolling away. The plate was partially covered with mud, but he could see that it was California and the letters C—8—Y were visible. There was no sound. Jo Jo realized the driver was coasting away. Strange. He scribbled the plate info on his palm with a ballpoint pen. He turned and walked out to the fountain.

As he approached the body, he thought it was a piece of sculpture. A student's, maybe. He was standing right over it before he realized that flies were already landing on it. The odd brown color was dried blood congealed over the whole surface. It smelled of hot copper. Puddled water from the fountain reflected deep red shadows.

He spun away from the awful sight, projectile vomiting in a perfect arc. When next conscious, he screamed into his walkie-talkie for someone, anyone to come help. He was standing in the Taper lobby with no idea of how he had gotten there.

A.J. Prescott, the older guard from the Chandler Pavilion, was at his side in minutes. Prescott missed seeing the body in his dash to find out what the hell was spooking Jo Jo. Finally, from the hysterical fool, he managed to understand that there was something horrible out on the plaza.

He went out to take a look and a minute later, ashen, he returned, picked up a phone and called 911. He pushed Jo Jo into his office chair, pulled a pint of Old Crow from his hip pocket, gave Jo Jo a slug, then finished it off. He didn't bother to hide the empty bottle, just tossed it into the office trash can.

Prescott was a cynical, sixty year old, ex-cop. He knew he'd catch hell about the liquor but fuck 'em where they breathed. It ain't every night you find a skinned, fly-covered, human scarecrow on the Chandler plaza. Man needed a drink to deal with that. 'Sides, security jobs were a dime a dozen for ex-cops. Thompson fired him, he'd not miss a paycheck. Fuck 'em. They settled down to wait for the black and whites. Three minutes later they heard the sirens screaming.

"It's our boy again, but I'll bet your pension this guy ain't Asian, too damn tall. Even without a head you can tell this guy must be six foot two or better."

Jimmy was crouched over Donahue's body with Brenner and Doc Jensen.

"If you're right, this makes another variable in the victim mix. Three Asian men, one Asian woman, now a non-Asian man. What the hell is going on? This isn't the way it's supposed to work." Doc looked as exasperated as he sounded.

Jimmy, "Yeah, Doc, we know. Women, kids, homosexuals, men, boys or little girls. One category per killer, but this guy doesn't fit the mold. This case will be giving our FBI shrink friends a fit. Maybe broaden their outlook a bit."

In the background, the forensics team, cops and ambulance attendants were standing around waiting for them to get out of the way so they could get on with their jobs. Uniformed cops were all over the plaza, scouring it for any bits of evidence. Little evidence markers dotted the pavement like party favors. Under the blue-green glare of the emergency lights, the caked blood looked black, charred.

No one could stand to look at it. Tough, cynical, twenty-year veterans on the job were working to keep a belly full of sour coffee from erupting. There was a stir at the crime scene tape where the uniforms were holding back a few reporters and spectators who were out at this ungodly hour. Now four forty-five AM. Out of the group walked Captain Dan Nolan in full uniform. He headed straight for Jimmy and Brenner.

"What's that S-O-B doing here?" Brenner asked no one in particular.

Jimmy, "Out for his morning—?"

Nolan interrupted. "Morning, Gentlemen. What have you got here? Another Skinner victim?"

Brenner and Jimmy stared at Nolan in disbelief. What the hell did he think they had? They exchanged looks trying hard not to crack up.

Doc looked up at the ambulance attendants. Thank god they were guys. "Okay gents, bag him up and take him in. I'll be right behind you."

To Jimmy and Brenner, ignoring Nolan, "I'll start on him as soon as he's at the morgue. Come by when you finish up here, maybe I'll have something for you."

"Thanks, Doc, we'll be there." Brenner nodded to Nolan and said to Jimmy, "C'mon, let's go talk to this security guard. Jake said we got a break this time, somebody got a partial on the van."

"Just a minute Lieutenant. Is there anything I can do to help here?" Nolan was purpling with the effort it took not to lose his temper and further emphasize to the watching cops his lack of authority at Brenner's crime scene.

Brenner smiled at him with a look reserved for something found on the bottom of a shoe, "Sure Captain, hang in for a bit and we'll brief you. Once we've talked to the witness. Why don't you go over and keep the press happy?"

Nolan opened his mouth to argue then realized that he was holding a weak hand. If he interfered at a Skinner crime scene in front of witnesses, Brenner would hang him out to dry with the Chief. To save face, he stalked off to talk to the reporters gathered at the perimeter.

Jimmy, "Man, what a piece'a work."

Brenner grimaced. "Yeah. Bastard makes my skin crawl. He's desperate to stay at his pay grade, always thinking of his alimony."

"Easy, Mark, easy. He'll step on his own dick soon enough. Just give him time."

Walking to the Taper lobby where Detective Jake Benson was pouring coffee into Jo Jo, Jimmy and Brenner passed two uniformed officers having a smoke with A..J. Prescott. Brenner recognized Prescott.

"Hey, A.J., what're you doing here? You working security out here?" He reached over and shook the startled man's hand.

"Lieutenant Brenner, how the hell'd you recognize me? I ain't seen you in ten, no eleven years. How you been keeping?"

"Well enough, A.J., what'd you see out here tonight? This is Jimmy Santos, you guys know each other?"

Jimmy nodded to the security guard as A.J. said, "Nah, don't know him, heard a him, that hot dog detective, used to be in the paper all the time. No offense, Santos."

Jimmy thought, right, noticing the use of his surname as a slur.

"So what'd you see A.J., anything?"

Brenner slid that in to short circuit the hostility he sensed between the two men. "Nothing Lou, I was checking the far side doors on the Chandler when the kid started screaming into the walkie. I hustled over here, didn't even see the body till he pointed it out. I came over from the Chandler along the driveway, body over there in the dark."

He pointed toward the fountain. The technicians were rolling a gurney toward the open rear doors of the ambulance.

"What's going on; Carson said this was the fourth or fifth in a series. That true?"

"Carson talks too much. Keep this to your self A.J., those press folks would just love to have that number confirmed. We don't need anymore grief from them." Even in the harsh shadowy light it was obvious that Brenner was furious. "Hang on here for a bit till we've talked to Jo Jo, we may have another question or two for you, okay?"

"Sure, Lou, my shift ain't up till eight, anyhow. Good luck, looks like you're gonna need it."

As they moved toward the Taper lobby, Jimmy couldn't resist, "What an asshole. He always that way?"

Brenner stopped, "Nah, he was a good cop. He, his partner and another black and white arrived at the same time at domestic dispute call out in East L A. They were flipping a coin to decide who was going in when the husband came out firing an automatic shotgun. Three of the guys died, didn't have a fucking chance.

"A.J. was shot up but he managed to blow the bastard away. When he got out of the hospital a month later, the Mayor pressured the department into suspending him without pay for sixty days. Said he and the others hadn't followed LAPD procedure. No warning to the perp, or some such shit. A.J. pulled the plug. Could make a man bitter."

Jimmy, "Jesus."

Brenner, "Yeah. Let's talk to Jo Jo."

———

Jo Jo was sitting in the ratty office chair. Enjoying being the center of all this attention, he was still deathly pale and reeked of the vomit splattered on his shoes. His breath added Old Crow to the stink.

After the introductions, Brenner hit him with it.

"You been drinking on the job, Jo Jo?"

"No way, Lieutenant. A.J. insisted I have a belt after I saw that thing out there—I never drink on duty. Old Thompson, the boss'd have my ass for that.

Never know when he's gonna show up, you know?"

Jimmy, quietly, "Tell us about it, Jo Jo."

Jo Jo looked down at the floor, rubbed his hands together, then used one to smooth his hair down. He fidgeted, squirming in the chair.

"Well, I—I, this guy, see, he was out on the plaza, musta been doing something to the body, stood up. That's when I first saw him."

Brenner, "You didn't see him carry the body out there? Where were you?"

"I was right here, in this chair, right where I'm sitting."

Jimmy, guessing, "You doze off, Jo Jo? That why you didn't see him at first?"

"Yeah, man, just for a second or two but don't let on to Thompson. I need this job. I ain't like A.J., he don't give a shit. I dozed off for just a second. When I woke, sat up, the guy was standing up out by the fountain. He looked around, real calm-like, then, cool as you please, walked back to his van.

"By the time I got outside, he was in the van and rolling away. That's what got me, you know, he didn't start the engine, just let it roll down the hill there. Weird. A.J. always told me, you see something weird, log it, so I did. I didn't have any paper so I wrote what I could see of the plate number on my hand then went out to see what this dude had been doing."

Jo Jo held his hand out, palm up. There, in sweat-smeared blue ink were the letters and numbers. His palm was grimy and the letters were barely legible but it was the most beautiful sight Jimmy and Brenner had seen in months. At that moment Jo Jo looked like a little boy hoping for praise from an older brother. Jimmy gave it to him.

"You did good, Jo Jo. Now stay with the van for a minute. Did you get a make and a color?"

Jo Jo beamed, "Both. It was black, '87, '88, a Ford. My brother-in-law's got one almost like it. He's been trying to off load it on me. What'm I gonna do with a van, man?"

Brenner, "Anything else you notice about it, Jo Jo, you know, dents, busted lights, anything at all?"

"Yeah, it was real clean, you know, like he'd just washed and waxed it, but it was scratched real bad down the passenger side."

Jimmy, "What kinda scratches—an accident, dents, what?"

"No, it was wide," he held his hands two feet apart to demonstrate, "like a band of scratches, stood out on that black wax job, you know."

Brenner, "Could it have been made by bushes, tree limbs, that sorta thing? I get them on my car when I go up fishing sometimes."

"Yeah, like that, soft scratches, not like when you drag along side something hard. Bushes would do what I saw."

Jimmy, "Okay, now, what did you do next?"

"I walked over to where the guy'd stood up. As I got there, I was thinking some art student had put a piece of sculpture out there. You know, so people would see it. Anyway when I got close enough to really make out what it was, I lost it. A.J. said I sprayed vomit twenty feet. I don't remember doing it. There's vomit on my shoes, so I must have, but I don't remember. Next thing I know, A.J.'s forcing that Old Crow down my throat and I'm gagging it up through my nose. Awful, man."

Jimmy, "Awful's just about right. A.J. should drink better bourbon. He said you got on the walkie and yelled for help. You don't remember that?"

"No, but I must have. I don't usually see A.J. till the end of the shift. He talks like he don't care, but he looks after that Chandler, man. Don't leave his station, 'cept for good reason."

Jimmy, "Brenner, you got anything else?" On Brenner's negative, "Okay, Jo Jo, you've done real good. I'll let your bosses know how good. We'll be in touch. Mark, let's go see what the Doc's got for us. Maybe a little breakfast on the way. My stomach's beginning to think my throat's been cut."

"Jesus, J.C., that's not funny. Let's roll."

28

In the car on the way to Doc's, Brenner called Callahan, his second-in-command at the squad. Callahan was still at home. "Hey D.C., Get your lazy butt into the office and run this partial for me. California, C—8—Y, '87, '88 black Ford van—Yeah, our first real break on The Skinner—Yeah, I know it'll be a bunch a vehicles, so what, how many you got now? Once you get a list, you know the drill, start checking owners—Right, see how many's in jail, dead, phony addresses, see what we got left.

Hit it buddy, we may finally be gettin somewhere—yeah, use all the help you need, any of the squad, pull Pete and Susannah off whatever they're doin. See yah in a coupla hours." To Jimmy, "It's happenin', I can feel it."

"Maybe, it's about time. If Doc Jensen just has something good for us I'll begin to believe it."

As they walked into the chill of the morgue, Doc's grin was visible around his mask. "Gents, we're going to identify this one. Name, rank and serial number. Look at this beautiful thing." Doc was indicating the corpse's right knee. The knee cap had been removed and, lying in what appeared to Jimmy and Brenner as a bed of gore, was a stainless steel socket. Doc carefully removed it.

"This little beauty turned up on the X-rays. No more than six or eight guys in town specialize in this kind of joint replacement. I'll send all of them copies of the X-rays and photos. One of those guys will recognize his work and bingo, presto, we get a name."

Jimmy, "What if it was done out of town?"

"Well, buddy, that's what makes this a real treasure. When I get it out and cleaned up, we'll find it has its own serial number and a manufacturer's code. It'll take few more steps. Manufacturer to distributor to surgeon or hospital. Everyone involved keeps track of these things, research, liability suits, you name it. We still wind up at the same place, the name of this guy with the stainless steel knee."

On Friday, September the tenth, Doctor Louis Scheeder confirmed that he had implanted that stainless steel knee joint in Mr. Michael J. Donahue on Jan. 7th, 1989 in Cedars Sinai Hospital at two thirty in the afternoon. Doc had identified, by name, a victim of the Skinner. The Media was about to have a field day.

29

Alison and Jimmy were talking in her home office as the Saturday night cocktail party hummed in other rooms around them. Alison's home was a perfect example of the California Craftsman Cottage; lovingly restored by a previous owner and beautifully furnished. Alison was renting with an option to buy. Buying a home was a new idea to her but her business manager was trying to keep some of her Cut Artist money from the IRS. Quirky Alison touches personalized each room. In the side arches between the living and dining room she had hung an empty window sash painted in a rainbow of colors.

It was a B-list group—a few stars, producers, an agent or two, friends, colleagues and crew from Seascape; an unusual spectrum of the business, stars and technicians. It was early yet, still quiet, not yet booze- and dope-driven. It would heat up later but Jimmy bet not too much. Alison didn't seem the type to encourage or welcome a raucous crowd.

Jimmy was wandering the room checking out the floor-to-ceiling bookcases. Gesturing to the full shelves, "You've read all these?"

"Over the years, they go back to high school, can't bear to part with any of them. Old friends, you know?"

"Where was that, high school?"

"A small town in Minnesota, south of Minneapolis-St. Paul. Wabasha, on the West bank of the Mississippi. Cold winters, black rock cliffs, eagles hunting, great people, the river...Up there it's not so big. Friendlier, frozen in winter, swim in it in summer—I think I sound homesick."

"It happens sometimes; stress, loneliness, home can look pretty good to you. You've got a lot to deal with right now." Jimmy perched on the edge of her desk and lit up. Smoke drifted into the light pools.

Alison, watching the smoke, "And you? Where did you grow up?"

"Monroe, Georgia. No one's ever heard of it."

"Do you visit?"

"No. Four brothers scattered all over, Mom and Dad died in a boating accident fifteen years ago. Not much reason to."

"What happened to your southern accent? I only hear a trace occasionally."

"The Marine Corp. I was first stationed in Newport, Rhode Island. My accent was so thick no one could understand me or me them. Couldn't order a hamburger or find a bathroom. I had to lose it in self-defense. Twenty five years in L.A. just about finished it off."

Jimmy dropped into his native accent that was always a micron below the surface. "'Sides, when ya tawlk lak this, everbody thanks yer stupid. Speshly iffn yer'a guy."

Alison laughed, "Okay, okay, Let's join the party. I don't know about you but I could use a drink."

"Lead on."

The younger contingent had 'N Sync hammering out of Alison's stereo. Jimmy had no idea what it was—loud, thats what. Must be getting old, he thought. Forty-six was creeping up on him and seemed on his mind a lot these days. Jimmy and Alison stopped at the bar. Vodka and cranberry for Alison, Jack Daniel's and ice for Jimmy. Several folks were in the backyard, smoking. Jimmy wanted to join them.

Alison introduced him to the Seascape's actors, who were holding court in a corner. Her assistant, Erik, caught her attention and, before he could pull her away, "Jimmy Santos, Erik Watkins, my assistant. You met at the office. I couldn't function without Erik."

Jimmy said hello to the short dark-haired kid. They shook hands and, beaming, the kid pulled Alison away, holding her elbow and talking directly into her ear under the throb of the music. Jimmy spent a few minutes with Jerry Martin. He told Martin what he ethically could about the Skinner investigation. Jimmy couldn't talk to many people about it though everyone wanted the inside dirt. He said hello to several other people; a couple of producers, the production designer.

An aging star, Irving Gould, was telling war stories from a large leather club chair in the corner. A dark amber drink was at his elbow. He was half in the bag. Two eager young guys sat, one on the floor, one on a footstool, soaking in his every word.

"Jimmy, join us. I saw you come in. This is Ron and the one on the floor is Dwight—or David. Something with a D. Anyway; I was just telling the boys about your escapade with Charlton down in Tijuana. Remember? As I heard it you pulled him out of a whorehouse and back across the border one step ahead of the Federales, Moses and the Mexican Hookers. That would make a hell of a—"

"C'mon Irving, don't spread that around again. The tabs had enough fun with it the first rumor round. Charlton was working on a picture down there and some mutt was trying some phony blackmail. I just made sure he got back without any hassle. That's all there was to it."

Ignoring Jimmy, Gould continued his story as Jimmy moved off, thinking, alcohol-fueled parties and viscous gossip; the stuff of old Hollywood. The parties of working-class kids who had gotten to Hollywood through studying and hard work, not by knowing somebody and having a degree in 'film.'

This generation of film makers was blissed out on spiritualism, sunshine, health food and bottled water. Nothing could make them lose that sweet smile of serenity. What happened to raising hell, occasionally? Getting angry? Taking a horse to Chasen's, for God's sake? A room full of these serene smiles reminded Jimmy of a Hari Krishna congregation. But that's the Biz these days. Everybody going along to get along, at least on the surface.

Hours later, the last goodbyes said, promises of lunches, calls and dinners made, the final guest carefully staggered down the driveway. He watched as Alison armed her rudimentary security system, the idea of a goodnight kiss on both their minds.

They moved into it naturally. As it threatened to become more, Alison pushed away gently. "Not tonight, please. Too much other stuff humming around in my head."

Reluctantly, Jimmy stepped back. They said good night and Jimmy headed the Jag for home.

Home for Jimmy was the ground floor of a beachfront duplex condo on the Peninsula, a half-mile-wide sliver of sand that runs from Washington Boulevard in Venice south to the Marina del Rey Channel. To the west of the Peninsula is the Pacific Ocean and beach. The eastern boundary is a channel from the Pacific that feeds the Venice canal system.

Many L.A. residents agreed with Jimmy that the Peninsula was the best place to live. Ocean breezes keep the air cool and, by L.A. standards, clean. He had bought it at the bottom of the seventies depression. L.A. property values sank and nobody wanted to live that close to, then, crime-ridden Venice.

The building was no-style California sliced at the waist before WW2 and divided into two dwellings, up and down, improved by decades of character-adding amateur remodeling. All the rooms on his ground floor overlooked a stucco-walled garden, the beach and the ocean. Tons of books; books everywhere, paper and hardbacks, art books, history, anthropology, archaeology; trash and treasure, he'd read it all. Somehow it all came together to reflect his twenty years on the streets of L.A. and his personality.

Jimmy's upstairs co-owner was Lise Hansen; a sixtyish widow, energetic and active in causes. They looked after each other and their house. Once again Jimmy had forgotten the faucet washers Lise had asked him pick up. Damn, he thought, as he opened a beer, she's gonna be pissed. A late night radio talk show murmured in the background, half-heard, something about pollution from hog farms. Hog farms...

When Jimmy was a kid, his dad had told him a story about Jimmy's grandfa-

112

ther who lived in Barwick, a tiny town in Deep South Georgia.

Seems Grandpa had a violent temper and a neighbor who could not or would not keep his six young pigs in their pen next door to Grandpa's yard. Once or twice a month the pigs would escape, root up Grandpa's vegetable garden and destroy Grandma's flower beds. Grandpa repeatedly asked the neighbor to keep the pigs inside his fence.

Early one morning, Grandpa heard the pigs again rooting up his carrots and tomato plants. He went into the garden with his Smith and Wesson revolver, shot all six pigs through the head, and threw them back over the neighbor's fence.

Autumn mornings, when he was twelve, almost thirteen, Jimmy would get up before daylight, leave the house silently carrying his 22 rifle and slip off into the woods near his house. The dark, the sharp crisp air and the solitude made the world his special place. The first light would give shape, form and color to the woods. He would find a spot—usually the base of a big oak—sit down, wait and watch.

After fifteen minutes or so of silent waiting, the wood's life began to return. The cry of a bird, a cricket chirp, a blue jay skittering, scolding from tree to tree, a crow sailing through to investigate. Then if he was patient enough, a squirrel would dart across the edge of his vision. Then another high in the trees. Jimmy sat. Waited.

Minutes would go by. The squirrels grew bolder. Often one would spot the foreign creature in their midst, anchor himself to a tree limb—Jimmy always thought of it as a him—and tail whipping, head bobbing, begin to bark. Not doglike but a combination of a screech and a bark. A chattering sound, a hacksaw-through-a-tin-can sound. Still Jimmy waited. Any movement would raise the alarm. All the squirrels would vanish. When Jimmy refused to move, the squirrel would grow bored and go on surveying the forest floor.

Jimmy would then, slowly, almost imperceptibly, begin to bring his rifle into firing position. Elbows braced across his knees. His Dad and Doctor Ivey, both crack shots with a rifle, had taught Jimmy to shoot as they did; aim at the limb under the squirrel. If the limb was of any size and the squirrel still felt threatened, he would lie flat, clinging to it. The aiming point was the limb at the junction of tree and squirrel. A hit here would kill the squirrel by concussion. No big hole in the meat. Jimmy squeezed off the shot. The branch exploded and the squirrel fell to the leaf-covered forest floor.

Jimmy sat motionless. He had learned that if he didn't move, the wood's life would almost instantly return to normal. The sound of the shot, so sharp, short and violent, was so foreign that it was ignored. Another squirrel, chattering, popped out only feet above where his fallen cousin had been. Jimmy inched his sights up to the new target.

He squeezed off the shot in his mind but didn't pull the trigger. Dad's rule in the Santos household: if you killed it you ate it. Jimmy was the only one in the family who liked squirrel stew. Even the way his Mom fixed it with onions, sweet potatoes and green peppers, one was enough.

31

Brenner called Jimmy at home. Early. "Can you get here about an hour before our meeting with the Chief at ten?"

Jimmy, scrambling for his phone and groggy, said, "You got it. See you at nine, nine fifteen."

When Jimmy arrived Brenner briefed him on his thoughts and what they should do. They kicked it around for a bit back and forth.

Jimmy cracked a grin, "Okay, lets go do it."

The Chief and Nolan were in the conference room when Brenner and Jimmy arrived. A stenographer sat at a corner table, pad, pen and tape recorder at the ready.

The Mayor, the City Council and the Police Commissioner were all taking a beating in the press; constant negative references in the news to the long negative history of the LAPD. This meeting was sure to be the Chief's cover-your-ass response to the powers that be. After a few halfhearted pleasantries and comments on the brutally hot weather, the Chief got to the point. He shifted uncomfortably in his chair, looking down at the empty pad before him,

"Mark, Jimmy, Captain Nolan has some concerns about the Skinner case. He brought them to me and I thought it best that he pass them on directly to you." He pointedly avoided an endorsement of these concerns, sat back in his chair and nodded to Nolan to begin. Nolan, sitting ramrod-straight in his chair and looking Brenner in the eye, assumed what he thought was a posture of command; he looked like a man in gastric distress. He deliberately avoided looking at Jimmy.

He said, "I think we have several problems with this investigation. One, it is proceeding on the basis of too many assumptions. You're assuming that the perp is Mexican-American Veteran. You're seriously considering some Aztec connection. That is preposterous. You're assuming that all the victims are Vietnamese. If that idea officially got to the press it would cause panic in that community. And you are proceeding on the assumption that there is only one killer. Again this idea is untenable. One of the Vics is a woman, another a white male. Surely those are copycat killings. You have at least two, maybe three killers and a serious leak in your investigation. Greater involvement by the FBI could help find the leak.

"Number two, I fielded a call from Doctor James Tilley at the VA hospital. He is very concerned that, without any firm evidence, you're trying to hang these murders on a current or former veteran. That calls into question the reputation of the hospital. He broached the subject of confidentiality, patient civil rights and hinted at lawsuits and injunctions. He is further concerned and confused that Mr. Santos and not an official member of the department approached him with this possibility. And that brings me to my third problem: Mr. Santos.

"Our department is embroiled in one of the highest-profile cases in its history. We should solve, and be seen to solve this case on our own. This unofficial consulting arrangement between Lieutenant Brenner and Mr. Santos is cause for grave concern."

This last said directly to the Chief. Nolan continued, "We have no control over Mr. Santos. When he was on the job, Mr.Santos was a high-profile publicity-seeking detective. I see no reason to believe he has changed. Furthermore, we have no way of qualifying the current benefit, if any, of his help to the department. I think Mr. Santos should withdraw from the case."

Jimmy eased back in his chair and spoke directly to the Chief.

"Fine. When's a good time? Now?"

The Chief looked like he'd just swallowed a bad oyster. He hadn't planned on this reaction. He figured Jimmy and Brenner would put up a fight, there'd be a lot of yelling, table pounding and name calling, then as boss he'd propose a compromise, everyone would agree and life would return to the uneasy status quo.

Not this. Not Jimmy resigning. The press would have a field day. Their guy leaving the case would make page one. Six and eleven leads. God, what would Brenner do? The Police Commissioner and the City Council would fire his ass. He'd leave thirty years of police work branded as a moron.

The Chief, "Wait a minute, wait just a goddamn minute, lets talk this—"

Jimmy grinned. "No, uh-unh, Chief. If you guys want me out, let's do it nice and clean. We'll issue a joint press release. Something like 'On the advice of Assistant Chief of the LAPD, Captain Dan Nolan, today the Chief asked for and received the resignation of consultant Jimmy Cagney Santos. Mr. Santos has been assisting Lieutenant Mark Brenner in solving the Skinner case.' That should do it, don't you think?"

Brenner, "You should add a paragraph saying, "Lieutenant Brenner asked to be reassigned to other duties. He has recommended to the department that Captain Dan Nolan replace him as Whip of the Special Cases Squad and assume command of the Skinner case immediately."

Nolan, "What? That's all a lot of bull. We can't issue a press release like—"

Jimmy interrupted, beginning a slow grin, he looked straight at Nolan, "Dan, If the press department is too backed up to issue the press release, I'd be happy to do it through my office. We have a few contacts."

His threat was clear to all in the room.

The Chief popped out of his chair. His face was red purple, his breath coming in short gasps as he leaned across the table and croaked,

"Shut the fuck up. All'a you shut up. There ain't gonna be no press release from anybody." He turned to the stenographer. "That'll be all, Ms. Turner, thank you. Take the tape and when it's transcribed, give all the copies and the tape to my secretary."

Ms. Turner made a hasty exit. The door closed with a soft clunk. Jimmy grinned. Brenner sat poker faced.

Nolan made one more try, "Chief, I think we—"

The Chief leaned across the table, right in Nolan's face, "I told you to shut the fuck up. Nobody gives a fuck what you think. Now get your meddling ass out of here. I want to talk to these guys. Alone."

Nolan, ashen, looking like he'd been slapped, stalked out and slammed the door. Class all the way. The Chief slumped back into his chair. Elbows on the table, he propped his head on his hands. Jimmy lit a Camel. Brenner leaned back and smiled at Jimmy. A full minute went by in silence. Then the Chief, as if from far off, "Okay, here's what we're gonna do. You two clowns are gonna solve this fucking case. And soon! There aren't gonna be press releases from anybody but me and they are gonna be few and far between till we catch this prick. Are we all clear on this?"

Jimmy stubbed his smoke out in an empty trash can. "What do we do about Nolan?"

Chief, "He's my problem. He's got some dirt on a City Council Member. That's why we had to go through this charade today. He's been poisoning the well for weeks. He'd screw up the investigation and create a PR disaster to feed his ego. I needed some ammunition to show what a dummy he really is. I can't get rid of him but I can keep his ass out of your way, most of the time. If he gets to be too big a pain in the ass let me know. I'll do what I can."

Brenner, "Thanks Chief. We'll deal with him and we'll catch the Skinner."

"Do it. And Santos, don't smoke in my office again. Got it?"

"Got it, Chief. Ciao."

After in Brenner's office Jimmy said what they were both thinking.

"Nolan's gonna be one dangerous SOB. You're gonna have to watch your back—and mine. I'll do the same."

———

Much of the animosity between Jimmy and Nolan grew out of an incident that formed the last of the 'Jimmy Stories' while Jimmy was carrying a LAPD badge.

It happened as Special Cases pulled the plug on a gang of Chinese immigrant smugglers. Acting on a tip to the Chinese-American member of the squad, the team had hit the smuggler's ship, docked in San Pedro, at four AM.

A fog horn moaned out in the channel where the lights on a string of low lying bait shacks floated like a shot from a Fellini film. Headlights from the black and whites threw stark shadows over the dark rippled water. The ship was a rusting, filthy, high-sided freighter registered in Panama. The team had achieved total surprise with the raid and below deck was thought to be secure; dejected immigrants filed down the gangway into the harsh lights and waiting vans of the INS under the guns of the LAPD.

From nowhere, a smuggler appeared on the freighter's bridge with a sawed-off, single-barreled shotgun gaffer's-taped tightly to his hand. The muzzle taped to the captain's neck. He was oil-grime dirty, dressed in ragged jeans, a ragged khaki work shirt and sandals. With deranged hair and missing four bottom teeth, the rest green, he looked like a creature that had come aboard around the rat guard.

Dripping sweat, his wild eyes flickered over the scene. Two detectives, Dan Nolan and Mike Foccachio, who were securing the bridge were caught flat-footed. Jimmy was on the bridge but out of Smuggler's sight.

Smuggler screamed at Nolan and Foccachio, "Back off you motherfuckers, back off or I'll blow this son-of-a-bitch to hell. Get outta the way—get offa' the bridge. Throw yer guns inna water. I'm outta here or this is a dead man." Spittle flew from his mouth.

Nolan and Foccachio tossed their pistols over the side and, hands in the air, moved down the ladder to the main deck, where they scurried behind a steel locker and stayed there. The cops and Brenner on the dock saw that Nolan and Foccachio were hiding, leaving Jimmy behind and alone.

Smuggler continued screaming, "I wanta car to the airport and a plane ready when we get there. I wanta—"

Jimmy was twenty feet away and slightly outside his line of sight, his .9mm Beretta in his hand. Before the guy could get himself and everybody else totally jazzed up about a hostage situation, Jimmy shot the shotgun.

He hit it just in front of the chamber sealing the barrel. The impact of the .9mm slug ripped the disabled shotgun from the scared shitless captain's neck. The smuggler pointed the crippled weapon at Jimmy and fired. The shotgun blew up, tore his hand off and peppered his face and chest with shrapnel. With his good hand, he clawed for the pistol in his belt. Jimmy knocked him down with a shot to the thigh and the team, joined sheepishly by Nolan and Foccachio, finished mopping up.

LAPD brass gave Jimmy a ration of shit about procedure, endangering the hostage, the whole nine yards of bureau speak. Jimmy knowing full well they were happy he'd wrapped it up quick with only the smuggler damaged and a hostage situation avoided. He let them go on till they exhausted themselves on bullshit. He grinned his lazy Georgia grin, "Shit, your 'hostage' was one of them. Besides, Commander, you know I'm a pretty good shot."

Jimmy didn't give much thought to Nolan or Foccachio's behavior on the ship but the squad was merciless. They never let the two detectives forget that they had hidden and left Jimmy alone. Human nature being what it is, the two detectives hated Jimmy for the incident.

32

"Sondra Newton. She was the most beautiful creature I'd ever seen. I was at a busy Atlanta restaurant with friends when she came in. I was on leave from the Marine Corp, visiting a college roommate. She came in and I couldn't take my eyes off of her and she was reciprocating from across the room, even though she was with some guy. The electricity was incredible.

She headed for the ladies' room and I followed. I scribbled a note on a napkin. Asked her to please call me and signed it. When she came out of the loo, I handed it to her, smiled and ducked into the men's room. We continued to flirt across the room until she and her date left."

Alison was leaning across the table smiling. She and Jimmy were finishing dinner at The Palm on Santa Monica Blvd. She'd asked Jimmy about his ex-wife.

"Well, did she call?"

"The next day. Said it was because I'd said 'please' in the note. We met at a restaurant that night, a Friday; spent the weekend in a motel. Monday afternoon I had to report back to my post at the Naval Air Station just outside Atlanta. She was in school at Emory University.

"We spent every weekend together for three months. She graduated and decided to go home to L.A., Hancock Park, to plan our June wedding. She wanted a big formal wedding with me in dress blues. By then I'd learned her dad had big bucks and was some kinda power in L.A. That worried me; but I was still blown away that this beautiful woman was interested in me. I would have walked through fire if she suggested it.

"I got to L.A. and quickly realized that her mom and dad didn't approve of her getting married, the Marine Corps, a Georgia redneck son-in-law, you name it. Mr. and Mrs. Newton hated the world and me, mostly me. None of it was good enough for their Sondra."

"So, what happened?"

"We had the June wedding. Sondra had a will of granite and daddy was a wuss. The Mayor, most of the city council, a Senator, three Representatives and four hundred of the Newton's closest friends were guests.

"I got too drunk to remember most of the reception. I came to in Acapulco. She wanted to stay in L.A. and do graduate work at UCLA. I had to finish my Marine Corp tour in Atlanta. I still had about two months to go. During that time she came East twice and I flew to L.A. once."

"Sounds okay so far. Except for her parents. What happened?"

"The real tip-off came when she insisted we live in a huge garage apartment at the Newton's mansion. Close to Mummy and Daddy. Then a friend from the Corps threw a birthday party for me up at his house in the Valley. Sondra seemed a little on edge all evening. On the way home she said, 'I've never been in so modest a home.'

"I thought she was kidding. Not so. She was dead serious. She'd spent a life, to age twenty five, completely swaddled in money. Not a clue. No idea how you lived on an income not in the Fortune 500. Once or twice, I had tried to tell her about what life was like growing up in a tiny Georgia town with other poor kids. A family of seven living on a sergeant's pay. She would just tune out immediately. Would never mention it.

"What finally tore it was my joining the LAPD. Entirely too blue collar, totally 'déclassé.' The Newton's had apoplexy. Sondra wouldn't even talk about it. The day I was accepted at the Academy, I came home and found all my stuff in the driveway. Taped to a suitcase was a letter that said I would hear from the Newton's attorney and that I was not to contact Sondra. Without too much regret, I took the hint and got on with my life."

"Have you seen her since?"

"Once," Jimmy took a sip of cabernet and hesitated, memory taking hold, "An actor friend that I was advising about a role bought a table at a World Wildlife Fund benefit. He insisted that I use two of the seats. My date and I were the only two at the table who were not TV celebrities; the cast of Cyber Run." He paused.

Alison smiled encouragement. "So, come on. What happened?"

"The evening was in full swing when I looked up and Sondra was standing at my elbow. I got it together and introduced her to everyone at the table without mentioning our prior matrimonial status."

Jimmy's eyes wandered and the hint of a smile touched the corners of his mouth as he remembered.

"Sugar wouldn't have melted in her mouth. My date was dying to know how I knew her but didn't ask. At least not then. A week later I heard she was dating the Cyber Run stud. Poor guy. Now that you've heard more than you ever wanted to know about the life of Jimmy Santos, how'd you meet Mr. Wildlife Photographer?"

The question hung there while a waiter took their orders for dessert and coffee. Two cappuccinos, tiramisu for Jimmy and crème brûlée for Alison.

Alison seemed hesitant, "You really want to hear about my ex?"

"Sure, if you want to talk about it."

Alison sank back in her chair and smiled.

"We were pretty young. Film school. Mark, a cinematographer, shot all my student projects. We spent more and more time together. He wanted to save the world and thought wildlife documentaries were the way to go. At graduation he wrangled a National Geographic grant to go to Africa. Filming Baboons. By then, I was all pumped up by his enthusiasm and drive. He asked me to go with him and be his wife. All the same night. The rest, as they say, is history. In a week, we were on a plane to Johannesburg as Mr. and Mrs."

"You didn't like Africa?"

"I loved it. Camping out of a Land Rover, tracking Baboons through game parks, it was awesome. But I woke up one day and realized I had given up my dream. I got interested in film because I wanted to tell stories. Dramatic stories, funny stories. People stories, not monkey stories. I'd gotten so involved in making Mark's life work that I'd lost me. I'd turned into the 'little helper' instead of a director.

"We spent a rocky couple of months after that. I tried to make him understand that I wanted to work from a script about people with real actors who—occasionally, anyway—would do as you asked. I wanted to be director, not a camera assistant. When I saw nothing was going to change and he was going to spend his life doing what he wanted, I split."

Alison's memories of that painful time threatened the evening's mood. Jimmy quickly changed the subject.

"Cut Artist, how did you make that happen?"

Grateful for the rescue, Alison launched into one of her favorite stories.

"I fell in love with a script that an ex-classmate couldn't sell. Not knowing any better, I hand-carried it to Brad Jansson. Found him on location in Wyoming. He was bored and wanted to take me to bed. He read the script, also loved it and agreed to do it with me directing. With that as a package, getting an agent was easy and we sold the package to Sony."

"Damn, that's a great story. There are people in this town who'd give their right arm to have pulled that off." Jimmy was avoiding the obvious question—

did you sleep with Jansson? Rude, none of his business. Plus he'd heard the location rumors.

Alison covered his hand with hers. "Thanks for not asking."

Jimmy blushed and cracked a smile. He shrugged. No other answer seemed called for. Coffee and dessert arrived and the conversation turned to less personal, more relaxed topics.

33

Dusk. An appliance store on a rundown street in San Pedro, dusty window full of twenty synchronized television sets, all showing color pictures of Donahue. The Priest watched. Every lead story on the van radio was a variation on "Mike Donahue Butchered, found at the Music Center, Skinner Accused." Every news stand's headlines screamed Donahue. The radio in his cave, Donahue, Donahue, Donahue. Son-of-a-bitchin' bigot sure got the press, thanks to me. And the damn fools don't even know why. Don't have a fucking clue.

Wrong place at the wrong time, my ass—what about all his bigoted bullshit on the radio every day, priming his redneck listeners to hate my People. A dead man whose entire career had thrived on selling race hatred. The Priest rolled over in his sleeping bag and flipped his radio from CAL-K-LUV to NPR. Mozart hummed from the tiny speakers. Sleeping bag, damned joke that was. It was three AM. He had slept maybe three hours a night since Donahue had been identified. The news flowed over from Southern California to the nation. CNN and the networks carried it on every news broadcast. Every story tied Donahue to the four other victims but nobody cared about them. CAL-K-LUV didn't mention them at all. With them it was all Donahue all the time. The other victims had no names. They were Asian. They weren't celebrities.

That Donahue was a national celebrity because of his grisly death no one noticed. A virulent, racist bigot made nationally famous by being beheaded, skinned, his black heart carved out. The Priest dozed, tossed, then dozed some more.

He woke as daylight filtered into the cave and the idea was just there, fully formed, sitting like a gargoyle smiling in his brain. Tell them! Tell his people! Tell the race-baiting bigoted bosses at CAL-K-LUV. Tell the world. Maybe then they'd get the message. Maybe then they would understand.

34

"Jimmy, I think that's a reach, given what you've got to go on."

"Yeah, yeah, I know but it makes it's own kinda sense."

Jimmy was back in Rod Fulo's office at UCLA. They were batting around ideas on the Skinner. Jimmy paced. Fulo leaned back in his office chair, enjoyed one of Jimmy's Camels and shot down ideas as fast as Jimmy could express them.

"Look at what we've got. Four Vietnamese victims and Donahue. You said yourself that these have all the earmarks of sacrificial victims. What's the connection between the VC and Donahue? I don't know. Yet. But it's a place—" His cell phone chirped. "Shit, excuse me," He answered the phone. "Santos."

"Jimmy, Brenner. We've just gotten a call from CAL-K-LUV, Donahue's radio station. They got a call from some guy claiming to be the Skinner. They are broadcasting his statement on every newscast. They've faxed over a transcript of the call—guy looks legit, seems to know all the right stuff. Man's a nutcase, alright. Where are you and when can you come in?"

"I'm in Fulo's office. Lemme give you his fax number," He gestured to Fulo who wrote the number on a scratch pad and turned it so Jimmy could read it.

"Send the stuff here. We'll go over it. He can help with interpreting—then I'll come to you. While you're at it, fax the note and a copy to Tilley at the VA. Maybe we can build a fire under his ass. Let's get a copy of the station's tape to the FBI."

"You got it. See ya."

Five minutes later they were reading the fax. Fulo looked at Jimmy in amazement.

"Looks like your theory was bang-on, Jimmy, this guy thinks he's a new Aztec Warrior-King. Nutty as a fruitcake. Look at this." Jimmy sat on the edge of Fulo's desk and quickly scanned the fax. Then he read it again more slowly.

People of the Mexica, hear me! I speak to you as Ahuitzotl, your Priest-King. The time has come to throw off the yoke of Cortez. It is time to restore the greatness of the One World. Time to reclaim the place of our people as the favorites of the Gods. We must never again submit to the white man. Hear me, obey me, throw off centuries of oppression of our great Nation. I have begun the sacrifices. I have offered up the blood of Vietnamese warriors to Huitzilopochtli, Blue Hummingbird!

I have sacrificed the bigot Donahue so that you might live. His blood has splashed into the sacred Eagle bowl that you might be free. His black heart have I eaten to give me power over his hate. His skin have I danced in to the great Huitzilopochtli.

I have flung their bodies into the heart of the Anglo's cultural arrogance. I spit on their pitiful pretensions to culture. Join me. Demand your rightful place as Mexica; People of The One World. Demand your rightful place as the center of the Universe. It is yours. You must reclaim it. My sacrifices will show the way. I, Ahuitzotl, Priest, demand this of you.

"Jesus," Jimmy indicating the fax, "He's laid it all out for us. Do you see anything here that hints at who he is? What's Ahuitzotl? This guy's statement is inciting Mexicans to murder."

Fulo took another one of Jimmy's Camels, "The easy one first. Ahuitzotl was the blood thirstiest of the Aztec Warrior-Kings. He sacrificed eighty thousand victims to open a new temple. Enemy towns destroyed, all the adults slaughtered and forty thousand children scattered throughout the empire to be raised by strangers. Get the picture?"

"Yeah, not a nice guy. Whats the One World?"

In their excitement, Jimmy and Fulo were both pacing. Circling each other like boxers. The professor's usually calm office seemed charged with electricity.

"The Aztecs considered themselves the center of creation. Their world, their empire, was the One World. Cortez burst that bubble, or so we thought. This guy hasn't gotten the word. His phrasing is interesting. It's almost as if he were reading from Aztec glyphs, their picture writings."

"How the hell could he do that? Why do that?"

"Why? Maybe that's how he thinks, how he's learned to think in terms of what he calls his people." Fulo jumped from idea to idea. "Notice he says, 'our people,' that may mean he is Mexican, or Mexican-American. Not a lot to go on. But his use of language makes me think he may be a scholar who's gone off his nut. Who else would have this ability to phrase in a dead language."

"Yeah, maybe. It's possible." Jimmy avoided shutting down Fulo too hard. He needed his ideas even when he didn't buy them "This perp is a fighter, a

126

strong, silent killer. His victims have been strong, fit people. Not pushovers. Taking them required strength and speed. Not exactly the basic description of a scholar."

"You're letting your prejudices get in the way."

Jimmy ignored this. "Whats is this about The Priest?"

He went to the books on the mission table and began to riffle the pages. Nervous energy released in activity.

Fulo took the book from him, flipped to a remembered page and pointed to a brilliantly colored drawing of a temple sacrifice. "Priest-Warrior-King: a typical trilogy in Aztec hierarchy. The king performed many priestly functions, including sacrifice." His pointing fingers held his Camel, smoked down to an inch long. Its smoke curled up from the vivid drawing in eerie memory of ancient temple fires. "He was also expected to be a great warrior. When Ahuitzotl's brother, Tixoc, proved a wimp, Ahuitzotl poisoned him and took over the throne."

Jimmy folded the fax and tucked it into his jacket pocket. "Well, this priest is inciting people to murder."

"No Jimmy, murder is the job of the Priest. Not the people. The people only watch and participate in the feasts. It's the Priest you must worry about."

With this sentence Fulo renamed the Skinner.

35

The media exploded. The Priest had given CAL-K-LUV a scoop. Though he called all the Spanish radio stations with the manifesto, CAL-K-LUV had the audience. The national and cable networks picked it up from CAL-K-LUV and credited them. It became the lead story on every local and national TV news broadcast and headlined all the papers; The New York and L.A. Times, the Post, USA Today, Register, Daily Mail all carried a variation of the Priest's story. It even made The Guardian. Sidebars tried to set the Aztec stage. Most were inaccurate, abbreviated, stupid and misleading.

Experts in Aztec lore popped up like earthworms after a spring rain. Some enterprising reporter discovered that Fulo had been advising Jimmy and the onslaught at his offices became fierce; Fulo was approached two, three times a day. He refused them all. Jimmy's office phones didn't stop ringing with requests for interviews. The press had no luck there either. Police department phones all over L.A. rang constantly. A flood of useless tips. All had to be checked against back-held knowledge of the crimes. Civilians terrified. Vietnamese most of all.

The Mayor called a special closed session of the City Council. They emerged six hours later with a weak, unanimous declaration calling for calm and assuring the public that the LAPD was doing all humanly possible to find The Priest. The Press blistered them with an unanswerable barrage of questions. Every reporter in the crowd realized this story could make their career and they were out for blood.

The Police Commissioner, the Chiefs, Brenner and Jimmy stood behind the Mayor. He introduced them, but all had been expressly forbidden to speak. It was the Mayor's show, top to bottom. He fumbled, evaded. His face kept changing color like a chameleon on a plaid blanket. The press ate him alive.

They all left the meeting room through a cordon of LAPD officers, reporters screaming at them for real, concrete answers. They got none. That night's newscasts showed the Mayor, pasty-faced and shifty-eyed, dodging question after question of substance, then dashing from the room protected by thirty five police officers. This coverage ran over and over on all the stations. Not since the aftermath of the Rodney King Riots had the heat on the LAPD been so brutal.

Brenner, "What a fucking bloodbath! I figure I got about forty-eight hours to come up with something on this motherfucking Priest, or I'm going to be coming to you for a job." Brenner looked wiped out as he sat talking to Jimmy in his cluttered office. "It'll take the downtown boys that long to weigh the odds, put the finger on the guy least able to do them harm if he's fired and doesn't go quietly. You can bet that is going to point that finger at me."

"Relax, Mark, I'll pay you twice what the city does, you got your pension time in and you'll get to meet all those stars you think I work for. Besides, you got an edge; as point on this, you'll get any lead that breaks. That is, if Nolan or some hot dog in the department doesn't go for it on his own. That's your biggest danger. The brass fire you now, they're just admitting another mistake."

"Something's got to break soon. This shitbird can't keep all the luck. I got a feeling he made a big mistake going public. All we need is one person who puts it together and drops a dime."

36

"Okay, here's your espresso, now what in the hell has got you so excited this early in the morning?" Jimmy sprawled in Brenner's hard office chair and watched him grin. Brenner sipped and grinned some more, making Jimmy wait for it.

"I got a call from Atlanta this morning. A Colonel Michael Graham, National Guard at Fort McPherson down there."

He paused and lit one of his little black stogies. "So?" asked Jimmy, pushing him along. He hadn't seen Brenner enjoying himself so much since the The Priest case started.

"Well, Colonel Graham saw the Donahue story on CNN this morning. They're three hours ahead of us, Atlanta is, seems he gets up at 4 AM. Army life, Jesus! Anyway..."

"Damn Brenner, will you quit enjoying this so much and get on with it. You didn't call me down here at seven-thirty-damn-AM for a lesson in time zones. What'd this Colonel have to say thats got you grinnin' like a possum eatin' briars?"

"Well, the Priest story rang a bell with the Colonel. Late in the war he was in Vietnam, a Lieutenant in Military Intelligence—hold the cracks about oxymorons. Anyway, Graham was stationed at the firebase at Dakto where he kept hearing rumors of some guy in the jungle killing VC and cutting their hearts out. Whole platoons of them. Terrorizing the motherfuckers. The VC even had wanted posters up for this spook. Whoever, he was a hero to the GI's and a PR bomb about to explode all over the US Military.

"Long and short of it, Graham found the spook. The guy wandered into

Dakto. Graham arrested him, doped him up, wrote up a highly irregular medical report, put him air-out-soonest to a VA mental ward in 'The World.'

"Graham was trying to avoid another atrocity story that would embarrass the US Military. Period, end of report, or so he thought. Now on CNN, he hears about some guy doing people in the jungles of L.A. The heart thing did it. He thought there was enough similarity that we should know about it. Might be our guy. So he called."

Jimmy was bow-string-tight in his chair.

"He have a name?"

"No, it's been twenty plus years. In addition, the guy's records were a mess. Graham was never sure what the guy's real name was. He remembers the guy was Mexican-American, a Marine. Name Hispanic. He remembered, this nut's nickname was The Priest. Graham said it made his skin crawl, cause the wacko made reference to his people and how he was a Priest to his People. A real spooky character. Links up with your Aztec theory, don't you think?"

"Fulo likes it. Did Graham file anything on it? Any records we can check?"

"Nah, way too sensitive. Can you imagine the shit hittin' the fan if this had landed at the L.A. Times. Christ, Fonda and the hippies would've had a field day. 'US Marine cutting the hearts out of Freedom Fighters.' Nah, he just wanted to disappear this guy. Bastards lucky he wasn't fragged and reported as KIA."

Jimmy lit a smoke, "Graham have any idea where this 'Priest' landed, what VA hospital?"

"No, this was just days before they started getting the hell outta there and Graham forgot all about it until CNN this morning. Didn't sound too pleased about remember'n it this morning either. He musta' been spooked."

Jimmy punched out his Camel, "How about you call our FBI buddies, see if they can track down flights out of Nam? Graham may be able to pinpoint a date. Close enough, anyhow. Could be a bear, that close to our pull out. Maybe they can backtrack and get us a name and destination."

"I'll go see that jackass Tilley at the VA hospital again. Somehow this just feels right. The perp might be getting a disability pension. If he's not screwed down tight, he might not wander too far, want to stay close to the money. If Uncle Sam had dropped him in New York, maybe he'd be decorating Lincoln Center instead of LA's Music Center."

"Ok, I'll get on it. Should find out today if anyone spotted somebody tailing Donahue. Somebody must'a seen something. This nut didn't just stumble over Donahue in the dark. Jesse's over at the highway patrol. Two CHPS on drunk patrol stopped a van on the night Donahue bought it. They called in responding to the APB on the van."

Jimmy stopped in the door. "Call me if that pans out and you get any kinda description of the driver. I'll be on the cell."

Jimmy got his car rolling. He called Millie and asked her to set up a meet with Dr. Tilley at the VA Hospital. He was psyched. The hunt. That's why he loved doing this.

It was a beautiful Georgia Saturday morning in the late fall of '72. Jimmy was a sophomore, home for Thanksgiving break from the University of Georgia. After the huge Thanksgiving meal had settled, Jimmy and Doc Ivey loaded two one-hundred-pound bags of cracked corn into the back of Doc's red International Harvester Scout.

They drove to a four-acre field where the season's corn had been harvested. Jimmy, through the rear hatch, thinly spread the cracked corn over the ground. It was illegal as hell. They were baiting the field for doves.

Doc always got a kick out of discussing the dire consequences of being caught by a game warden. Fat chance, thought Jimmy. The field was in the middle of nowhere, and besides, Doc owned it.

Just before daylight the following Saturday morning, Doc, his two brothers and Jimmy, armed with shotguns, took up positions around the perimeter of the field at a hundred and fifty yard intervals and settled down to wait.

Just after good light, the doves began to come whistling in. The shot guns began to talk. If everyone timed it just right the birds would be turned to fly in circles over the edge of the field. A scared dove can hit about ninety miles an hour and these were sure scared birds.

One broke out of the flight and flew straight over the field at Jimmy. Sixty feet off the ground and high-tailing it. Jimmy drew a bead, allowed for a good lead and fired. The bird crumpled in mid-air and its momentum carried it straight to Jimmy. He stuck out his left hand and caught the dove before it hit the ground. Jimmy stood there with the warm dead bird in his hand.

He thought, what the hell am I doing? After that bright morning, Jimmy limited his hunting to criminals.

37

Jimmy was back in the office. Millie was catching him up on the morning's messages. "Did you shut your phone off again? I've tried two or three times to get you." Jimmy pulled his phone from his pocket and checked it.

"Shit, musta done it after Brenner's call in Fulo's office. Sorry about that."

"Someday that's going to prove a bad habit."

"Yeah, yeah."

"Doc Jensen set up another meeting between you and Dr. Tilley. Tilley wants a very clear idea of what you need before he'll commit to giving you anything. Doc made him sound like a tough old bird, ex-bird colonel in the Marines, or something."

"He got that right."

Jimmy was in Dr. Tilley's office at the VA hospital. He laid out the essentials of the call from Colonel Graham in Atlanta.

"This is what we think we've got so far: a Mexican-American vet, flown from Nam to the US on a med-evac flight. According to Colonel Graham, the guy was a full-blown wacko, he may have washed up here in L.A. He's doing these victims in a manner that suggests Aztec ritual—"

"Hang on Mr. Santos, Jimmy, you're still giving me nothing but think, maybe, suggests. Do you have anything solid that leads you or the police department to believe that your criminal is a patient here at this VA Hospital? Or was a patient? In fact, anything positive at all to support your leaps in logic?"

Jimmy sat on Doctor Tilley's hard metal chair and smothered an urge to strangle the ramrod-straight figure across the desk. The guy enjoyed being an uncommunicative jerk.

"Doctor Tilley, you've got what we've got. Everything points to a disturbed vet on a murderous rampage. He's killed and carved up five people we know about and will keep on doing it till we stop him."

"But you don't even know if the man was sent here; if the man you're looking for is indeed the Colonel's wacko, as you so elegantly put it."

"True, but if we're right and he was, you and your doctors could shortcut the time it will take to find this guy." Shit, shouldn't have said shortcut.

"Our duties here don't include providing shortcuts for the police or anyone else, Mr. Santos. Our duty is to our patients and to their privacy. Please remember that."

"But surely Doctor, your duty includes doing anything you can to preserve human life. This bastard is killing at the rate of two a month. He's cutting out their hearts while they are alive and watching. He won't stop until he is caught and put away."

"I mentioned this subject at our last staff meeting, but with so little to go on, no one would comment. With your permission, I'll lay out the enlarged scenario at our meeting tomorrow. If it rings a bell with one of our doctors who has treated someone fitting this profile, and he or she is willing to talk about him, I'll be in touch. You could try for a court order forcing us to talk to you; but you won't get one. Your area of inquiry is too broad. You'll just have to wait. Now if you'll please excuse me."

Jimmy pounded his fist on the steering wheel. Hard to do and talk on a cell and drive at the same time. "Doc Jensen, you got to do something with this asshole Tilley. Phone him up, go see him, something. This Graham tip feels too right to keep running into Tilley's fucking cliche-draped stonewall. The man is impossible."

"Easy, Jimmy, the man may be difficult, but he could hang himself out to dry if he was too eager to help. He's got years of training in cover-your-ass, in case you've forgotten. He may want to help, but he's going to let one of his staff stick their neck out first. Give it a day or two and I'll call him. By then one of his Doctors may have broken the log jam. And, it's just possible that the guy's never been near VA L.A."

"Doc, a hundred bucks says you're wrong."

"You are on Jimmy, just for the hell of it. I think you're right. See you."

38

It was late Friday afternoon. Susan was on the intercom. "Jimmy, there's a guy on line three, says his name is Mustafa. Swears he has information on the Priest. You want to take it?"

"Who? Oh yeah, I'll take it. Hey Mousie, how's the revolution?"

"Fuck you man, why you always gotta be such a wise ass? I call tryin' to help your sorry ass and you gotta diss me."

"How are you gonna help me, Mousie, and whats it gonna cost me?"

"You working on that Skinner thing, you know, the Priest, right? Well I might just have some information you could use. You wanna come down here and talk about it."

"What information? What do you know about the Priest? And I repeat, whats it gonna cost me?"

"I can tell you where to find this guy. Come on down and we'll talk."

Mousie hung up and left Jimmy listening to a dial tone.

---

35 minutes later Jimmy was in San Pedro. He had broken every speed limit and several times driven in the breakdown lane to get through the Friday afternoon traffic. Jimmy pounded on the door of the neat little house next to the bodega. The Che poster stared at him with unblinking eyes.

Mousie opened the door. "I figured you'd be here man but damn, this is quick service. This Priest dude must be givin' you pigs a hard time. Come on in, the brothers'r out today. Uh, this is Mshobe—you met her before."

The interior of Mousie's house was as surprising to Jimmy as its neat exterior. Floors, walls and ceilings were white-stained wood. The living room space flowed uninterrupted through the dining room over a counter into the kitchen. African sculptures and reproductions of prehistoric cave paintings enhanced the stark white space.

"Cut the shit, Mousie. What've you got and what do you want for it?"

"I'm just tryin' to do my civic duty, Mr. Santos, sir. Ain't no crime in that now is they? Sides, I'm kinda jammed up with your good buddy, Cunningham, over at Harbor Division. Thought you and I'd work a little trade."

"What kinda jammed up? Who've you killed this time?"

"No, no, no, nothing like that. This is a minor beef, if Cunningham'll bounce it that way. If he don't and makes a felony beef outta it, I'm looking at a mandatory twenty-five-to-life as a three-fall guy."

"Whats the beef?"

Mousie got up and began to pace. He wouldn't meet Jimmy's eye. "Say man, you want a drink, a beer, anything?"

"Cut to the chase Mousie. This ain't a social call."

"Okay, okay, relax. Well, I got to thinking 'bout all that money you made me give away just sittin' there at that church. I thought maybe I could sweet talk that old pastor into sendin' some of it back my way. He got all huffy and called Cunningham. Told him I was tryin' to con him. Called it extortion." Mousie perched his butt on the pass through counter and continued selling. "Now, Cunningham and the DA can play it a coupla ways. One means my goin' back in the slam for a long time. I figured if you put in a good word 'bout how I helped you catch this Priest guy, maybe they'll drop it to a misdemeanor. I'll do six months in county and everbody's happy."

"What the hell could you know about the Priest?"

"Somethin' worth somethin'. Why'd I try to make up something like that, man? Hell, I know you gonna check it. I know you smart, I ain't gonna run no con on you with me lookin' at hard time."

"That phone working?" Jimmy pointed to the kitchen wall phone.

"Yeah, man. I pay my bills."

Jimmy picked it off the wall as he looked up Harbor Division's number in his notebook. He punched in the numbers. "Detective Cunningham, please. Jimmy Santos calling. Hey Jack, Jimmy—fine, you? Look, I'm here with your good buddy Mousie. Yeah, that Mousie. He says he's got some info on The Priest to trade for a break on his extortion beef."

Jimmy watched Mousie squirm as he listened to Cunningham,

"Get what you can Jimmy. We got jack shit that'll stick on that extortion complaint. DA and I thought we'd throw a scare into Mousie, make him keep his head down for a week or two. Good luck, buddy."

Cunningham hung up and Jimmy kept talking into the dead phone.

"Yeah Jack, I'll tell him. Bounce his sorry ass right back up to Quentin. Gotcha. Take care." He hung up and turned to the pacing Mousie and a nervous Mshobe. "Okay, you got a deal. So let's have it."

Mousie talked, fast. "Mshobe, here, had been down to the beach a coupla' times. Heard this dude tellin' stories about ole Mexico. She tole me about it when the news broke about this Priest dude cutting up all those people. We went back the next weekend. I thought you might be interested. Seems he's down there every weekend."

39

Sunday afternoon. Cabrillo Beach. The sun was creating a glorious light show through the western clouds. Shafts of sunlight slipped under the trees and cast long shadows across the grass. A sea breeze cooled the people gathered to hear The Priest and rustled the palm fronds overhead. Two boys and their dad were fishing off of the rocks at the foot of the cliffs.

Strange mood, thought The Priest. Something out of harmony here. He smoothly continued his story about the Aztecs' last King, Moctezuma, and his torture-murder at the hands of Cortez. The group had too many men in their twenties and thirties, leaning casual but alert, watching for something. A tall, black-haired Anglo strolling up from the beach. Another one, overweight, smelling of cop, coming around the corner of the museum. TV—I saw these two at the Mayor's press conference!

Still talking, The Priest gently took the little six year old girl from his lap. He put her on the ground in front of her mother. As she stood, he pinched her, hard. She jumped forward, screaming, and knocked her mother over, both tumbling backward into the crowd. Every eye focused on them. The little girl screamed her lungs out.

In a continuous movement, The Priest turned and dashed west for the looming cliff face. The story group erupted as three men jumped up, 9mm semi automatics appearing in their hands as they chased The Priest. Shouting, Spanish and English. The two Anglos, guns drawn, joined them. A hundred confused, panicked people. It was like a suddenly disturbed flock of geese. Frantic, erratic movement with no direction, no logic.

No one could shoot. Too many civilians. Women screamed, crouched over their children. Some of the men tried timidly to delay the cops, tripping one, stumbling into the paths of two more. The panic spread outward.

Clots of tourists on the cliff side walks stopped to see what was happening. Why the screams? Cars on the nearby drive screeched to a halt. A red van, beer-drinking driver looking at the panicked scene, slammed into the back of a low-rider. A fist fight erupted.

The Priest slammed gawking tourists from his path, slashing through the vegetation, then cut toward the water and the jagged, brush-choked cliffs that came down to the sea. He flew up the walls of rock and sand, using every bit of cover, each gully, each clump of vegetation. The fisherman and his sons watched in open-mouthed astonishment. The tall Anglo was a hundred feet behind The Priest, not giving up, but not shooting, yet.

The Priest climbed, turned into a curving, steeply-sloped cut in the cliff face. His breath came in gasps, his hands bleeding from the coral cliffs. Sweat poured into his eyes. His mind was racing.

How had they known to come here? What else did they know? Gotta get away from them. Can't let them interfere. No! His foot slipped and he slid back, almost falling. No! He scrambled, got a handhold on a petrified coral outcrop and pulled himself higher up the cliff.

Must make a diversion. Stop the chase. He ripped a table sized boulder loose, sending it careening down the cut.

Jimmy turned into the cut in the path of the onrushing boulder. He was halfway up the hundred foot cliff. A fall would be fatal. The boulder rushed at him, guided by the jagged walls of the cliff. He tried to jump aside.

The boulder bounced and clipped his right hip and sent him spinning backward down the cliff. Falling fast, he snagged a scraggly bush and ripped it from the earth. Bits of coral and dirt filled the air and blinded him. Still falling, he made a desperate grab for an exposed root with his left hand and slammed to a stop.

He destroyed his jeans and the skin on his knees and lost a chunk of palm skin to the root. The fall knocked the breath out of him. He lay gasping as broken coral bits rained down the cliff face. The boulder splashed into the ocean, narrowly missing the fisherman's sons. The Priest disappeared over the cliff top.

———————————

Jimmy and Brenner had selected a few Hispanic members of the Special Cases Squad to infiltrate the story group. While it sounded like a solid tip, it didn't seem to warrant the whole squad. Cunningham and Harbor Division had signed off on it. A smaller unit could pull off the capture and not risk endangering the hundreds of sun worshippers sure to be at the beach on a hot Sunday afternoon. Jimmy and Brenner would signal the takedown when everyone was set. They'd never had time to get set. The Priest had smelled the trap and bolted.

Most of the story group had melted away by the time Jimmy, Brenner and their troops regrouped on the beach. Questioning the few people remaining in Spanish and English produced little or nothing of value.

"He comes every Sunday, tells stories, eats, drinks a little beer, then goes away." That's all they knew or were going to tell. They were not anxious to help the cops find a prized one of their own. In truth, they knew little more.

Brenner, "What the hell happened to you?"

"I shoulda shot the prick."

Jimmy frowned at Brenner. He was disgusted with himself and their screw up. His jeans and shirt were shredded from the belly first slide down the coral cliff. The medic had cut open the leg of his jeans and bandaged his ripped knee. He was now bandaging Jimmy's hand. The antiseptic stung like hell.

"You couldn't do that. Too many civilians around and we don't know for sure about the guy. Except he sure can move. Like a damn deer."

Jimmy gave him another dirty look, "Tell me about it."

Brenner, "José, collect the beer cans where the suspect was sitting. Get 'em into the lab. Have them checked for prints and a DNA test on any saliva they find. Let's spread out, see if there's any sign of his van. Parking lots, alleys, whatever. Maybe we can pull something out of this rat fuck. Ramirez, call it in, get an alert out on his van."

Brenner wasn't hopeful, and right to be skeptical. The Priest had parked up in the hills and walked in. He was driving north before Brenner's team started the search.

Skin jumping, mind roiling, adrenaline pumping, heart racing, The Priest guided the van cautiously up the 405. The same questions boiled through his mind over and over. How the hell did they do that? How did they get so close? How did they know where he would be?

He'd recognized Jimmy after he'd spotted Brenner and the two images coalesced into TV images. The hunters of the The Priest.

Did they know about the van? Was he safe driving it? The questions tumbled in on top of one another, cascading flood of thoughts drowning him in fear. He mustn't be caught. Too much work to do for his people.

He got off the 405 south of the airport. Here, if he had to, he could jump out and run on foot or dodge down an alley. Christ, they were so close!

No sirens followed him out of San Pedro, none on the 405. Not sure of themselves, then. No heavy backup. He kept checking his rearview mirror for pursuit. Thought they'd take him by surprise, corner him at the beach.

Thank the Gods he'd recognized that detective, Santos, Jimmy Santos. Son-of-a-bitch was one of the People. One of his People. Why is he an enemy of the Mexica. He'd make the perfect sacrifice, and soon.

It was getting dark. The Priest drove in behind one of the fast food shacks that littered the PCH just north of Sunset. He parked and sat. He waited. Nothing followed him in. He was safe, for the moment.

After hard dark, he removed the Beretta from under the seat and shoved it into his belt at the small of his back. Stuffed his maps in his hip pocket. He wiped down the entire van—removed the plates, shoved them deep into a dumpster, walked to the beach and west toward his cave.

How to find Santos? How to track him, capture him? Find his hunter before he was found. Show the world the power his mission gave him. The power his mission demanded of him.

Sacrifice Santos, the traitor-warrior, and present him at Parker Center—Police Headquarters, heart of the LAPD world.

Fuck you, Anglos! Fuck you, Santos! His mind raced his steps as he fled north to his cave, his sanctuary.

Jimmy leaked the almost-capture to a TV news anchor who'd done him favors in the past. She did him proud.

"Unidentified sources close to the LAPD investigation of the Priest's killings speaking off-the-record today disclosed a major break in the case. On Sunday an LAPD task force narrowly missed capturing a major suspect in the case. They are moving quickly to identify this man and expect to make an arrest in the next few days. Chief Rowland of the LAPD refused comment on this report citing the ongoing investigation."

Jimmy figured this might take some heat off Brenner, give them a little breathing room and worry the hell out of The Priest. That it was mostly smoke didn't bother him at all.

40

Brenner conducted a briefing on Monday afternoon in the Priest case room. Jimmy, Captain Nolan, ten detectives assigned to the case, the FBI profiler, two FBI agents, a rep from the county sheriffs and the CHP office listened. They were crammed into the small windowless room, walls covered with crime scene photos, a rotation duty chart, evidence charts and notes and arrows connecting various bits. They sat on steel folding chairs. Brenner paced in front of a scarred steel desk.

"The guy on Sunday looks like our man. We've talked to all the people who were there. This is a regular Sunday gathering, almost like a church service. He tells stories about the Mexican past. They think this dude is an Aztec Shaman. He encourages this idea. It all squares with Jimmy's and our UCLA prof's theory that our perp is well-versed in the Aztecs. It also squares with the perps statement to the news media. Two other bits from the story group: One guy is almost sure the perp is a Vietnam Vet. No one has a clue where he lives." He paused to light a cigar.

Nolan jumped in like a teacher reprimanding a student. "Lieutenant, new department regs forbid smoking in the building. Please don't." Brenner viciously stubbed out the cigar.

Jimmy, ignoring, "What do we have on the van?"

Brenner, "The CHP's who stopped a van on the night Donahue was snatched describe the guy we saw on Sunday. Their description of the van matches Jo-Jo's, the one we have from the Donahue killing. He's been smart and careful so far. He'll probably ditch the van. He's gotta figure we know about it if we knew enough to reach out to him on Sunday. We should keep an eye out for it but he won't be near it."

A young plainclothes detective slammed into the room. "Lieutenant Brenner, we've got a name! Oops, sorry."

Brenner, "Thats okay, Dave, what'cha got?"

"The lab just phoned in. The beer cans you picked up at the beach. Good partials on one and two clear on the other. They ran them through the computer. The Feds kicked back an ex-Marine. Francisco Villa. They're pulling his records, will send them here ASAP. Looks like he left Nam in the spring of '74."

"Good news, finally. Okay guys, take the back trail. You got a name now, find out what plane he left Nam on. Where did it take him? Plug this confirmed vet info into your profiles. Donaldson, you get on to the DMV. Find out all you can from them. Particularly about his van. Address maybe. Run this name through VICAP and NCIC. Jimmy, you and I'll take the VA. Maybe with a name and a military record, they'll finally loosen up. Be willing to give us a hand."

Nolan, "It won't sit well with city hall if you antagonize the VA Hospital. Make sure you check with the Mayor's office."

Working to keep a straight face and obviously not meaning a word, Brenner replied, "Sure thing Captain." He turned to the others. "You guys from the Sheriff's office—soon as we get anything on that van, I want you to find it, capisce? This is looking good. Something breaking our way. Any questions?"

Jimmy, "I got one for Cap'n Dan. You got any words of wisdom for us on how to catch this guy? I mean, other than keeping our lungs healthy and staying in touch with the Mayor's office?" He lit a Camel as he said it.

Nolan. trying for dignity, "Very funny Mr. Santos. You get paid extra for your humor?"

"You forget, Captain, I don't get paid." Jimmy blew the smoke into the air as the men around the table tried not to crack up.

The Sheriff's rep, "Knock it off guys. What about this 'arrest in the next few days' news story, you LAPD guys holding back on us?"

Jimmy, "Nah, they are just making shit up, grabbing headlines. Some stringer in San Pedro musta heard about the dust-up last Sunday. Put two and two together and got five. The station made it seem viable by assigning a 'source' to it."

Brenner looked over at Jimmy and barely suppressed a grin. The briefing split up and Jimmy and Brenner headed for the VA Hospital. They didn't check with the Mayor's office.

41

"He is a Marine Corp vet who left Nam in the spring of '74. Here's his picture from the Pentagon file. Name, Francisco Villa. Now, can you help us?" Jimmy sat quietly and let Brenner do the talking. Maybe he and his badge could dent Tilley's armor. They were in Doctor Tilley's VA office.

Tilley, "Well I don't—"

"Doctor, this information is a direct result of our personally hearing this man, Villa, talking to a group of Mexican-American citizens last Sunday. The picture is from the Defense Department. The Mexican-Americans believe he is a Shaman. They believe he is this man who calls himself The Priest. A man we know to be a killer, a mass killer. A man who went on the radio and claimed responsibility for these killings." Brenner was losing it. He took one of his little cigars out, realized where he was, and sat twirling it in his big fingers.

Jimmy, "Doctor, please, this is no longer conjecture. This is hard evidence. We need you to take this info to your doctors. Or let us talk to them. See if any of them know this man, have treated him. If they are willing to talk to us about him."

"It's still a big problem for us. Patient rights don't just go away because you have some tenuous evidence. We must—"

Brenner, "Doc how about this. You lay it all out for your people. Let them decide. We'll leave our contact numbers with you. If one of them contacts us directly, you can keep the hospital out of it. Will that work?"

"Perhaps. One of them could be acting as a result of the media coverage. That might be the answer."

Bingo, thought Jimmy, Brenner's given him a way to cover his ass if the shit hits the fan. Blame it on the media and leave somebody else's ass out in the cold. Good old bureaucratic do-si-do.

Brenner, "Good. Here's a card for each of us. You or any doctor can call either or both. Mr. Santos has the full confidence of the department."

They were in Jimmy's Jag on the way back downtown.

"Jesus, what a putz."

"Couldn't sum him up better myself," replied Jimmy.

That afternoon Nolan, acting through the LAPD press office, went around Brenner and Jimmy and released Villa's name, a computer-enhanced photo and a bio to the media. Got himself five minutes on the six and eleven news. Wanted for questioning in the investigation of The Priest killings. No charges filed. Just questioning. Blah, blah, blah.

The release mentioned The Priest's Vietnam service, his hometown and hinted that he may have spent time at the VA Hospital. Nolan's action proved that he could not only be a pain in the ass but dangerous. Regardless of who released it, the press packet served to involve the public and, more importantly, to dangle bait for the doctors at the VA. Predictably, it created a media storm. The Priest's name and photo led the local and national news and would for days.

42

A week spent at the cave, in the woods, on the beach. A thin mental veneer of peace formed. The trap at Cabrillo Beach had been too close, too goddamn close. They knew too much.

Van abandoned. He needed transportation. He took the bus into West L.A.. Hung around the Mexican worker pickup points at Sawtelle and Pico.

Chavez going down to Mexico for a couple of weeks, maybe a month. A hundred bucks from his dwindling cash rented The Priest a beat-up '79, dark blue Toyota Tacoma. Use it, keep it running while Chavez was in Mexico.

Find Santos. Not hard; TV coverage, a name and a phone book. Techstar Security, 1678 North Maple Drive, Beverly Hills. Hang out in the neighborhood with tools in the truck. Occasionally sweep leaves off the sidewalk. Move the truck. Keep the parking entrance in sight. Sweep some more. Use a stick with a nail in the end to pick up trash. Put it in a bag. No one paid the slightest attention to him. The Priest was invisible. Two days later, there he was: Santos, driving a green '82 Jag pulling in at eight thirty-five AM.

The Priest felt a hot wave of hatred that this man, one of his people, was his hunter. Traitor to the Mexica. Warrior-Hunter of The Priest. He wanted to scream to the Gods, to the sky, the trees, the Earth Mother.

See this traitor to our people. Wait for my sacrifice. His heart will bleed for his treason. His heart's blood will wash over the Temple stones and splash into the sacred bowl in sweet atonement. We'll take his power, use his power, defeat our enemies.

He got in the truck and waited. Two hours later Santos drove out of the building. He didn't notice the Mexican driver in an old pickup truck behind him; L.A. streets are full of them.

For four days The Priest followed Jimmy. He found his house on The Peninsula. He saw where he parked when he visited Brenner. Followed them to lunch at Barney's Beanery. He followed him to a meeting with Fulo. He had no idea what Jimmy was doing at UCLA. Curious.

The Priest knew he was taking a risk following Jimmy. Often, he lost him. Let him disappear. Better than risk being spotted. Constants in Jimmy's life developed. His house, the office, the police station, his girlfriend's. Jimmy could be picked up anywhere. Patience. No time limits, no schedule. The second day, The Priest followed him to Alison's and slowed to watch her greet Jimmy at the door.

He kept rolling. Beautiful woman. Girlfriend? Santos' woman?

A couple of the guys knew him, figured he needed a day's work. No problem. They were doing the yard on the uphill side of Alison's. He studied Alison's house. Go slow.

43

Jimmy answered the phone at his desk. "Hello, Santos."

"Mr. Santos. My name is Bartholome Annucci, Bart for short, I'm a psychiatrist at the VA hospital here in L.A., just got back to work after a vacation in New York. Tilley briefed the staff on your request about this Priest business. I think I may be able to help."

Jimmy jumped in, "What kinda help? Do you know this guy? When can I see you?"

"Some of my Hollywood colleagues tell me you can keep secrets. You must realize the ethical bind I'm in. I won't talk to the police. I'll talk with you only on the basis of deep background, nothing for attribution. If that's acceptable, come out anytime this morning. I'm in an office right down the hall from Tilley. Name's on the door." He hung up.

Jimmy scribbled the name on a scrap of paper and dashed out of the office. On the way out to the VA hospital he called into the office to let them know where he'd be. He didn't notice the blue pickup truck that followed him from his garage.

———

Jimmy wound his way through the labyrinthine corridors of the VA hospital. Cheap fluorescent lights, dirty walls; only the dirty, glazed terra cotta floor tile relieved the grayness, but even these reminded Jimmy of old, dried blood.

After three previous trips to Tilley's office, Annucci's office was a pleasant relief. Jimmy noticed that Annucci did all he could to eliminate military rigor and grayness from his office. Opposite the door was the window wall, looking out into a small courtyard filled with L.A.'s tropical plants.

The room was dominated by book cases. Plenty of psychiatry, psychology and human behavior volumes but also history, art and fiction. Several collector's series of classics, Dickens, Balzac, Scott and Stevenson. Jimmy also noticed many volumes in Latin, Greek and German.

After they had introduced themselves, Jimmy was drawn to a collection of two dozen small bonelike objects on Annucci's desk and bookshelves. They looked like little sawed-off people.

Jimmy pointed to them. "What are those?"

"Reindeer antler people. Inuit—they make them for sale to the tourists. It happens with shrinks; a patient will give you a little gift. If you keep it in the office, other patients see it and assuming you collect them, give you another. Pretty soon, you are collecting them. That little family's been growing for about fifteen years."

Slouching in Annucci's visitors chair, Jimmy wondered if this wizened little man was the key that would unlock The Priest case.

Annucci came right to the point, "Let's say there is such a man as you described to Tilley, who had been a patient here. Further, for the sake of argument, let's say he was a patient of mine. From Tilley's rundown, there seems a strong possibility, even probability, that this hypothetical patient is your Priest, a killer who will kill again. This is what makes me inclined to talk to you. I'm on very shaky ground here, ethically. So here's what I want to do. Run it down for me as you did for Tilley. If it's as convincing from you as I've conjured in my head, we'll talk."

Jimmy did.

"Okay. God and the American Psychiatric Association help me. I don't really know if what I can tell you will be helpful. You'll be the judge of that. I have—had, he hasn't shown up for the last two months—a patient who fits your description to a tee. He's forty-five but looks younger...Lets get out of here. New hospital regs, I need a smoke, and I'll bet you do too. Talking about a patient is making me nervous as hell."

Outside the door to the parking lot, Annucci got his pipe going and Jimmy lit a Camel. Annucci indicated a nearby bench and they sat.

"Francisco Villa is a tormented man." He told Jimmy about the Priest's grandfather, his belief that he was an Aztec Shaman, his life through high school. "His grandfather constantly preached to the boy his inherited greatness. Imagine, if you will, growing up Mexican-American in West Texas in the

1960's. You go to school believing you're the greatest thing since the mighty Montezuma. You're six years old.

"You are dirt poor. Sixty-five percent of your classmates are Anglos. How great do they make you feel. How great do they think you are? Spic, wetback—these are some of the milder insults you put up with every hour of every school day. You are never chosen to play on any team. None of the Anglo girls will talk to you. Your teacher barely tolerates you. You wind up in the outcast, small group of Mexican-American students, hunker down and try to survive.

"But everyday when you go home and Grandpa force feeds you greatness. He's honest, well-meaning; believes every word of what he's saying. Villa is too timid, too sensitive to tell him about his treatment in school. Doesn't want to embarrass the old man.

"So he represses it. Holds it inside. Six, eight years this continues. Enough internal conflict to make this sensitive boy vague about reality. Now we jump to the late 60s. Villa joined the Marines. Am I telling you more than you want to know?"

Jimmy, "Not at all. The more I know about this guy, the better chance I have of putting his ass away."

"Right." Annucci got his pipe going again and continued. "1969, Villa is shipped to Vietnam. For the first three or four months, no activity in his file. Then, notes about him being MIA for forty-odd days. Three weeks later he's missing again. This becomes a pattern if you're looking for it. Obviously, nobody was. Somebody should have asked, what's he doing out in the bush weeks at a time, by himself. Eventually a young Lieutenant did. Interviewed Villa, sedated him and sent him here. Villa having only the vaguest of reasons why."

Jimmy, "Do you have any idea what he was doing out in the bush?"

"From other patients and doctors, I picked up fragments of rumors that I'd dismissed until this Priest business came up. Jimmy, they seemed like dope-generated revenge fantasies. Now I'm not so sure. During the time Villa was in Nam and, particularly in the region where he was assigned, rumors flew thick and fast about something in the jungle killing VC and cutting their hearts out. It was real enough that the VC distributed wanted posters on what they called 'The Phantom Warrior.' Sound familiar?"

Jimmy, "Jesus. Graham was the young lieutenant you mentioned. He's the one who doped up Villa and put him on a plane to the States."

"I think you're right. That brings us up to the point where I meet Villa in 1976. He'd been talking to Dr. Margaret Bumford before he was transferred to me. Villa always called her 'Ole Bitch.' You can guess from that their relationship was less than therapeutic. With me, after a while, he began to open up a bit. Enough that I learned something of his early life as I've related it to you.

Not enough that I can point you in any real direction. I don't know where he lives, for instance. Rough—outdoors, I'm pretty sure. Probably has no real job. He wanted library books, so he used my address for a card."

"What kinda books?"

"History, particularly Mexican history."

"Which branch of the library? Maybe some lead there."

"I doubt it, but it's the branch here in Westwood, the one closest to the hospital."

"Any further ideas on where I might start to look for this guy?"

"No, not really. Early on, I had hopes that he and I were accomplishing something. Then, something knocked the props out from under him. He went into a tailspin. Began missing appointments, very secretive when he was here."

"When was this? The shift in his behavior."

"Three and a half months ago. Early May, Cinco de Mayo. There was a drive-by massacre in Olvera Street. He was there. Three of his people, as he called them, were killed. Nine were wounded and hurt very badly. He was very upset. Not least by the cavalier attitude of the cops and the media—just three more dead Mexicans, ho-hum. He was livid over that."

"Did he mention what he was doing there? Olvera Street, I mean."

"Storytelling. Aztec stories. That had become the focus of his life. He started doing it and found that people loved to hear them. I had high hopes that eventually that would be his key to recovery. His introduction into the world he'd always held at bay."

"One further question for now, Dr. Annucci. Do you see any sexual component in these killings?"

"Not from what I know of them. If it's Villa, and I think it is, he's doing exactly what he said he's doing. Trying to attract the favorable attention of his Gods. He's killing and sacrificing for his people, the Mexica. Misguided, horrible—frightening, even—but on some level, to him, honorable, understandable, productive. He truly believes that he is a Priest-Warrior of his people and that his actions will eventually bring them great blessings. This is the key to understanding him."

"Any idea how I can contact this Grandfather of his?"

"All I have is a name and PO box in Texas from his personnel file. Not much help, I'm afraid. But I'll give it to you."

"It's a place to start. Thanks, Doctor. I know this wasn't easy for you, but it's a big help. Maybe we can get this psycho off the streets soon. If you think of anything else, here's my card, please give me a call."

As Jimmy climbed into the Jag, the presence of a blue pickup truck parked in the shade barely registered. Seeing a lot of those lately, he thought. Dismissing the thought, he drove back to the office.

The Priest had parked in the dappled, tree-shaded corner of the VA hospital parking lot. He left the truck baking in the sun and pretended to take a nap under a tree. Through half closed eyes he watched the psych wing. It was his fourth day of tailing Jimmy. How the hell did he know to come here? Who is he going to talk to? How much did they know about him?

He watched as Jimmy and Annucci came outside and sat down. Sweat was running into his shirt collar and down his ribcage. Not all of it was from the August heat. His thoughts continued to race.

Annucci, betraying me? Annucci knows nothing. Told him shit. Some ancient history. Nobody, not even Annucci knows about the cave, the Temple. Nothing that will help the traitor Santos.

He saw Jimmy look at his truck. Careful, he thought, be ready to run. When Jimmy drove off without any move toward the truck, The Priest finally quit holding his breath and breathed deep. Must stop Santos. Must sacrifice him, and soon. His woman.—get to him through her. She is key. Soon. Soon.

Tied together. The Priest remembered Paco's stories of warrior duels. Favored captives were awarded the most honorable death: two warriors, the captive and the victor, were tied together—arm tied to arm. The victor armed with a vicious obsidian blade, the captive with only a sword.

Fight to the death. Santos had the LAPD, The Priest, his cunning. The Priest longed to encourage his people but the danger was too great. He must stay in the shadows till he could sacrifice Santos.

Santos talking to Annucci and setting the trap at Cabrillo Beach haunted him. He'd wake screaming in the cave, Santos holding a nightmare knife at his throat. He'd have to wait. Almost caught him on that run up the cliff face. Smart, too, a dangerous enemy. A warrior.

Capture and sacrifice his woman first. Make Santos wild with grief and rage. Divert his energy. Confuse his focus. Throw him off balance. Make him careless. Then, take him. Sacrifice him! Only then could he claim his place as Savior, Warrior-King of his people. Soon. Soon. Now watch his woman and wait.

44

Jimmy was in his garden watering neglected plants, plucking off dead leaves and blossoms. They always suffered when he was on a case. He had a cold Tecate and a Camel going, only a fragment of his mind on the plants. He was totally unaware of the beauty yards from his elbow.

The Pacific was slamming into the sand, waves rolling far up the beach, hissing songs of sand and saltwater. A stiff onshore breeze buffeted the seagulls and pelicans, backlit by the setting sun as they worked the crashing waves for supper. Summer was drawing to its imperceptible close over Southern California.

He had turned down an invite to join the cops for a 'quick one' at their watering hole near Parker Center. Alone and obsessed with the Priest again, he thought.

Donahue? As they said in Georgia, the guy probably needed killing. He was the vocal tip of the pervasive racism in L.A.

In the South of Jimmy's youth, it had been the blacks. Here it was the Mexicans. Vilified, misunderstood. Doing all the jobs that no one else would or wanted to do. A constant and growing presence that scared the hell out of the typical, ignorant redneck. Somebody to blame for the difficulties of living.

He finished fussing with the plants, dropped into his favorite deck chair, put his feet up and continued to worry. One of Southern California's finer sunsets continued unnoticed.

What was the killer saying through these dump sites? Was it 'look at you? Look at what you are doing' to—? That is the real question here. It's more, 'look at what you're doing to my people.' Going around in fucking circles again.

He'd been involved in meetings all day about the Priest. The task force.

He and Brenner preferred to work with a small group, but politics demanded a task force. The public wanted to see action and, to them, a task force meant action. The Mayor insisted on giving it to them.

The Chief had taken the lead at the last press conference, careful to ensure that Brenner was standing at his right hand. Jimmy was stationed just over his left shoulder. The Chief answered all the reporters' questions noncommittally. Just enough meat to ensure that they didn't go for his throat. Brenner and Jimmy were there so that if, later, the media wanted blood, the Chief could feed them to the press as the fuckups. They were the ones who couldn't find The Priest.

The Priest's photograph on every newscast, in every newspaper. He'd let his hair grow since his Marine photo was taken. The computer enhanced photo showed it long. He chopped it off. A cap or hat and a pair of almost no-prescription reading glasses from a drugstore helped change his appearance. Still, so dangerous, media into the hunt.

Even his beloved beach was dangerous with all the news coverage. One stroller recognizing him could lead Santos and his fat Lieutenant friend to the area. No-go. Must keep out of sight during the day. Night, a friend. Suicide, trying to snatch Santos' woman from that studio. Too many people. Too much traffic. All inside the walls. Some other way. Must come up another plan.

Maybe go for Santos? No. Better keep him distracted, focus on his woman. Dangerous man. Distraction. Santos at his beach house. Isolated, in L.A. terms. Deception. A feint. Make Santos think he's the target. Confuse the bastard. Destroy his confidence. Yeah. Now move. Tonight.

Dark. A rare summer thunderstorm slashing down the beach—perfect. The Rain God, Quetzalquoatl, helping. The Priest lay on his belly against the low outer wall of Santos' beach garden. Black clothes, cap and gloves melded him into the shadows. Rainwater puddling under him. No movement on the beach. The house quiet except for an old lady occasionally crossing a lighted window on the second floor. Santos' car not in its usual space.

Inch by inch The Priest swung open the garden gate and slithered toward the ocean-side glass doors. Eight feet in, he was out of sight of the old lady's windows. Still on his belly, he reached the doors. No security system. Quick work with his Buck knife and he was in.

Silence. Stillness. Nothing but the tick of a clock, the hum of a refrigerator. Adrenalin screaming. Ocean hiss. A lightning flash lit the room. Silence. Stillness. Nothing but the tick of the clock, the hum of the fridge. Adrenaline still screaming. A lightning flash lit the room.

The Priest waited for his eyes to adapt to the dark. Using a small pen light he moved deeper into the house. Start with the desk. Nothing locked, cocky bastard. He went through every drawer. In each one he carefully examined the contents, then deliberately left them slightly rearranged. He put a small gift on the desk. Bedroom area next. Same drill. No mess. Nothing obvious. Kitchen, bathroom, living area all the same. He ignored the drips from his rain-soaked clothes. Headlights swept across the room as a car swung into the driveway from the street. In seconds, The Priest was out the glass doors. He slipped the lock closed with his knife and vanished over the wall into the storm.

Jimmy stepped out of the Jag and the hair stood up on his arms. He ignored the warning as he dashed to the door out of the rain. He allowed it to register as he keyed the front door and swung it open. A faint odor was the first clue. He pulled his Beretta and stood, waiting. His hand hovered over the light switch. Slowly his eyes adjusted to the deeper darkness in the house. Nothing moved. No strange sounds. The fridge hummed. No air moving from an open door. No broken window. Just that faint, foreign, man smell.

Something was out of whack. His house felt strange. He moved to the right of the door, reached for the light switch and flicked it on while the Beretta searched the room for a target. Nothing. Bullshit!

Something! He crossed to the beach doors—locked. His shoes crunched damp sand on the floor—wrong. Tuesday; the housekeeper should have vacuumed this morning. Scratches around the aluminum lock. Rainwater footprints. Water puddles. He carefully checked the rest of the house, anywhere a person could hide. Nothing. He put the Beretta away, got a Tecate from the fridge, lit a Camel and began a search. Desk first.

Twenty minutes later he called Brenner at home.

"Yeah, very slick. He went through everything in the house. No, nothing missing. No, Lise didn't hear a thing. Send out a print team, will you? Ask them to bring a comparison card with The Priest's prints—yeah, it was him. He left a calling card. A little Reindeer Man from Annucci's desk. Wants us to know he knows we talked to Annucci—I don't know, maybe wanted to see if I have anything lying around on the case. Fat chance—okay, I'll call you when they leave."

Two hours later, back on the phone with Brenner.

"On the toilet handle. A perfect thumb print. Took his gloves off to take a leak—Yeah, our boy all right. Gutsy prick. Maybe I should hire a private dick and some body guards, whadya ya think?"

Jimmy called Alison and they talked for half an hour. His day. Hers. Sick of all the security. Been ten days, now. Progress on the picture. She told a funny story of a young actor, insecure and talking endlessly about his motivation. Sometimes she wondered if she weren't better off with the monkeys.

He mentioned The Priest's visit. Told her there was nothing to worry about, just a look around. The Priest had made it obvious...a threat, maybe. He was a long time getting to sleep. What in the hell did The Priest hope to gain by searching his house. Distraction? Showing off? Spooky motherfucker.

45

Alison was in her home office, sorting through casting photos, when the phone rang. "No, I'm up, come on over, I'll put the coffee on—No, don't tell me till you get here. See you in about fifteen minutes—Yes, I miss you too."

She went out to the kitchen and began making coffee, her mind on Jimmy. Their relationship—God, how she hated that word. Someone should come up with something better. Did it describe what was developing between them? Jimmy was such a loner, so closed off. Charming, witty, understanding, attentive when he was around. Then he'd vanish for days. No calls, nothing. Then, like tonight, out of the blue, he'd call, acting as if his three day absences were perfectly normal. Slightly sheepish, but not apologetic. No explanation.

I'm almost as isolated as when I was with the cinematographer-husband who only wanted to film Baboons. Well, not quite.

Most mysterious of all, Jimmy'd obviously been thinking of her. Maybe the whole time. Is this his idea of normalcy? Must be. She knew it was not hers. She was on the phone to her friends, even casual ones, often. Liked to keep up, participate, touch base. Her insecurity? Maybe. God knows Jimmy wasn't insecure. Confident, warm and straightforward were the descriptors she would choose to for him. The electronic peal of the doorbell startled her.

Midnight. Overcast sky, a black, black night. No breeze moved. The Priest parked his truck two blocks away from Alison's. He killed the dome light, opened the door and slid into the darkness. Dressed all in black—jeans, sneakers and cotton sweat shirt, thin black leather gloves, his Beretta in the back of his belt.

His trip through the quiet backyards was slowed only once by a noisy poodle, yapping on a screened-in porch. Frozen in place by a flicked-on light, The Priest watched as a stooped old woman scolded the dog and let him run joyously back into the house.

Cautiously, he melded into the shadows ten yards from Alison's living room window, from which the voice of Patsy Cline floated. Sheer curtains were drawn. One lamp on. A flickering light from a fireplace.

The Priest settled to watch. Night after night, this had become the pattern. He was drawn irresistibly to this nighttime watching of Jimmy. Hating Jimmy. Jimmy, his enemy, one of his people, a Mexica, his hunter. A man who had everything The Priest did not. Sleepless nights spent watching, planning, hating. Jimmy, his woman. Soon. Soon.

"You could go home to Minnesota for a while. Till we catch this fucker. You'd be safe there. This guy sent me a pretty clear message that I'm a target; you may be next." Jimmy was trying to convince Alison to get outta Dodge. She wasn't buying.

"Nope, nada, no way. I've got a movie to prep and a contract that says I start shooting in a week. And if I don't, Sony and Torchlight will sue my butt off. Oh, and I should mention, I love doing my job. I won't dodge the hard patches. I have fifty people asking a hundred questions a day and it's only started. Soon, it'll be a hundred an hour. There's casting, music, an editor to choose, the writer to babysit. Sets and locations to find and discuss. I can not, will not leave. We have to find another way."

"I can talk to Jerry Martin. He'd cut you some slack. Hell, he wouldn't want you hurt or—"

"Jimmy, no, I don't want that. I won't accept that. This is what I do. Part—a large part—of what I am. My work is damn important to me. Just as yours is to you. You're not leaving, so enough about my running. It ain't happening. I'm staying in Los Angeles and making my movie. Whats your plan B?"

"You are one tough lady. Damn it..." He paused, thinking, angry, frustrated. With himself, he realized. Frightened for Alison, The possibility that she could be hurt. I've finally found a woman I'm in love with. Get your shit together and protect her. Devise a plan that will ensure her safety, on her terms. "Damn it, there is no really good plan B. Bodyguards twenty-four hours a day. My people. More people at your office, here. Cops where and whenever Brenner can schedule them. I'll bring Martin to help cover you at the studio. That's what we can do. It may not be enough. But we'll make it work."

"It will. Nothing indicates he even knows I exist, and this bastard kidnaps first. He's not a distance killer. With all those people around, he'll never get close to me. No way. And if he tries, it gives you and your people a chance at him. Have you thought of that?"

"Yeah, I've thought of it. Scares hell out of me. You as bait—no way. And there's nothing that says he can't change his M.O. The pressure on him may be great enough. Who knows what he'll do?"

Alison stopped Jimmy's pacing by putting her arms around him. She looked up at him. "Hey, it'll be okay. We'll get through this. Did you mean what you said on the phone? Not just trying to calm a frightened lady, were you?"

Jimmy pulled her to him, tight. Spoke into her brown hair. "Damn right, I meant it. Yeah, I meant it, mean it. Damn it, I love you. There, I've said it. I don't want anything to happen to you—careful, you're gonna break a rib."

After a long, very satisfying kiss, Alison said, "You want to start that 24 hour watch tonight?"

Jimmy smiled and kissed her again.

Alison, "I guess that means yes.

46

The next morning, at daylight, The Priest was sitting in his truck up the hill from Alison's house. He was slouched down under his steering wheel when the teamster pulled up in front of her house. Santos' car was gone. Two minutes later, Alison came out, got in and they drove off. The silver Volvo would be easy to follow. Wait. As the Volvo left, another car pulled out of Alison's driveway and followed. The Priest recognized one of the Santos-supplied bodyguards driving. At Laurel Canyon the two cars turned south. The Priest let one car get between them and followed.

This early in the morning traffic was light. He'd have to be careful not to be spotted. They turned west on Sunset and then south again on La Cienega. The Priest kept two or three cars behind and followed them easily down to Venice then west to Overland where they again turned south.

He almost missed their turn into the gate at Sony, just crossing the intersection as the light changed. He continued south on Overland thinking about what he had seen.

A guarded, movie studio gate. Was Santos' woman an actress? How could he find out? How long would she be in there? Was Santos' man always with her? He hooked a left on Culver Boulevard and drove around the block. Another guarded gate on Ince and another on Washington.

No way to watch all three. He took the right turn back onto Overland and parked in the shopping center lot at the corner, behind the Denny's. Time for some thinking and planning. He knew her name, Alison Reed. Find out from there who she is, what job she does for Sony Pictures. A place to start.

An hour later he sat in a computer carrel at the Inglewood branch of the L.A. Public Library. 'Movie people' typed into the search engine quickly turned up Hollywood.com and the Internet Movie Database. There was Alison Reed, director, complete with credits. Another hour at the keyboard reading back issues of Hollywood Reporter and Variety and he had the name of the picture Alison was working on and knew roughly what the job entailed. A boss, highly paid, according to Variety. That explained the driver. Santos must be responsible for the bodyguards.

He returned to wait outside Alison's house, parking three blocks up the hill. The Priest hid in a bamboo thicket across the street. He could remain in place and find out what time she returned home. These canyon homes were easy to watch. Board fences, trees, bushes, tangled vines and rough topography offered many places to hide.

Santos' woman was never alone. The driver, bodyguards. Santos with her at night. All night. Cops on increased patrol through the Canyon streets. He had to get onto the movie studio grounds. How?

The next day he began watching the studio gates. Wearing his raggediest clothes, and with an old and shapeless straw hat pulled down over his eyes, he parked in the shopping center on Overland. Faking the shambling walk of the homeless, he stopped in a liquor store and bought a cheap bottle of wine. Cloaked now in the anonymity of Mexican dereliction, he crossed Washington Boulevard and wandered down the sidewalk to a position opposite the studio gate. He sat down in plain sight of the gate guards, had a long swig of his wine and leaned back against the low concrete block wall taking in the morning sunshine.

Nobody paid any attention to him. He was again invisible. The morning went slowly by, a constant stream of cars in and out. All visitors stopped at the gate for a brief conversation with the guards. Some, those with employee stickers, drove right onto the lot. Most parked in the multi-story parking garage immediately inside the lot to the right.

There was little foot traffic. Occasionally someone would walk out and disappear in the direction of the shopping center, reappearing later with coffee or shopping bags. A few beautiful girls left the Washington Boulevard bus, walked down to the gate and were admitted. Toward lunchtime a couple of pizza and other lunch delivery guys were passed through the gate. Some on bicycles.

About twelve forty-five an LAPD car made a second pass down Overland and gave him a hard look. The Priest slowly got up and shuffled off and around the corner onto Culver. Patience, he told himself. Just take it easy and watch.

He settled again across the street from the east gate on Ince.

Right in front of the MGM building, it provided a better view into the lot. Fifty yards in, a Mexican ground crew was working on the landscaping. Maybe that could be made to work for him. He was musing on this when a huge black security guard came out and politely asked him to move along.

The Priest moved. Ten minutes later he took station across from the Washington gate. This one was much quieter—mostly pedestrian traffic. Several late lunch deliveries from busy Venice Boulevard only a block to the north. He spent three hours watching, seeming to doze in the sun. By the time he staggered off at six-thirty, he had formed a plan.

The next morning, in his homeless gear, he was in place across the street from the Overland gate when Alison's two-car caravan pulled in. He watched as they drove into the bowels of the lot. A hundred yards in, the cars parked. Alison got out and disappeared with her bodyguard behind a huge grey building marked with a number 9. The drivers drove off to park. Now I know where she is. Time to move. He went back to his truck and changed clothes.

An hour later, he approached the Washington gate dressed in clean jeans, sparkling white tee shirt, a Dodger's baseball cap and sunglasses. Not a hint that of the bum who had hung out across the street yesterday. He carried a large flat pizza box. A few polite words with the gate guard and he had directions to Building 9. Stage 9, the guard called it. Smooth, no problema.

The Studio covers a huge two-city-block area, as much as eight or ten acres. Gigantic sound stages, set building and costume shops, one- and two-story office complexes, temporary offices and dressing rooms in trailers, parking lots, trucks, cars and buzzing golf carts all interconnected and supported by streets humming with hundreds of people making multiple movies. The Priest followed directions and wandered through the maze of buildings. The sun was pounding down and bouncing off the high pale grey walls. Some of the black-topped alleys felt like ovens.

He approached the stage door. Alison came out and walked the few steps to her motor home, her bodyguard two steps behind. They both glanced at him, registered 'delivery boy' and ignored him. The Priest kept walking as if to the next stage. No one paid any attention to him.

In a deserted alley he spotted a trash can, a broom and long-handled dust pan. He stuffed the pizza box into the trash can. He slipped on the wrinkled denim shirt tied around his waist, reversed his Dodgers cap, picked up the broom and dust pan and worked his way back toward the stage. He spent the next couple of hours working in the vicinity of Stage 9, easily mimicking the lazy shuffle of the bored grounds workers.

Mid-afternoon, Santos showed up. The Priest saw him walking toward Stage 9 from the parking structure. Jimmy walked as if he was completely at home in the bustle of the studio. The Priest turned slightly away from him and continued cleaning the alley where he was working. Santos checked at Alison's trailer and, not finding her there, waited with others outside the stage door. When the flashing red light went off and a bell rang they all entered the stage. A few minutes later, Santos, Alison and her bodyguard emerged. Jimmy and Alison sat in director's chairs outside Alison's trailer, where a fitful breeze made the air cooler.

The bodyguard wandered off in the direction of the canteen truck. Careful to remain unobserved, The Priest watched as Santos and Alison chatted in the shade of her trailer's canopy. Accepted by the movie crew, Jimmy waited patiently when she was called away to the stage or interrupted by the constant stream of people with questions. After an hour together and a kiss goodbye, Santos left.

The Priest continued watching. Alison and her bodyguard made several more trips between the stage and her motor home. Actors and technicians swarmed the area, several productions shooting so no predictable patterns. Golf carts zipped busily around. People everywhere; popping in and out of doors, motor homes, around corners, no discernible rhythms. The place was bustling with the business of making movies. Not a prayer in hell of snatching Alison here. He drifted off down an alley, dumped the broom and dust pan and nonchalantly walked out of the Overland Avenue gate.

47

"We have to get a warrant. If you thought getting info from Tilley was difficult, wait'll you try to talk something outta there." Brenner and Jimmy were in Brenner's office at the end of another frustrating day. Nothing was coming together fast enough. Not a peep out of The Priest. Nothing on the van. Nada. Zip, zero progress.

Jimmy, "My idea is this. Annucci mentioned this guy's heavy use of the library. Maybe some idea of what he was reading or researching will lead us somewhere. Every time you check out a book, they read your card and your book's barcode with one of those scanner things. It's fed into their computer. They should have a record of everything he has checked out. Let's go for it. Get a warrant. Go to your friendliest judge, lie a little if you have to."

"I don't think it'll be a problem. You want to glom onto everything this guy has checked out?"

"Yeah, send it over to the office. Let me go through it. Lightning may strike. Nothing else is ringing any bells. Did you reach Graham again?"

"Yeah, he confirmed what we thought. Villa is the nut he whisked out of Nam. Never thought to hear from him again. Thought the VA would deep six him into a funny farm for the rest of his life. We shoulda been so lucky.

"I'll send Susie Chan—she's our computer whiz—over to Judge Bolting in the morning. He'll sign a warrant for her. Then she can go out to Westwood and hassle the librarians. She'll get the stuff and bring it to your office. You gonna be there?"

"Have her call my cell. I might be out at the studio with Alison but I can meet Susie at the office when she's got the stuff. Keep your fingers crossed."

"You should have heard the bitching and moaning from those old biddies." Susie had obviously had a fun morning. "They first tried to tell me they didn't keep track of what people read. Too much data, violation of privacy, first amendment violations yack, yack, yack." Then, when I pointed out that Brenner wrote up the warrant allowing me into their computers to look and that I was capable of doing just that, they said the computers were down. I pointed out that the checkout desk was in full swing, computers working just fine. They realized I was not going away until they complied with the warrant.

"When I compiled a list of the stuff they said they didn't keep track of, they made me go into the stacks and dig out all this stuff myself. Long and short of it, here's the take. Four shopping bags full. They wanted me to remind you that you only have them for two weeks on the circulation stuff and a week on the research material."

"Yeah, right. This stuff is now evidence in a multiple homicide case. I'll write 'em a nice thank you note. Looks like I've got a long night ahead. Thanks Susie, you done good."

One AM and Jimmy was still at it. Books all over his office. Empty coffee cups, full ashtrays, remnants of a McDonald's supper cluttered his desk. A Camel smoldered in an ashtray. Three of the four bags stood empty on the sofa. He was starting on bag number four. His direct phone rang.

"Speak—what the hell are you doing up at this hour?"

Brenner, "Been going over the whole case again, thought I'd see if you've come up with anything."

"Mexican history. Latino history in L.A. Focus seems to be on anything Aztec. One thing though, a lot of these books have bits of sand in them. Like they'd been read on the beach. One had a leaf in it. Might be worth getting a botanist to look at it. I can't identify it. Might give us something."

"Good idea. We've got a guy helps out the lab now and then. We'll get it over to him tomorrow. How much longer you gonna keep at it?"

"Got one more bag to go through, then I'll call it a night. Anything new on your end?"

"Nada. Same old, same old. This guy's luck is holding. Talk to you. Good hunting!"

"Ciao."

Jimmy got up and stretched out the long muscles in his back, poured another cup of coffee from the dwindling thermos and started on bag number four. Same kind of material at first. Then, almost to the bottom, it changed.

It seemed to be travel books and atlases. All well-used. California, L.A., northern Mexico, South Texas, the Angeles National Forest. Eclectic collection, thought Jimmy. The battered Rand-McNally Atlas of California fell open to a double spread page of North L.A. and the Angeles National Forest.

Jimmy sat and stared at it. Where did this fit? Did it fall open here because of use by The Priest?

It's a public book. Why would it have to be him? Jimmy adjusted his desk light for a closer look. There seemed to be a very faint pattern of smudges. Pencil erasures? Fingerprints? What the hell is this about? Who made these? He decided to send it over to the lab tomorrow, see if The Priest's prints are on this page. He closed the atlas with the eraser end of a pencil and set it aside.

The next book down. Gold. A well-used copy of "Insight Guides: Los Angles," held the by-now expected grains of sand and, when he held it by the binding to shake out the sand, a tiny piece of paper that fluttered to the floor. He reached for it. Then stopped.

He dug around in his desk drawer and found a couple of toothpicks. Using them as tweezers he put the paper on his desk. A receipt. Barely legible, from the Fernwood Market on Topanga Canyon Road. How about that. Bookmark maybe. The Priest's? One more for the print lab. He teased the receipt into an envelope with the toothpicks and sealed it. Same with the little pile of sand and the leaf fragment. Three flat envelopes. Small haul for a night's work. But maybe, just maybe the first step on the path leading directly to The Priest.

48

The Priest case room seethed with activity and tension. Five detectives manned active phone lines. The Sheriff's office had found the van. North side of the PCH, two miles east of Topanga Canyon Road. Forensics had towed it in and gone over it—no prints, wiped clean, lots of blood evidence, hair and fiber samples in the back. The exterior wheel wells gave up mud and plant matter. All of it went under the microscopes.

Nobody doubted that it belonged to the Priest. Four different blood types and counting. Plates missing but make, model, scratches and color matched Jo-Jo's and CHP's description.

Jimmy realized that the location was only a few miles from the address on the receipt found in The Priest's library book. The accumulated sand fit also. He was still waiting on info regarding prints on the receipt but had results promised within the hour, with the botanist to report in by the end of day.

In anticipation, Jimmy pulled Liz off the Alison detail. She and Bart were to suit up for the beach. Begin east of the van location and work west, interview all available people on or near the beach, show the Priest's picture around. Brenner had two detectives assigned to the same general area working the highway strip and the canyon road.

The FBI called in. The plane that brought the Priest back from Nam had landed and offloaded at Edwards Air Force base, 100 miles north of L.A. Another bingo. Coming together, goddamn, it was finally coming together!

At the end of the day, gloom returned. Liz's team reported no joy on the beach interviews. Same from the detectives. No one noticed a lone Mexican walking around L.A., period. The Priest had invisibility built-in, a kind of racism at work. Liz mentioned a group of surfers who congregated in the Topanga Canyon Road area of the beach, so Jimmy and Brenner recruited three young undercover detectives from Narcotics to surf for the next few days, join the existing group and keep an eye on the beach. Get close to the surfers, try to jog their memory. Possibly spot the Priest.

The Prints on the receipt matched the Priest's. The botanist report stated only that the leaf was from a plant that grew along the Pacific coast, primarily, but not exclusively, in the area from Manhattan Beach to Santa Barbara—too large an area to be useful. More to follow on the samples from the van.

In the rush to get all this info out, the vaguely-marked atlas was buried in the lab under a pile of unrelated paperwork and forgotten.

49

Liz, her team and the detectives had just missed The Priest. At daylight, he had climbed into the blue pick-up truck and headed for Alison's. Another day or two following her might pay off. Nothing to be done with Santos, yet. Let him stew over the break-in.

Wonder if they found that print on the toilet handle? Probably, Santos seemed like a smart mother. Just not smart enough. What'd he think of his little gift from Annucci, that bastard.

The morning's trip had started as usual—down out of the Canyon, south on the way to the studio. But the driver took the Santa Monica freeway east. The Priest followed. He closed up the distance and hung in the lane behind Alison's tail car. Where are they off to this morning? Something new in the mix. The Priest followed on Vermont until they peeled off into a lot on the south side of the USC swimming pool.

He parked around the corner and, wearing his crushed straw hat and sunglasses, ambled back to watch. The three-quarter acre parking lot formed by the space between the pool complex and the four-story wall of the stadium was full of bright white trucks, all with movie transport logos, a gaggle of varied-sized mobile homes and people buzzing around everywhere. Think 'circus come to town' and you wouldn't be far off.

The area, bathed in Southern California sunlight, swarmed with the controlled, choreographed chaos of an early, first morning film location. People streamed in from the street carrying clothes on hangers or rolled other racks full of costumes from the wardrobe truck. Trucks were being unloaded, lights, cable and pipes sorted. Camera carts and dollies were readied for the day's work. Food was being ordered and served fast from a long menu on a whiteboard stuck to the side of a catering truck. Eggs, bacon, toast, oatmeal, burritos in a bewildering variety. Breakfast outdoors. Coffee, always coffee, the blood of a movie's crew. Lots of action at the coffee table, laden with pastries, bagels, donuts, fruit and walk-around food, hot water for ten varieties of tea.

Security stood around with coffee eating donuts, occasionally sorting out vehicle tie-ups. Several officious looking youngsters strode around, mumbling into walkie-talkies while studying the day's call sheet.

There were smiles on most faces, a bounce it their step—out of the studio, finally. After weeks cooped up in the dark, conditioned air, they were working in a bright, seventy-five degree, sunlit Southern California morning. Would be for days. Life didn't get much better than this.

The pool complex comprised two pools. The shallow, empty one supplied with steps was the site for two large catering tents filled with movie folks scarfing down breakfast; eggs and everything from French Toast to grits and sausage, bagels and cream cheese to bananas and apples. They crowded around eight-to-ten person tables wrapped with plastic cloths, stapled to hold against the wind, on too-low white plastic folding chairs.

The westerly pool, an Olympic size, contained the film set. It was filled with carefully filtered, heated water. Here, the greens crew was putting the finishing touches on the set, planting moss, lichen, small dead grasses and weeds on plastic rocks. A scenic artist was touching up scratches and dings created as the other crews worked. The crafts service table, being set up on the apron opposite the set, would soon be loaded with coffee, soft drinks, water and numerous snacks for easy access by the shooting crew.

The set was an exact duplicate of a fifty-yard stretch of the rocky Oregon coastline. Painted fiberglass over wooden structure, it started in the water and climbed westward into the bleacher section to a height of fifty-five feet. Near the top, scraggly evergreen trees and larger plants completed the illusion. Divers in the water were positioning a small boat and a camera raft at the shoreline. The Priest could see that if the camera were close enough the effect would be totally realistic.

The Priest continued his circuit. On the northwest corner a gate was open and unguarded. A USC Mexican grounds crew was cleaning up fallen palm fronds from the recent storm. He joined them. The morning was already getting hot and they were sweating out last night's cervezas. He helped two guys who were struggling to hoist an overloaded trash can into the back of a truck. A few minutes conversation and he had a garbled rundown on the movie crew.

Yes, they were here yesterday and two weeks before that building the set. They would be here for three, maybe four more days. Filming a scene where the hero and girlfriend crash the small boat onto the rocks. Big wind machines.

Machines that made big waves. Very generous people, gave away food and Cokes. No cervezas though. Only at day's end after we have gone home.

The Priest continued around the periphery of the site. A small crowd of neighborhood people and students had gathered in the parking lot to watch. He joined them. The set was again to the west. On his right, was a small village of motor homes. Ten or twelve set up in lines of three with alleys for access in between. Two wardrobe trucks had lines of people waiting outside. There was a constant bustle of activity around the others.

He noticed that the youngsters with the walkie-talkies were constantly referring to legal-sized sheets of paper that they carried in pockets or pouches, as they scurried around the motor homes. Schedules? Plans for the day?

As he wondered about this, Alison left her trailer with her ever-present bodyguard. She made quick stops at three motor homes and then walked over to the set. There, she was joined by six other people and, with much hand-waving and pointing, was obviously holding a meeting about the day's shooting. That finished, she returned to her trailer. Her bodyguard took up station outside on a director's chair.

Ten minutes later, an actress in period costume left her trailer and chatted with the bodyguard before wandering over to the crafts service table. The bodyguard watched her every step of the way and to stare as she created her organic breakfast. When she glanced his way, he quickly looked down so she wouldn't catch him staring.

She returned to his post in the sun and he found another director's chair for her. They continued to chat as the chaos swirled around them. The Priest watched them. Body language spoke volumes; Mr. Bodyguard was very interested, Ms Actress was reciprocating. A distraction. Good.

Fifteen minutes later one of the Walkie-Talkies knocked on the door to Alison's trailer, then waited for her outside. Alison came out wearing a half wetsuit and walked to the set with bodyguard and Walkie-Talkie. Ms. Actress tagged along. Another twenty minutes and Alison was on a raft at the edge of the set with the camera crew lining up a shot.

The Priest watched it all. Much better chance for a snatch here. Fewer people than the studio. More relaxed. Bodyguard distracted. He drifted over near the food table. One of the security cops waved him off, but kindly. No one too uptight in the warm sunshine and soft breeze. A movie crew happily working outside in good weather.

One of the Walkie-Talkies came over to the small crowd and requested their cooperation when filming began. Quiet, no flash cameras, no recording devices. As she turned to leave, her copy of the schedule fell to the pavement. She kept going. The Priest waited until he was sure she was not returning, then picked it up. He walked over to a pick-up parked in the shade, climbed up and sat on the side of the bed. Good view of the set. He opened the folded paper and studied it.

It took a few minutes. Careful reading showed that beginning tomorrow the company would be working nights, arriving at the pool at four PM. By now, The Priest knew that the company often worked ten- to twelve-hour days. All night. Opportunity. He decided to spend the day watching. Stay in the shadows. The bodyguard might have his picture close at hand, if not memorized. Careful. Careful.

50

"Man, this place is a mess." Jimmy and Brenner were recapping yet another frustrating day. The case room was indeed a mess. New laws to the contrary, ashtrays overflowed on half a dozen desks, smoke hanging in the air. Discarded newspapers, fast food wrappers, bits of dead Big Macs and Whoppers littered desks. Someone had missed the trash can with a discarded, half-eaten burrito, which lay splattered on the floor awaiting the patient cleaning crew who struggled to keep order in this most disorderly of rooms. A varying fifteen to twenty harried law officers with the biggest case of their careers spent little time worrying about their surroundings.

Only Susie Chan's desk was clean and neat. Must be that computer geek thing, Jimmy thought.

"You had any further thoughts on your visitor?" Brenner lit another of his black cigars.

"Just what we talked about. I think he's coming unglued. Thinks maybe he'll rattle me. Obviously wanted me to know it was him. Annucci confirmed he was missing the bone man. He feels Villa may be reacting to the pressure."

"We're so damn close. I can feel it. Like a boulder balanced at the top of a cliff. One tiny shove, swoosh, down it rolls."

Brenner spit this out around the smoke from his twelfth black cigar of the day. He had begun counting. His teenage daughter was giving him increasing hell about the smoking.

"Swoosh. What the hell kinda word is that for our leader to be using? Swoosh, Jesus. Next you'll be saying shazam. Then where'll we be?"

"Still sitting here on our ass, hoping for a break in this goddamn case, that's where. Don't you ever go home? Spend some time with Alison?"

"Time with Alison, fond memory. She's so busy with that damn movie, I'm lucky to see her an hour a day. Man, I thought cops kept crazy hours. She leaves the house at five-thirty, gets home at ten then does homework for two or three hours. Hasn't slept more than four hours a night in a month. Tomorrow, she starts shooting nights through the end of the week. Then I'll really never see her except when I go to the set. It's a bitch."

Mark gave Jimmy a skeptical look. Who's he think he's kidding. "Ah, the course of true love."

"Fuck you. Back to work for a minute, then I'll buy you a beer. There's something gnawing at me about this beach connection. Too many pointers in that direction. Yeah, I know nobody has turned up a thing up there. Still, I've got this itch. Let the team know that I'm gonna be up there tomorrow. I'm gonna spend the day combing that neighborhood and the beach area. I think it's worth the effort. Tell our surfer bunch to ignore me. They don't know me if I come around asking dumb questions. Maybe I can shake something loose that others have missed."

"Done. You won't get any argument from me. Let's get outta here and have a cool one. Feels like Miller time to me."

"You got it. A couple, then I'm gonna drop by USC."

51

Night. Shadows. Friends. The Priest wore black sneakers and jeans, a navy blue sweatshirt and a black baseball cap pulled low. Deep shadows hid his face. His black belt pouch carried his blowgun and darts. He smiled when he realized he blended in with both spectators and crew. The crew was big on jeans, sweatshirts and baseball caps.

The Priest watched as the movie company created a tempest in the USC pool. The wave machines agitated the water. Rain towers, twenty feet high, sprayed gallons of water in torrents. Huge fans whirled the water in gale-driven fury at the rocks. Manmade lightning flashed. The tiny row boat with two stars aboard tried to make landfall on the fake rocky shore. The actor jumped overboard and tried to pull the boat up onto the rocks.

The boat got swept away from him, crashed. The actress was dumped into the swirling water. The actor dived in to rescue her. They swam to safety.

Safety divers hovered. Time and again some detail went wrong. The storm was shut off, the boat and its wet, cold wet actors were dried, changed and make-up restored, re-set. Alison, the camera crew and their raft were repositioned and they tried again and again. Alison now wore a full black wetsuit as protection from the night cold.

Only a few spectators still watched. Boredom and the hour had driven most to their homes; it was two fifteen AM. The Priest's cover was dwindling with the crowd.

The high-contrast lighting on set provided cover in the black shadows. Lighting on the scene focused everyone's attention there. Beyond the set, harsh directional work lights made pools of intensely bright light and areas of blackest shadow. When the last of the spectators went home, he would watch from those shadows. It was the first of four filming nights. A reconnaissance mission for The Priest.

At three, after Alison once again called "cut" and held a short conference on the camera raft, the crew dragged the raft to the side and pulled the boat out of the water. The actors were wrapped in blankets and hustled off to their trailers. Alison, a Walkie-Talkie and her bodyguard headed for the food tent and the coffee pot.

The crew swarmed in to reset lights and tie down the boats. Safety divers flopped on the pool sides like weary seals. The Priest had watched the same furious activity each time the company prepared to film a new sequence. The changeover activity totally engaged the attention of most of the crew. At the same time, any idle crew members seemed the least involved, taking a brief period of relaxation. Now was the time when the bodyguard always drifted over and chatted with Ms. Actress. Alison often drifted off by herself, totally absorbed in her thoughts. The crew left her alone.

Some of the crew never joined this activity. The Priest noticed that the drivers and a few of the food service people always stayed on the sidelines. At night they occupied the shadows, sitting in their vehicles, napping, smoking, filling the time with idle chatter and gossip as they waited for dawn. When it came time to make his move, these would be the dangerous ones. Hidden, maybe watching. The night crept on toward dawn. The rhythm was established and noted.

Set up a shot. Film it until all satisfied. Organized chaos while breaking down and setting up the next shot. Repeat. When the night sky began to turn the grey of morning the First Assistant Director shouted "that's a wrap!" The signal to everyone to go home.

Everyone galvanized into action. Lights shut off. Cables coiled and loaded into trucks or left in place to wait till dark. Yells of "turn the damn light back on, I'm still working here." Equipment carts banging together in the dark. Vehicles starting. Coolers on the trucks opened and beer passed around. The security cops were the first away, their work day over with one left asleep in his car to 'watch' through the day.

Alison headed for her trailer. The bodyguard watched her go, stopping for a final word with his new friend. The Walkie-Talkie was stopped by an actor with a question. Alison was alone in the chaos of the end of a long night's filming. Weariness showed in her every step, unaware that her protectors had dropped away.

The Priest watched. He was twenty feet from her trailer door in the shadowed corner where a large palm and a dumpster abutted. The lights between the trailers had died with the generator's hum. Everyone's attention was on packing and going home. Now, he thought. If it's like this tomorrow, this is where I'll take her. Three more mornings to make it happen.

The Priest spent the day at his Temple. He needed the peace, the deep solitude found only in his magical place. He spent the day fasting and praying for help in his mission and for his people. He sang the ancient war songs. His chanting reverberated from the towering rock walls till late in the afternoon, Nahuatl echoing around the canyon. He left in time to get to USC at dark.

Another night of watching. Once, he dozed off as he sat in shadow with little happening on the set. He snapped awake when a crew member stumbled over him in the dark. The guy had slipped off into the dark to take a leak. Shouldn't have left the set; too embarrassed to say anything to The Priest.

This night a repeat of last night's rhythms. At dawn, The Priest was in position. Alison again wandered off from her watchers as everyone prepared to go home. The Priest approached her from his shadowy place under the royal palm. He brought his dart gun to his mouth to fire. A Walkie-Talkie, calling her, dashed around the corner of Alison's trailer. Stopped her with a question about the next night's filming.

The Priest faked a cough, ducked his head, palmed the dart gun and strolled by them. He turned and headed for the parking lot. Just another crew member going home. Close, very damn close.

Again he went north to his Temple. Important to get close to his Gods. Plead for their help. Their Guidance.

52

Jimmy arrived in the Topanga Canyon Road area early on the morning of Alison's fourth night shoot. He spent the morning conducting a car search for any possible place a homeless person could call home. He drove every road, checked each alley, walked the perimeter of all the parking lots. Nothing.

Armed with the picture of the Priest, he talked to business owners. Starting with the fast food place where The Priest had left the van, he worked the beach strip to the west. Nothing. He stopped at a seafood place for lunch. Afterward he started west from the fast food joint. Still nothing. Several people had already spoken to Liz and her partner and some mentioned having seen the photo on TV. Why all the fuss? What did the guy do? Jimmy kept it vague. No sense in getting people in a vigilante mood. No one remembered seeing The Priest.

He decided to start in the Canyon itself, with the market where the receipt originated. Three and a half miles up the Canyon was the Fernwood Market, an old quonset structure with a movie-style false stucco front painted a brilliant white. The two guys running the place were not sure. They might have seen the guy. Mexican, you know, didn't really notice them unless they caused trouble. Might be worth talking to the night girl, she might have seen him.

He started working down the east side of the Canyon road, house to house. Harder here; people uncomfortable opening doors to strangers. Residents in the canyon had a reputation for minding their own business and expected the same from the outside world. Not a bad attitude, thought Jimmy; made it damn hard to talk to them though. Again some mentioned Liz's questions from the day before. It became obvious that he had to do a night trip.

He started back up the Canyon on the west side. Slow going. None had ever seen the Priest. He worked his way up to the market at the high point in the Canyon. There he remembered the little roads that trickled off Topanga Canyon Road to the west. They were closer to PCH. He headed for them. Nothing happening this far up.

The first, off to the west, was Rodeo Grounds Road. Little more than a dirt track pimpled with large rocks, it meandered down a slight hill and crossed a dry stream bed, the road going through cattails and river grasses. A hundred yards from the PCH and he was back in time a century.

The Jag is getting a workout today, he thought. He eased it down and across the rocky dry waterway, climbed up the other side and spotted a cabin. It reminded Jimmy of the cabins found deep in the woods of Georgia. A tiny little place in bad need of a paint job, it sat way back in the trees. Its roof of rusty metal was tucked under a huge weeping willow. The remnants of a short and ancient gravel drive wove its way back into the overgrown yard.

Jimmy eased the Jag over the ruts and weeds that scraped on the undercarriage and parked under the biggest eucalyptus tree he'd ever seen. He sat for a minute or two trying to decide if the cabin was occupied. What the hell, I'm here, might as well knock on the door. Probably be met with a shotgun held by some marijuana farmer.

He climbed the rickety porch steps, carefully avoided a rotted floor board and knocked on the door. Behind the rusty screened door, the inner door was open. He knocked again. Still nothing. Recent cooking smells wafted out. A quiet gospel song was playing on a radio somewhere in the house but no one was answering the door. Writing it off as another zero, he started back across the porch. A small squeaky voice stopped him.

"Mister, you want something?" Jimmy turned to see a tiny, grey haired lady peering at him through the screened door. She couldn't be five feet tall and must be ninety years old. "You just going to stand there with your mouth open or can I help you with something, young man?"

"Er, yes ma'am. That is, I hope you can." Jimmy produced a business card and held it up for her inspection. She still had not unlatched the screen. "I'm Jimmy Santos, a detective working with the Los Angeles Police Department. We're looking for a man you might have seen here in your neighborhood. I'd like to show you his picture, if I could bother you for a minute, m'am."

"I can't read that without my glasses, but you've got good manners. A southerner? My name is Ellen Waldrop. Come on in, no bother." She held the screened door open for him. "I haven't had a gentleman caller in years. Give that old biddy down the road something to talk about. I've got some fresh iced tea in the kitchen. Light's better there too. For looking at pictures. Well, don't just stand there, you'll let the bugs in."

Jimmy followed her through the spotless little cabin to the kitchen at the rear of the house. It was a beautiful, simple warm room. Old; appliances from before the second world war, the fridge had a condenser on top. Old casement windows filled the back wall of the room, looking out to the woods and dry stream bed beyond. Many small panes of glass sparkled in the late afternoon sunlight that splashed golden slivers through the trees.

"I live mostly in this room. The windows make it so cheery. My birds are my only company these days." She pointed to three feeders she had hanging from the trees. "The squirrels and raccoons eat all the bird food if I don't run them off. I keep a close watch though. The birds know me. They stay around while I scare the squirrels off."

She filled two big glasses with ice, poured the tea then joined Jimmy at the table.

"Thank you, Ms. Waldrop. You must be from the South, too. Only Southerners fill a glass with ice for iced tea. Most people give you a little smidgen of ice that melts when you pour in the tea."

"I'm from Mobile, and it's Mrs. I was married for forty five years next month. He's passed on four years now. Wonder he lasted long as he did, the way that man drank. Sweet, though. Drunk as a lord and never an unkind word. Never missed a days work. Just had to have his bourbon. Let's look at your pictures."

Jimmy took The Priest's picture from his inside coat pocket and, for the hundredth time that day, showed it to a skeptical stranger. Mrs. Waldrop slipped on her gold-framed half reading glasses and held the photo to the light from the window and, as casually as you please, said, "Right out there." She pointed to the windows.

"I'm sorry, m'am, you've seen this man out behind your house?" Jimmy's voice was incredulous.

"Every once in awhile. Never bothers anybody. He walks along the creek bed back there like he knows where he's going. Been doing it for years. Probably thinks no one can see him 'cause he's down in the creek bed and the brush is so thick. I've never said hello. Don't know him, you know. Why do you want to find him?"

Fifteen minutes later Jimmy was in the creek bed behind the Waldrop house. The sun was falling fast and his shadow danced through the tall grasses far ahead of him. It would be too dark to see in minutes. Damn, goddamn. Jimmy cursed under his breath as he tripped again over an unseen hazard. A briar-armed vine tugged at his suit sleeve. An hour earlier and I might have found a trail. Tonight, nothing. Daylight tomorrow.

Jimmy talked with Mrs. Waldrop for another half an hour. He found out little more. He calmed her down, assured her she had nothing to fear. She seemed okay, having seen the man for years with no harm done. No reason to think anything had changed. Jimmy kept to himself that she didn't fit even the loosest interpretation of a victim's profile.

He went back to the Fernwood Market to talk to the night clerk. She took one look at the date on the receipt and said, "No way, I started work here the month after." Gave Jimmy the owner's name and phone number; maybe he could track down the previous clerk through him.

The drive down the PCH and across town to USC had Jimmy thinking. The hunt. Pressure. Alison. Disjointed thoughts tumbled, scrambled. Searched my house. Son-of-a-bitch. This is now personal. Me and you, Priest. It's just you and me. No task force. I'm coming for you.

He called Brenner. He was gone for the day. Good. Jimmy left a long vague message on his voicemail, a loose account of the day with no mention of Mrs. Waldrop.

Jimmy thought, swing by USC and spend an hour or so on the set with Alison. Then turn in early. Return to the woods at daylight. Just me and the quarry. Like the old days with a hell of a lot more at stake than squirrel stew.

53

Jimmy arrived on set as Alison was setting up a shot on the camera raft. Jimmy watched from the pool edge and chatted with her bodyguard, Bill. Wives, husbands, boy and girlfriends were often visitors to the set and everyone took them in stride as long as they stayed out of the way. Jimmy did. It was about nine o'clock and Bill reported all was running smoothly—no major hassles on the set and not a hint of the Priest. Little did he suspect that a hundred feet away in the shadowed rank of spectators the Priest watched him talking.

Jimmy, "Who are those folks over by the divers tent?"

Bill, turning to look, "Them? They've been here every night. Stand and watch Julia and the crew. A movie star, making a storm on demand and turning it off seems to fascinate them. No trouble. They just watch."

When the shot was lined up to Alison's satisfaction she left the set to the lighting and effects crew and joined Jimmy and Bill pool side. Bill left to talk to his actress friend. Jimmy and Alison relaxed in director's chairs and watched the crew work.

Jimmy, "Hi, pretty lady. Its a wonder your crew gets any work done with you in that wet suit."

Alison smiled at the compliment, arms high in the air and stretching, "Thank you, kind sir, I think. God, I'm beat. I feel like I've been run over by a truck."

She slumped down in the chair and stretched one leg then the other. Her black wetsuit was covered with a dark, lined windbreaker to ward off the unseasonable night's chill. A black baseball cap held her hair off her face.

Jimmy, "You gonna be at it all night?"

Alison smiled, "Yes, I think so. This is our last night here, we've got to get it." She continued stretching. "We'll do it, it's just that everybody is exhausted. Fourth night in a row. Working on water is a killer, even in a pool. Everything takes twice as long. Supposed to rain later. Any luck with the Priest today?"

"Maybe. Several things point to him having a place up in Topanga Canyon. I'm gonna spend tomorrow up there." Jimmy paused as he lit a Camel. "I met a great old lady this afternoon. She swears he walks the creek bed right behind her house. Didn't seem fazed at all. 'Course, I didn't go into any detail about him. I'll duck outta here soon. I want to be up in the canyon at daylight. That okay?"

Jimmy watched as Bill left his friend and made a slow circuit around the pool looking for anything unusual or out of place. He obviously saw nothing.

"Sure it's okay, I'm going to be marooned on that raft the rest of the night. Tomorrow, I'm gonna sleep all day." Alison stifled a yawn. "Excuse me, not the company. Thank God for Saturdays. Next week we're back on days in the studio. Life a bit more normal."

"Yeah, just sixteen hour days instead of twenty. How many more weeks of this till we can really spend some time together?" Jimmy rose and began massaging Alison's neck and shoulders. "Maybe a week up in Monterey. A little bed and breakfast I know. Great food, beautiful beaches, quiet, nothing to do but eat, sleep and make love."

Alison, "Sounds like heaven. Two weeks shooting to go, a week or so break while the editor makes a first assembly, lets make that a date?"

"You're on." He gave Alison a soft kiss. "I'm outta here. See you tomorrow afternoon. Take care of yourself."

"You too. Be careful tomorrow."

The Priest had drifted farther back into the shadows. The bodyguard was more alert with Santos onsite—his recent check of the set was proof of that—but it looked like he was leaving anyway. Jimmy was almost to the 10 freeway on Vermont when the ill-defined thought floated through his mind. Blue pickup truck. Now what the hell does that mean? It'll come back. They always do.

54

It had started pissing down rain, just enough to make everybody miserable. Thin mists of it glistened in the wash of the harsh lights. Unusual too, this summer night, was the drop in temperature; a chill permeated the set. Work continued. Tired, edgy crew members struggled to get through the fourth night of shooting. Jimmy had left hours ago. One AM, maybe four and a half hours to go.

The Priest watched from the shadows at the north end of the set. Here, the old admin building, the end of the spectator's stands and the diver's tent formed a labyrinth of bright light and shadow. An ideal place to watch unnoticed. Outside the work perimeter, but close to the action and Alison. The security guards were used to this stranger who just watched. He'd been there each day of the filming, stayed out of the way, didn't bother the crew.

Tonight. The word whispered in The Priest's mind.

The crew's obvious fatigue, the rain keeping everyone's head down, people darting from place to place, unaware of their surroundings; tonight was the perfect time. At the end of the night; the furious going home activity, wandering attention, no one with a fixed position. The night's long discipline breaking down. Confusing patterns of light and shade, hints of dawn mixing with work lights that often snapped off too soon. Work carts and vehicles moving in disorganized patterns. The time when Alison could vanish the longest with no one missing her. No place she had to be.

The Priest drifted over to the trailer area with the next flurry of setup activity. He'd arrived early this afternoon and parked in the east lot near the trailers. Working quickly before the crew arrived he'd pushed a dumpster in closer to Alison's trailer. This and the big royal palm provided good cover just outside the splash of work light. Nothing to do now but wait.

At four forty-five AM the First AD called a wrap. In spite of the chilly mist the work had gone quickly; the crew was released early before the sun drove them from the pool. A whoop of joy went up from tired throats. Full wrap out and a company move back to the studio. The kicked-ants-nest activity jumped into gear.

The Priest watched from the dark eastern side of the trailer area. When the flurry of activity began, he stayed in place until Alison was walking toward her trailer. Again the bodyguard hung back to make a date for later with his actress. The Walkie-Talkies were all engaged in getting the company on the move and with schedules for Monday's work. Alison was alone.

The Priest moved into the shadows at the dumpster. He slipped a dart into his blow gun and palmed it in his right hand. He pushed a four-wheeled tarp-covered dolly, loaded with empty boxes, out of the shadows. Looking like a busy crew member, he strolled slowly down the alley toward the door of Alison's trailer. As he cleared the dumpster, she turned into the alley. Ten feet away. She glanced up, startled at his approach. Fatigue etched her face. Her reactions were slow. A crew member wrapping out? A weary smile, the beginnings of a "good night." Then she recognized him.

He could see it in the terrified eyes. The dart hit just under her uplifted chin. The Priest caught her before she hit the pavement. He swept the middle boxes off the dolly, put Alison in their place and covered her with the dark tarp. He moved back around the dumpster and through the mottled light to his truck. A bad moment when a security guard asked if he needed a hand.

"Thanks, no problem. This stuff's light, see you Monday." He kept moving, no hurry. He lowered the tailgate of the truck, lifted Alison, wrapped in the tarp, into the open truck bed, closed the tailgate and drove off.

He had left the parking lot and was driving north on Vermont when the First AD realized Alison was not in her trailer. "Anyone got a twenty on Alison?" bounced around the set on the walkie-talkies. No answers. Again and again he asked for Alison's location. He ran down the list of Walkie-Talkies by name, checking. Still negative answers. You don't lose your fucking director on a movie set! Fifteen frantic, searching minutes later they all realized she was gone.

One of the Walkie-Talkies found her cap behind her trailer. The bodyguard got on the phone to Brenner. He couldn't face Jimmy, even on the phone.

55

Daylight and the low angle of the sun made Jimmy's tracking easier. It threw into high relief any irregularity in the dry, rocky stream bed. Jimmy had dressed in hiking boots, jeans, a plaid shirt and a dark wind breaker. He was going to be too warm later, but in the dawn chill he was fine. His Beretta was in a shoulder holster, his phone off.

Jimmy was behind Mrs. Waldrop's house trying to pick up the trail of the man she had seen walking there. The man Jimmy was sure was the Priest.

Topanga Creek is a seasonal stream; in winter and early spring when it rains in L.A. it is a fast moving flow of water. With heavy downpours it becomes a torrent, tens of thousands of gallons gathered by the hills and directed southward to the Pacific Ocean.

Now in early August it was dust-dry. The first sign Jimmy found was a partial toe print from a shoe or a boot. It looked as if the wearer had stepped on a rock that shifted slightly, dipping the toe forward. The print was in the rockier part of the stream bed and protected from the Santa Ana winds by the rocks around it. No recreational hiker would choose to walk here with the smooth sandy stream bed only a few feet away.

Gotcha, thought Jimmy. The toe print pointed north. Jimmy followed, stopping every five or ten steps to pick up other signs. The sun was now beating through the trees, the day's heat already building. Bugs were swarming, nasty little bastards. Birds sang. Jimmy moved off slowly toward the north.

An hour later, he was beginning to discern a pattern. Whoever walked up and down this creek had varied his path. He soon found signs that in the rainy season someone had walked parallel to the stream. Both sides. Both ways. A crushed clump of dried grass, a broken twig, widely spaced and faint. Other signs were in the creek bed itself. The print of the edge of a boot sole. A small stone rolled over with the soil-stained side to the sky. Jimmy silently thanked his childhood Doctor friend for his tracking skills. These were not signs you would find by accident. Tricky bastard wanted no path to his door.

Jimmy almost missed the first one. He was stepping cautiously over a broken sapling, dropped casually over the rocks by a flood, when something in its position made him stop. He backed off. Hair stood up on his arms, the back of his neck. Odd. What? The quiet. The angle. A cardinal flicked through the little clearing shrieking. Jimmy flinched.

He squatted and looked. Five minutes later, he saw it. The sapling had been cut down. The stump end, sculpted to look broken, was balanced on the bigger rocks. In the brushy tangle of foliage and vines, where the top touched the ground, something was out of place. He rose and moved toward it. A dented, rusted two pound coffee can.

What the hell is that doing there? Very carefully, Jimmy moved aside the brush till he could see inside. Egg size stones. The can was carefully balanced so that any movement of the sapling—maybe a kick by a careless foot—would dump the rocks onto another can below. A crude but effective alarm system. I must be getting close. This sound won't carry far.

How many more of these little surprises have you set up, asshole?

Jimmy moved back to the track and carefully over the sapling. He checked his back trail. Clever bastard made the trail more obvious over the alarm trap. Must move very cautiously now. Take the time. The S-O-B might be in residence.

The next one was a tangle of vines rigged to another can of stones, these sitting over an empty, rusty five gallon jerry can. Trip that one and wake the dead, thought Jimmy. Sound like a goddamned timpani. The unsuspecting hiker who tripped that noise would wet his pants. Not many would slip up on The Priest unannounced.

Watching for the alarm trips, Jimmy spotted the next one, a fine black monofilament stretched taut across the easily-traveled sandy creek bed. A broken clump of grass blown over it by the wind was the tip-off to this one. It hung unnaturally on the strand. Damn, if I hadn't caught the other two, I'd have never seen this one. Tiny tin cans, a pebble in each, were tied to the monofilament. The slightest jiggle would set them ringing. Jimmy drew his gun. Close, very close. The Priest could be up there. He stood. Five minutes. Ten. Fifteen.

Nothing but wood's sounds. Far in the distance the Pacific swished on the beach, birds and bugs and his quiet breathing the only live noise. No breeze. The sun hot. He scanned and rescanned the area. Nothing out of place. A quiet summer day in canyon country. Some atavistic sense told him he was very close. To what? What had he seen, heard that drove this feeling deep into his gut? Wait; stand still until you've figured it out. Look. Listen. The tension was making the sweat pour from him. His hand on the hot metal of the Beretta was slippery. Calm, calm down.

A scrub jay flashed from branch to branch scolding, the brilliant blue a tiny, flashing flag against the desert colors of the canyon. It disappeared up the hill into a clump of chaparral, tucked under an overhang of sandstone. Shadows blacker than they should be in that clump. Why? The jay was not just in deep shadow. It had vanished.

He moved up toward the thick brush. A step, wait five minutes and take another step. Still silence. Yes. Watch for trip wires. The shadows in the sunlight's edge had a glint; a flicker of light, reflection. Black plastic under the brush cover. A shelter? Wind-borne trash?

Jimmy concentrated on the dense jumble of chaparral, sage, dried grasses and tumbleweed. One cautious step at a time he moved up the scree strewn slope. No prints on the rock surface. Still total silence. Still only birds and insect sounds. Six feet from the clump, screeching, the jay burst out in a whirr of blue and black wings.

Nothing in there or that jay wouldn't have stayed so long. Not frightened 'till I spooked it. What the hell is this? A tunnel, partially dug into the hill and partially built of arched branches, covered with dense brush, tumbleweed, vines and dried grass. It seemed to go up and under a pick-up-sticks pile of logs and debris that clung to the hillside under the massive rock overhang. Light through the logs above filtered down almost imperceptibly into the tunnel. A nest, he's got a fucking nest up there.

Jimmy waited and listened. I've got to go up there. Right into his gun if he's there. Not a whisper of sound from the tunnel. Jimmy started up, Beretta in his right hand as his left probed the semi-darkness ahead for more traps. He crawled, pulling himself forward with his elbows. He moved only a foot at a time.

A spider scuttled under his left sleeve and up along his outstretched arm. He resisted an urge to smash it. Sand and dust dropped into his shirt collar. The sun heated the black tunnel, causing the dried brush to creak and snap. Oven-hot, heat radiating into his back. Sweat soaked his shirt and jeans. He expected a shot every second. Nothing. Finally, he found himself in a cave. Light from tiny holes in black plastic dimly illuminated the interior. Damp and gloomy, a fitting home for this night stalker.

He could see the entire space as soon as he was out of the tunnel. Roughly ten by twenty feet, ceiling height a varying seven feet. The same man smell he remembered from his house break-in. No one home. The floor was earth, the walls earth and logs and some boulders. The west side hugged the slope of the hill. Gouged into this wall was a rough platform which held a sleeping bag. Dug deeper into the wall, a niche held a few books.

Light beaming through the black plastic danced with dust motes. Tools, utensils and clothes hung from nails in the east wall. A couple of wood shelves nailed to this wall held basic supplies. A small table and stool completed the furniture. There was a camp stove and two lanterns for light. Jimmy lit one of them and took a closer look, all the time listening for any sound foreign to the canyon. There was the quiet sigh of a breeze and the creaks of logs and dead brush heated in the sun.

Hanging from one of the nails in the log wall was an old leather shoulder bag. Stuffed inside were The Priest's meager records: Francisco Villa's disability discharge papers, his VA reporting forms, pension check stubs, an old color snapshot of a tiny dried-up white-haired Mexican guy.

In the corner by the water bottles years of spills had softened the clay floor. Pressed into the damp clay was a boot print, a dead match to the boot print at the female victim's drop site. Double documented as far as Jimmy was concerned. A paper identity and the footprint. His killer.

Jimmy opened the dried food containers and searched under and through the sleeping bag. Looked in every pocket in every garment. Pulled the black plastic from any hidden surface and scrutinized it. Checked every square foot of the floor for buried hiding places. He found nothing of interest except the papers, the footprint and boxes of ammunition.

56

Jimmy was on the cell phone to Brenner. Brenner told him, "Alison vanished from USC," after giving him holy hell about having his phone shut off. Jimmy was down in the creek bed, fresh air clearing his head. Brenner asked what he had found.

"He's got another place. He must have. Thats where he's taking her. Not a shred of evidence here to indicate this is the sacrifice site. Nothing. No blood stains, no body parts, absolutely nothing. I've checked the area for half a mile around. He does it somewhere else, I'm sure of it. That's the place we've got to find."

Jimmy could hear his own voice rising, hysteria creeping in. No! No time for panic. Alison must be terrified. He and everyone had let her down. She needed him with a clear head. He had to find her, protect her.

"What, no, I've got to come in to the case room. I'll draw a map to this place for forensics when I get there. I've got to go over all the files from the top. Anything else from the movie set?"

Brenner, forcing calm, "All they found was the cap she was wearing. One of the security cops thinks he saw the vehicle; the first one to leave after wrap, twenty minutes before other crew members. He noticed it because the guy was so quick to get out of there. Nothing on the guy. Dark skin, dark hair, dark clothes. May have been the guy who hung around the last few days watching filming. It all adds up to the Priest. A blue Toyota pickup."

"Ah shit man, NO! I saw that truck. Dismissed it. It must be the same one that was outside the VA hospital last week. I've fucked up, big time.

"Cool it, J.C. You're not Superman. No one expects you to do the impossible. We got a partial plate. We're running it and have an APB out on it. Are you okay?"

Jimmy took a deep breath. If his panic was showing, not good.

"Yeah. See you in half an hour."

Alison terrorized. Stark, mind numbing terror. He'd been so quick, so strong. Picked her up as if she was a child. Wrapped her in this foul-smelling tarp and threw her into the truck bed as if she were a Raggedy Ann doll. Her head bounced against the steel bed with every pothole, and her elbow and hip bones crunched against the steel wheel well. She couldn't move—not tied, she could have understood that. Her body was free, loose even and flopping around like a corpse.

More terror flooded her brain. Couldn't move. Her eyes. Yes, she could see. She was sure of that, even though there was only grayness. A pinhole in the tarp over her nose was pinging light off her right eye. Yes. Light; she could see. What has he done to me? The heat under the tarp was increasing. The sun's heat was beginning to cook the oil smell of the old canvas and soak into the black wetsuit. She passed out.

She woke when the truck slammed to a halt, sliding her forward, her head crashing into the cab. She remembered everything: the fright when she had recognized him, The Priest, yes, thats what Jimmy called him. His hand coming up and the sting of something sticking on her neck. Beginning to fall. Trying to call the guard. Make a noise. Alert Jimmy, anybody that she was being kidnapped. Where was that fucking bodyguard, I'll kill him. But she couldn't make a sound. Nothing came from her throat. The muscles didn't tighten to make sound. Her mouth refused to obey.

Dreamlike, her mind tried to force her muscles to work, to move, to scream. Nothing happened. The truck made a hard right turn and she almost rolled over onto her face. God no, her brain screamed. I'll suffocate if I do that. Must stay on my back. No control. Oh God, don't let me suffocate in this truck.

Sweat ran from her forehead into her eyes, stinging and burning. A big sweeping turn and Alison realized they were getting on a freeway. The speed picked up and the ride smoothed out to something more comfortable. My God, I'm paralyzed and worried about the comfort of the ride. I'm losing my mind.

The truck ride seemed to go on forever. Alison drifted in and out of consciousness, losing all track of time. Once, when she came to, Seascape popped into her mind. She instantly dismissed its irrelevance. No time now!

The only escape from the terror, heat and thirst lay in oblivion. In one of her semi-conscious periods the swaying motions in the truck indicated the transition from one freeway to another.

She was out when they made the next big swing but semi-woke when the truck swung off a freeway and onto a city street, indicated by traffic noises and stop-start traffic. She came fully awake as a group of school children crossed in front, chattering across the street at a stoplight.

She could hear every word, understand every sentence as they innocently passed only six feet from her head. They seemed to take forever to cross the street. Straining every fiber of her being, she tried to call out. Nothing. She might have been trying to levitate the truck with willpower for all the good it did her. The children were gone. Jimmy, Jimmy!

Tears rolled from her eyes, unbidden. Then the truck was climbing, constantly upward. She began a slow slide, inching toward the tailgate. She felt her left foot touch first. I can feel, she screamed in her mind. Hope blazed until she realized that she'd been able to feel since the dart sting, she just couldn't do anything about it. Slowly she began to collapse into the tailgate. Left leg, then the right, obeying gravity and the centrifugal forces of the truck's motion. Her legs were crumpled and her head bounced against the wheel well. Tingles from circulation loss began.

The truck turned hard left and bounced horribly; it felt like a rocky, rutted dirt track. Alison was thrown willy-nilly all over the steel bed. The loose bumper jack clunked her on the head, then got jammed under her neck. The full weight of her hips was lifted and slammed down on her hand and wrist. Her mind screamed. Her face remained placid.

The continued pounding from the steel truck bed was sapping her will. Though she couldn't move a muscle, every one of them felt tortured. A gut-wrenching thrust from the truck threw her across the bed and into the other wheel well. She felt the muscles crunch in her shoulder and her knee bang into the steel wall.

The tarp became an enemy, threatening to smother her as it twisted and folded with her uncontrolled motion. Tears streamed, her hair wet with sweat and tears, her eyes now jumping uncontrollably. She was as flaccid as a pound of liver. I'm going to die. One fantastic jolt and her head came down on the jack. She passed out again.

She heard the truck door slam. Groggy, totally disoriented, every muscle aching, it took her several seconds to realize she was no longer moving, no longer being thrown around. She heard scraping, brushing sounds from outside the truck, then the sound of the tailgate being lowered. She felt a strong hand grasp her ankle and her body being pulled toward the ankle. Her mind screamed. Don't touch me, you bastard! A sense of pure violation flooded her. Get away! Leave me alone!

All thoughts stayed locked in her mind. A hand pulled the tarp away from her face and she looked into the eyes of The Priest. He looked totally calm. He moved with slow deliberation as he unwrapped the greasy canvas. When she was clear of the fabric, he picked up a leather harness and began to put it on.

The air. The beautiful clean air. She sucked it in deep, replacing the stink of the oil-smeared tarp. She could see the beauty of the mountains, the clear, cloudless blue of the sky. A tiny calm touched her until The Priest dragged her out over the tailgate and spread her arms and legs. He picked up her feet and backing toward her, fed them through loops in the leather harness. He leaned back, grasped her left arm, and pulled her toward his back. Her arm held over his shoulder, he managed to slide a belt around her waist and secure her tightly to him. Two more belts diagonally across her back and buckled to the harness held her to him in a classic piggy-back ride.

Her arms dangled and her head lolled back as The Priest began to walk off toward the mountains. The sweat-filled wet suit began to chafe. The leather loops around her thighs cut off circulation to her legs, which began to cramp and burn. Her bobbing head crunched her nose into the back of The Priest's skull.

57

Thirty-nine minutes after leaving Topanga Canyon, Jimmy was sitting at the case room conference table surrounded by files. His watch lay on the table within eye line. He'd drawn the map for the forensics team. They were on their way to the cave. Good material for the trial perhaps, but no help now in finding Alison. He'd searched too carefully to have missed anything at the cave. It was now ten forty-five. Twenty hours to go till sunrise.

The truck. The fact that he hadn't realized the significance of the truck haunted him. God damn it, he thought, if only I'd called Bill and asked him to check out that truck. If I'd checked it out. Alison would—stop it. As Dad used to say, "If a bullfrog had wings it wouldn't bump its ass." Get on with it. Focus on rescuing Alison.

He started with the first one. The one found in the LACMA Sculpture Garden. Page by careful page, he went over the case.

Every crime scene photo. Every autopsy report. Every interview. Not a single clue as to where the sacrifice was performed. Drop sites, that's all. Noon, one o'clock. At two, a uniform dropped a brown bag in front of him.

"You've got to eat something, Jimmy. Tuna on rye, fries and a Coke. Eat."

He thanked her with a smile and continued digging through the files as he ate. He had finished the last case file when Brenner came in.

"We've got every available person scouring the streets for that truck. A picture and description of The Priest and a description of the truck was distributed at every roll call this morning. LAPD, Sheriffs, CHPs and every local department within a hundred miles of L.A. We got a piece on the noon news. Asking the public for help. First time we've had any lead time on this bastard. You come up with anything?"

"Not so far. If the answer is here, why haven't we seen it before? Damned if I'm having any luck. About to start through the summaries." He glanced at his watch for the thousandth time. "Millie is bringing Fulo down here about three. Maybe another rundown on the Aztec angle will help."

Hours. He must have been walking for hours. She could hear his boots crunching over the rocky soil. Scrubby chaparral clawed at her legs, scratched at her hands. They reached a slow trickling stream. He walked into it and turned away from the sun. North, she thought. He continued upstream in that direction, occasionally leaving the stream to walk on the rocky bank. The sound and sight of water so close made her thirst pure torture.

Twice, she passed out. At least twice that she could remember. Her disorientation was so complete that it could have been three or four times. Blood ran over her lips and down her chin from her nose that kept colliding with the back of his head. Thirst had thickened her tongue and threatened to choke her. The wetsuit was soaking up the sun's heat and accelerating dehydration. Her legs were now completely numb, feeling and circulation a distant memory. Her fingers had begun to tingle from dangling vertically.

Overriding all was the terror. The acute awareness that her body was in torment and that her mind could only register it, not perform the most minimal task to alleviate a second of its misery. Her entire being was imprisoned in her skull, behind her eyes. It was like being dead and yet alive. The horrible nightmare where they are closing the coffin on you and your mind is screaming, I'm not dead! Don't seal me in here!

Jimmy!

58

4 PM. The forensic team chief called in. Jimmy was right. No bloodstains any-where in or around the cave. No fingerprints but The Priest's and Jimmy's. Definitely not a killing scene. 5 PM. Dark in two and a half hours. Sunrise in twelve. Three of them—Jimmy, Brenner and Fulo—were deep into the files. Jimmy's Camels and Brenner's cigars were stinking the air.

Tension was a palpable presence. Millie was pacing. The four walls of the room were covered with graphic depictions of the case in chronological order. Photos, maps, crime scene sketches. Summary reports were interspersed. Mil-lie stopped before one of those. She studied it with a frown of puzzlement.

"Jimmy, this CHP report. They stopped what they think was The Priest's van on the night Donahue went missing."

"Yeah, I remember. What about it?"

"If his camp is near the PCH and Topanga Canyon Road, and Donahue's ranch is up in the Santa Monica Mountains, what was The Priest doing in his van at two AM way up near Azusa? Probably with Donahue alive in the back."

Time in the room froze. They all got it.

"Going to his sacrifice place. Damn, Millie, I like it. Annucci mentioned The Priest talking about the mountains. His fascination with their wildness. What do you think, Fulo?"

"It fits. The Aztec temples were man-made mountains. Look like them to-day, those that are still overgrown. I like it too."

Brenner, "But what do we do with it? That's the Angeles National Forest up there. Tens, maybe hundreds of square miles of rough country."

Jimmy sat. Leaning back in his chair staring at the ceiling. Lost in thought. "What? What'd you just say?"

Brenner, "I said, tens, maybe hundreds of square miles—"

"No, before that?"

"That's the Angeles National Forest—"

"That's it, something about that area. Something I've seen or heard. What the hell was it?" Jimmy got up and started to pace, mumbling, cursing his memory. "God damn it, what the hell is it?"

The door opened and a lab technician came in.

Brenner, "What you got for us, Ariel?"

"Here's the preliminary lab work on today's stuff from the cave. More paper to add to your piles. Sorry we couldn't be more helpful."

Jimmy, "Hang on, just a minute. Lab report. That's—" He began to dig frantically through the lab report folders. "Here! Now—no, its not here. Goddamn it, I missed it every time."

Brenner, "What? What'd you—?"

"The lab didn't send back a report on an atlas I found in the library materials Susie got for us. Didn't send back the atlas, either. Come on, Ariel, lets go down to the print section, see if we can find it. Mark will you intensify the search in the north, near the mountains, say from Altadena over to Glendora. Millie, you can take Fulo home."

Millie and Fulo, almost together, "Not on your life. We're staying."

Jimmy, "C'mon Ariel. That atlas may be—shut the fuck up. Don't jinx it, Jimmy. Millie, thanks."

They dashed down the hall to the elevator.

7:25 PM. Jimmy, Ariel and two other technicians had torn apart the print and document section of the lab. Zero. No atlas.

Ariel, "Once more Jimmy, describe this thing."

Jimmy, exasperated, Christ these guys. "An atlas. Roughly nine inches by twelve. Two comic books thick. A map of California on the front. Dirty, dog eared. Looked ready for the trash. I don't know what else—"

Technician interrupting, "Oh fuck, wait a minute. Johnson was showing his secretary how to get to Palm Springs. Used a book just like that. Let's check their desks."

Five minutes later, there it was, top drawer, a desk in the fluids and gasses section. The lab report was paper clipped inside the back cover. The post-it Jimmy used to mark the page was still there. Covered in fingerprint powder. Jimmy scanned the report. Villa's prints. Erased pencil marks. The darkest smudge, a dirty Villa print on The Angeles National Forest border in the San

Gabriel Mountains.

Taking the atlas, Jimmy ran from the lab. He slammed through the door into the stairwell; no time for an elevator. He blew across the lobby, out on the street to the Jag and screeched off toward the 10 Freeway. When he settled into the fast lane and was hitting ninety-five he realized he hadn't told anyone where he was going.

Jimmy keyed Brenner's speed dial. Before it could ring he punched the off button. No. Tell him where I'm going and he'll have a swarm of cops, sirens and flashing lights in there. When I pick up a trail, then I'll call for backup. Keep it backup and not a bunch of trigger-happy SWAT guys stumbling around in the dark.

I'll find her the way I do it, one guy, alone. In control. Move quickly and quietly through the dark. Follow that son-of-a-bitch and nail him before he knows I'm there. Hang on, Alison, I'm coming.

59

He'd violated his own rules, rules that had kept him and his Temple safe. He'd taken Alison at dawn, driven to the mountains through the daytime traffic and hiked to his Temple, risking being seen by other hikers. Not a hitch. The Gods were smiling on him.

His Sacrifice must be blessed. He had gotten away clean and no one had a clue as to where he was. Inside the canyon, to the south of the Temple entrance, the rocky walls folded back on themselves and formed a cul-de-sac out of sight of the main Temple area and the Altar. Huge fallen boulders created a maze between the main canyon and this hidden pocket. Here, he had built a camp site. A canvas tarp, stretched and tied over the rocks, provided shelter from the blazing sun. A camp stove, a sleeping bag and an AK-47 with two extra magazines made up the furnishings.

He placed Alison gently on the rolled-out sleeping bag and used his buck knife to cut her out of the wetsuit, leaving her in only bra and panties. He filled a half-liter bottle with water and, holding her head up, allowed her to drink. When the bottle was empty, he laid her head back, stood and covered her with a light blanket. He walked out into the canyon to make his preparations for sunrise.

Calm, he is so unbelievably calm, her mind was screaming. The knife. Her heart had stopped. She was sure of it. When he had unsheathed and opened that shining blade, she'd ceased to breathe. This is it, her mind had whimpered.

Jimmy, where are you? The Priest had started out of her sight at her right ankle and slit the hot neoprene all the way up to her shoulder. In spite of the instant cooling relief, terror had blanked her mind.

When she returned to awareness, the wetsuit was off, she was cooler and he was holding a bottle of water to her lips. She could only swallow involuntarily but nothing was ever so welcome. Maybe he's not going to kill me. Why give me water if he's going to kill me? A faint glimmer of hope bubbled in her brain. She slid slowly into sleep.

Jimmy sped up the 605 to the 210 Freeway, praying all the way that the CHP was employed elsewhere. He took the San Gabriel Canyon Road exit north. 8:03 PM. He swung in under the lights of a Shell station and parked. He pulled a high-intensity narrow beam Mag-Lite from his glove box and again studied the map.

The finger smudge covered several square miles of mountains that could involve days of searching with platoons of men. I've got to narrow this down. He tried different angles of the light. Tried tipping the paper, rotating it. Reading it upside down. Nothing. Shit! He held it, single thickness, up to the light, the Mag-Lite behind.

A shadow, the tiniest darkening of the paper. A pencil had dug in, scarring the fibers. Maybe, just maybe. The backlit detail around the shadow faded out in the translucence.

He could see the mark but not read the map. He held the map against the glass of the partially opened driver's window and carefully transferred the Mag-Lite to his left hand, outside the car. He was able to backlight the shadow area against the hard clear surface.

He took a pencil from his shirt pocket and precisely marked the shadow on the front face of the map. He flipped the map over and found his pencil mark on the front. It fell on what appeared to be a dirt road. A road five miles further north and meandering westerly into the mountains.

"Gas, Mister?" Jimmy's heart damned near stopped. Concentration so intense he'd not heard the attendant's approach.

"No thanks, just stopped to check some directions. You from around here?"

"All my life. Born and raised right down there in Azusa. Can I help you find something?"

"This road here." Jimmy showed him the map. "Where does it go?"

"Nowhere, don't go nowhere. Just stops. That the road you're looking for? No houses on it, nothing. People use it as a starting place for mountain hikes. Nothing up there at night."

Jimmy almost ran over the startled guy's foot as he screeched away, yelling "Thanks!" over his shoulder.

Jimmy overshot the road on his first pass—hardly a road, more a dirt trail partially hidden by scruffy brush. He U-turned, pulled into the trail and stopped. He shut off his headlights. As his eyes slowly adjusted to the thin moonlight, he could see the trail slope upward and turn, a hundred yards away, gently to the north. There, the trees and undergrowth thickened.

The hills around him rose higher to the north and west. He was midway up the foothills of the San Gabriel Mountains. 8:45 PM. Barely rolling, he crept the car up to the edge of the tree cover and parked. He loaded his pockets—two extra magazines for the Beretta, the Mag-Lite, the phone—then quietly opened the car door, got out and closed it gently. On foot from here.

The moon was six diameters above the horizon. He had hours before it set. Except for the shadowed areas, it provided enough light to walk. Moving slowly, carefully, he started North, keeping to the shadows at the roads edge. The dark blue truck could have driven through here. The many wheel tracks in the sandy trail made it impossible to sort one from another.

60

"Where the fuck is he? Goddamn it, Ariel!"

"He looked over that map, scanned the lab report and ran out of there like his ass was on fire. Didn't say a word. Just ran. Down the stairs, didn't even wait for the elevator."

Brenner, Millie and Fulo were still in the case room. When Jimmy hadn't returned after thirty minutes, Brenner had called down to see what the hell was going on. Ariel innocently replied that Jimmy was gone. Brenner had, not politely, ordered his ass to the case room.

"Fuck, all we can do is wait. He'll call in. He's gotta."

Brenner was furious. He knew Jimmy might go after The Priest on his own. Get himself killed on his own, most likely.

Millie, "Can't we call him?'

"Try if you like." He indicated the phone. "He won't answer. We'll have to wait till he calls us."

Jimmy had been walking for nineteen minutes. The luminous dial on his watch showed 9:05. Late, goddamn it's getting late. This is my only chance, the only clue I've got.

Nothing but night sounds. The breeze rustled a palm frond, hissing through the undergrowth. The day's heat radiated from the sandy track, making sweat run freely, even at this hour. An owl hooted way up the trail. A mosquito buzzed his head. Behind him, to the south, the glow of L.A. spread from horizon to horizon.

Seventy-five yards ahead, moonlight glinted off a shiny surface. He stopped. Taking minutes to go a yard, he stalked the glint of moonlight. From ten yards away he could make out the silhouette of a pick-up truck. From five, the color. Blue.

Still nothing moved. He waited another five minutes. Still nothing. The truck had been pulled off the trail behind a stand of mountain laurel and scrub fir.

The driver had brushed out the wheel tracks where it left the trail. He hadn't been as careful with footprints around the truck. Jimmy crouched and examined them, shielding the Mag-Lite with his hand. Jimmy had been running on gut-think and hunches. Everything pointed to a second place, a killing place, here in these mountains where The Priest would bring Alison. This was proof. These footprints were the same as those at the woman's drop site and in the cave. Made by those black combat boots described by Paul Sayer. There was a deep groove across the left heel, looked like a red hot poker had pressed into the rubber.

These prints were as good as a fingerprint to Jimmy. This was the truck he had seen at the VA and on a side street at USC. No more hunch; certainty. The Priest was here in these mountains. The prints twisted deeply into the sandy soil at the tailgate and moved away up through the underbrush toward the mountains. Jimmy followed far enough to ensure no one was in hearing range, then returned to the truck. He climbed into the truck, rolled the windows tight, dug out his phone and keyed Brenner's cell number.

Brenner, reading the caller ID, picked up on the first ring. "Where the fuck are you?"

"You're gonna have to listen close. I can't talk loud. I'm up north, just west of San Gabriel Canyon Road. I—"

"Goddamn it Jimmy, I can't hear you. What?"

"Mark, you're—put me on speaker and turn up the volume."

Brenner did. The hiss was annoying. "Jimmy, try now."

Concentrating on the speakerphone, no one noticed the corridor door opening or Dan Nolan stepping into the room. He stopped just inside the door, crossed his arms, leaned against the wall and listened. Despite the hiss and crackle, Jimmy came in loud and clear.

"Look, I'm up here at the edge of the San Gabriel Mountains. I don't know how close The Priest is, but I know he's up here. If you have to call me later, I'll tap the phone to answer—are you getting this?"

"Yeah, staticky, but go ahead, I'm digging out a map. How do you know it's him?"

"The truck, footprints. He's here."

Brenner knew Jimmy's tracking skills. If he said the man was there, he was there. "I've got the map. Where exactly are you?'

"Before I tell you, you gotta promise not to call out the cavalry. You bring them in here, this prick will kill Alison and disappear into the mountains."

"I don't like it, but okay. I can't help if I don't know where you are. Now give it to me."

"I'm in his truck, about two hundred and fifty yards west on a dirt trail running off San Gabriel Canyon Road. The trail is fifteen point seven miles north of the 210 Freeway on the west side. It's—"

"How the hell—"

"Later, there's no time now. Hand-pick a small squad. The K-9 unit has a German Shepherd that tracks silently. Bring it. I'll leave my handkerchief in the truck. Use it for the tracking scent. Follow me up into the mountains. Stash an ambulance at the intersection of the trail and the main road. Leave all the vehicles there. Mark, I can't emphasize this enough. If your backup unit comes thrashing around in here, The Priest is gonna kill Alison and vanish. Don't bring a man more than you have to."

"Roger that. We'll come in like Apaches. Watch your ass."

"See ya." The speaker phone went dead.

10:17 PM. Jimmy started up the mountain after Alison and The Priest.

Brenner was the first to see . "What the fu—What are you doing here?"

Nolan straightening up off the wall, "I see your buddy is up to his usual grandstanding tricks. Another grab for the headlines, huh? The one-man rescue. His favorite."

Brenner, "Look, Captain, Jimmy knows what he's doing. He's there on the scene. If he says we should go in quietly, that's what we're gonna do."

"Right, do it his way. Be a real shame if he fucks it up and gets himself and his girlfriend killed. Good night, Lieutenant." Nolan left the office.

Millie turned to Brenner, "So that's the famous Captain Nolan. Is he really going to leave you alone to deal with this?"

"I don't know Millie, it's not like him to walk away, but I don't have time right now to worry about him. I gotta put this team together and get to Azusa. Let's go down to my office. I'd guess you're not going home now."

Millie, "You got that right."

Brenner should have followed his instincts and challenged Nolan. Ten minutes later, he was in his office marking up a map of the Angeles National Forest and ordering the duty helicopter and SWAT team to mount up and be ready to fly in thirty.

61

The boot prints led away up the trail. The moon cast its pale light. The temperature was dropping. It's gonna get damn cold up here, thought Jimmy, shrugging the black windbreaker up on his neck. The only sounds were those of the desert night—the breeze moving through the scrub vegetation, an occasional night bird call, the soft scrunch of Jimmy's footfall on the sandy track. Nothing from The Priest or Alison. The trail was gradually getting steeper. He could feel the increased pull on his calves and thighs. Fatigue was becoming a factor; only adrenaline was keeping him going. He'd been up since before daylight and endured a day of increasing tension. He glanced at his watch. 10:39. Damn.

His thoughts raced. Somewhere up ahead, he's got to get off this public trail. He's not heading for a place the public can find. Gotta watch for it. Thats when it'll get trickier. He put the Mag-Lite in his hip pocket and once more checked the Beretta. Damn nerves, he thought, third time I've checked that since leaving the truck. I've got to get that under control. No time now to let the imagination run, to think about what he's gonna do to Alison in just a few short hours.

There. Mistake. The print of the right boot had dug and twisted in the sand as the Priest had turned off the public trail and walked through the chaparral in a more northerly direction. North by Northwest, good title for a movie, thought Jimmy. Though hidden from the pale moonlight more often, the track was easier to follow because it was alone in the sandy shale. Too easy, thought Jimmy, as he remembered the tricky trail up through Topanga. Thirty yards later, he proved correct.

The trail vanished on a flattened area of sandstone. Printless rock spread out for seventy five yards in every direction. Bastard knew this was here and uses it to confuse his trail, mused Jimmy. To change direction? That's what I'd do. He's been heading north, northwest, bet he swings off to the west here. Jimmy used precious minutes carefully searching the westerly perimeter of the rocky surface, his guess proved correct as he picked up the boot prints moving off to the west. He followed with increasing confidence. Remembering the map, Jimmy thought, the Bear River is up ahead about three miles. He's going somewhere near there.

Brenner had his team together. Brenner, the dog and handler, and three Special Squad team members. All dressed completely in black with handguns and vests. Brenner had a twelve-gauge Remington pump shotgun, Callahan and Susie Chan had M-16's and Brill, ex-special forces, who was the best shot in the squad, had a night scope equipped Robar, SR-60 sniper rifle. On their belts they all had handcuffs, walkie-talkies, six cell Mag-Lites and night vision goggles. Each cop used black tape to secure the hardware on their belts to avoid noise. Fulo and Millie were in the back and would stay with the vehicle. They were all in a department van speeding east on the 10 Freeway, with Callahan driving. The van radio was tuned to the LAPD emergency frequency. It was quiet.

An EMS ambulance was right on their tail. Brenner had called in a lot of favors to put the rescue team together without notifying the department. His thoughts raced. His ass was going to be in a sling if this didn't pay off. But Jimmy was right, though. Go in quiet. Go in fast. The German Shepherd whined softly, voicing the tension in the van.

When they pulled off San Gabriel Canyon Road, Callahan saw Jimmy's Jag and pulled in behind it. The team quietly spilled out of the van and began assembling their equipment. The van police band radio blasted the silence. Brenner dove into the front seat and spun the volume down. He just managed to hear, "—urbank control, this is PD Helo 171, altitude 3000, heading 075 at 90 knots, proceeding to target area."

"Roger 171, 075 at 90. Good hunting."

Brenner shut the volume all the way down and in a low whisper,

"That son-of-a-bitchin' Nolan. He's sending a helicopter up here."

Susie, "How—?"

Brenner, stalking around in a tight circle snapped,

"That was an LAPD helicopter call sign. The heading from takeoff is toward us. It's probably got a SWAT team on board if I know Nolan. We gotta move, people. Let's hit it."

He opened his cell phone and hit Jimmy's speed dial number. It signaled the vibrate function on Jimmy's cell. Miles away, up in the canyons, Jimmy opened his phone, held it tight to his ear and tapped on its microphone with a fingernail. Brenner got the signal and, speaking in a whisper, "J.C., Nolan's put a chopper in the air. Heading this way. Probably got a SWAT team on board. They just took off. Do you read me?"

He heard Jimmy's tapping, then the signal went dead.

"C'mon people, single file. Jerry, you and the dog out front, then me and Brill, then Susie, Callahan. We gotta find Jimmy and the Priest before that chopper gets here."

Silently, they moved out toward the night black mountains.

62.

Jimmy closed his cell phone and silently cursed. How the hell had that bastard known where to send a chopper, a SWAT team? No, not send. The prick would be right up front with the pilot. He's gonna get Alison killed unless I can find the Priest before Nolan spooks him. He checked his watch. 11:12 PM. Gotta move. Now I'm racing the sun and the helicopter. A few minutes later, he found the spot where the Priest had stepped into the Bear River.

Which way? North and higher in the hills. He'd bet on North. Jimmy turned and waded very slowly upstream. He capped the Mag-Lite with his hand and allowed a sliver of light to wash over the water. Twenty steps later he picked up his first sign—a rock underwater had been rolled over. Its color difference from its neighbors was all the clue Jimmy needed. Yes! Forty yards further north he saw where the Priest had stepped out of the steam onto the rocky shore, crushed a small weed, and continued north through a tiny patch of sand. Jimmy thought, he's really not expecting anyone to follow. He's just moving from habit. Old jungle habits. Hide your trail where possible. Don't make it easy.

Jimmy's thoughts turned to Alison. Did she know about the sunrise deadline? God, I hope not. Couldn't remember mentioning it to her. She's gonna be terrified enough. Just stop it.

Concentrate on the track. Move! Don't think about anything except what you can effect. You can't help Alison till you get there, and you can't do anything about the helicopter. So just concentrate and move! He continued upstream listening to the gurgle of the nearly dry river.

With the lights of Pasadena off the starboard side, the chopper pilot started climbing. He needed more altitude to get over the mountains. The brightly-lit city was dropping away under the plexiglass bubble. As in all choppers, the engine and rotor blade noise in the cockpit was deafening. The pilot, Nolan and the SWAT leader were communicating through thick headsets and microphones. The pilot pointed ahead through the windshield and said to Nolan, "Sir, show me that map again."

Nolan twisted in the co-pilot's seat and pointing to the map on his knee said, "We head for this intersection and spiral out from there."

"Sir, we need a narrower search area. It's gonna be dark as hell down there. We can't find two people in those canyons."

"You've got the searchlight, don't you?"

"Yes sir, but all that's gonna do is warn the perp that we're coming."

"There are two teams on the ground. We'll find them and let them point the way." He resumed checking the magazine in his Glock-9.

"Whatever you say, sir."

With that, the pilot seemed to turn his full attention to flying. He was thinking, stupid bastard, for all his rank he's gonna get somebody killed tonight. Doesn't have a clue what he's doing.

63

Twice since arriving at the Temple, The Priest had pricked Alison's neck with a dart covered with his poison. Once at mid-day and again after dark. Each time, he had given her water. The dart stings had washed away any faint hope that the Priest had plans other than sacrifice. If possible, her terror was increasing with the darkness. There's no way Jimmy can find this place in the dark. I'm going to die here in these mountains and no one will know until they find me at some godforsaken tourist trap.

Jimmy, Jimmy, JIMMY, her mind screamed his name over and over. As midnight approached, The Priest entered the lean-to. He filled a small pail with water, unsheathed and opened his buck knife. He carefully cut away her bra and panties. With the gentleness of a good nurse, he began to wash Alison. There was nothing sexual about it. He was tender, methodical and thorough; preparing the sacrifice to his Gods. It was the worst moment of Alison's ordeal. She fainted.

When she came to, she was lying, back arched, over a flat cold stone. It cut into her shoulder blades and the tops of her thighs. Her breasts were arched toward the black sky, feet not touching the ground. Her head hung so that she saw the world upside-down. Her fixed, open eyes saw the torchlight flickering on the rocks.

She could hear the Priest chanting in some guttural language. As he moved into view she could see that he was naked. He had painted his entire body black and cut his earlobes. Blood ran down over his shoulders, chest and arms.

He carried a black knife in his right hand, its blade glittered in the torchlight.

Directly behind her head and near the canyon wall was a crude wooden rack. It held the grinning skulls of the five victims who came before her.

Closer, she stared upside down at a human skin stuffed with straw. The straw poked out of the badly-sewn shut eyes and mouth. God, she thought, just get it over with.

64

The Priest's trail continued to follow the course of the river and climbed up along the steep hillsides cut away by the ancient flow of water. Jimmy could see evidence that the trail had been used before. It resembled the game trails animals create in their daily roaming. Careful now, he thought. This is probably the only way the Priest can get to his sanctuary. He's been up and down this many times.

Traps. Gotta be. Just like at the cave. He spotted the first one about fifty yards on. A seemingly loose tangle of dead chaparral and cactus stuck out of the uphill rock at ankle. Jimmy stopped and examined it with the hooded light. The brush was a trigger. A careless kick or a tangled foot was designed to set off an avalanche of boulders balanced up on the hillside.

This was not just a noisemaker but a trap designed to kill. The unsuspecting hiker would be carried off the trail and buried under tons of rock in the riverbed below.

He carefully stepped around the trigger and hastened up the trail. He'd gone about twenty-five feet when he thought, Brenner. He and the dog will stumble right into that trap. He went back to the downhill side of the trigger. He took a page from his notebook, scribbled a warning and pegged it into the trail surface with a twig. Damn, he thought, I'll have to mark everything I find for them. Better hope I find all the Priest's little goodies.

Time, damn it, taking time. 11:51 PM. In spite of the chill night he was beginning to sweat. The pressure was getting to him. Too many people counting on him. Too little time. When am I gonna hear that chopper? Just shut up and move, goddamn it. Move! The moon was further down in the west, its cool light striking at a flatter angle across the trail.

That's why he saw the next trap. He'd stopped, dripping sweat and breathing hard from exertion and tension. He was wiping the sweat from his eyes when, ten feet up the trail, he saw a slight disturbance in the surface texture. A faint, almost invisible line trickled across the trail. The slope rose steeply over loose rocks to his right and dropped off sharply to the river on the left. How the hell does he get around this, he thought. Over the rocks, the only way. But very careful. It may be a double trap. Climb up on those rocks and bam, the hillside comes down on you. Another killer.

He again hooded the Mag-Lite in his hand and moved up to examine the trigger. It took about ten minutes. It was a triple trap. Any passage along the trail, below it or over the rocks would trigger a rockslide. Jimmy shook his head in reluctant admiration. Bastard is very, very good, and very paranoid. No way he could know anybody would be tracking him. I must be getting very close.

The only way to continue on this trail must be behind me and I missed it. Backtrack. Find where he branched off. It's gotta be there. He found it, but it took a long fifteen minutes.

The Priest had passed a low rock jutting from the upside of the hill and continued on to the trap's trigger. He'd deliberately left faint bootprints. Then, walking backward in those same prints, he'd stepped up onto the jutting rock and climbed. The safe trail was parallel to the one below. It continued north.

Jimmy left another written warning for Brenner and resumed tracking the Priest. He was much too close to the Priest to risk the cell phone. He just hoped Brenner's dog handler had some woods savvy and would pay attention to his warnings. He spit on several rocks on the alternate trail. His reinforced scent trail would help the dog. It was all he could do. It was now 12:37 AM. Only four hours to go.

They were making good time. Even in the dark and with the increasing incline of the trail, they had the advantage on Jimmy. They only had to follow the silent-but-eager German Shepard and his handler. Brenner was breathing hard, the little cigars taking their toll. He had stopped at the Priest's truck and called the Chief at home.

Brenner had given the Chief a complete rundown on the situation and why they were proceeding with a small team. He begged him to get through to Nolan by radio and order the fool to abort, not endanger them all by blundering onto the scene with the chopper and a SWAT team. The moron had not a clue where he was going or what he was up against, and was endangering the lives of ten or fifteen people plus the chopper.

The Chief, after chewing Brenner's ass for not notifying him sooner, seemed to see the sense in Brenner's argument. Brenner could almost hear the wheels turning as the Chief weighed the option of a failed chopper-SWAT operation against a failed ground team. Which could he best defend on the six o'clock news? Brenner thought, when you get right down to it this son-of-a-bitch is just another politician.

Brenner kept trying until the Chief interrupted him, "Shut the fuck up. Get off the phone and go find Jimmy and the Priest. I'll make a decision and call you back."

Brenner had explained the tapping phone business and then shut the fuck up. He was still waiting to hear a decision. It was tearing his guts out.

65

The trail had trickled down to a narrow track, barely three feet wide, dropping sharply off to the left. It continued up and disappeared around an outcrop of rock high above the river. From somewhere ahead, Jimmy was picking up the faint smell of burning pitch and intermittently what sounded like drums. Close, very close. Perfect spot for another trap. Here, high on this narrow ledge. He risked the masked Mag-Lite for a few seconds. Nothing. Gotta be here, he thought.

He stopped and listened, taking in all the sensory information. The hair on his body began to rise. Oh yeah, something's here, big time. An involuntary glance at the luminous dial on his watch; 2:08 AM. Find it and move! He eased down on his haunches and let his eyes go unfocused, moving his head left to right. He tried to pick up something with his peripheral vision, which was most sensitive in the dark. Nothing.

He sat motionless for ten minutes and looked. Left, right, again. A soft breeze wafted down the canyon, ruffled his hair and the chaparral on the trail edge. An owl hooted down by the river and thirty yards up the trail a rabbit popped out of the low vegetation. Still nothing of the trap he was sure was here. He had to go around that large rock ahead to continue. The trail there narrowed to about two feet. That's gotta be the place, he thought. He stood slowly and creeping forward approaching the rock. Still nothing. With in-finite care he moved toward the rock. Nothing. He reached the rock safely and breathed a sigh of relief.

He started to step around it when every hair on his body stood in protest. He stopped with one foot suspended in the air, frozen in place. Just around the bend was a recess in the rock face. Hidden there was a pile of stones, stacked to look like the natural scree from a long-ago slide. He examined the rock he was standing against. A large piece of rock was delicately balanced in place at just the right height to use as a handhold to swing around the larger rock narrowing the trail. The trigger. Jimmy eased away from the obstructing rock and hugged the drop-off edge. He stepped around the narrow place, took two further steps and looked back.

Clever bastard. He understood what had been planned to happen. Anyone expecting a trap would relax on reaching the big rock safely. Then they'd grasp the balanced rock, swing around the narrowed place and bring down the stacked rock scree in a trail clearing roar. Bastard really liked his privacy. He again marked the trap for Brenner, then continued north on the trail.

Fifty feet up the trail, the drumming sound increased. The faint smell of burning pitch drifted out of a brush-choked crack in the rock wall. The crack looked impossibly narrow. As Jimmy stood and looked at it, he thought he saw the faintest glimmer of light deep in the crack. Still thinking the crack looked too narrow for an entrance, he checked fifty feet further up the trail. Nothing remotely possible as an entrance. He moved back to the source of the drumming and the burning smell. Behind and below him was the large pool in the Bear River. The rabbit had long since deserted the trail. He was alone and staring at the wall.

Finally, seeing no other option, he silently squeezed through the brush, turned sideways and edged into the cracked rock. It was deceptive. Only the outer edges of the crack were tight. Like two oversized, dull knife blades. Once past them the space opened quickly. Wide enough to walk through. The drumming sound and the smell increased; a flicker of light touched a high rock outcrop. Jimmy could feel the rhythm of drum beat. Deep bass notes, volume low.

Instead of continuing, Jimmy cautiously backed out, went back down the trail to the downhill side of the last trap and left Brenner another, longer note.

He returned to the canyon entrance, drew the Beretta, crouched and moved forward. Ten yards in, the light source began to flicker on the rock walls and the smell grew stronger. Jimmy moved cautiously from rock to rock, hugging the shadows. Moving forward only a few feet in minutes. He took a full minute to raise his head over the rock between him and the main canyon. When his eyes cleared the rock, he stopped. Before him lay the Priest's Temple.

Centered in the Canyon, Alison lay face up on a large stone altar block. Naked. Her head was to his left and the south side of the canyon. Her long brown hair swept the ground. Stripes of red and white paint circled her body like a python. Her face was painted white with huge black circles around her eyes.

The Priest, naked, body painted black and blood running over his shoulders, danced and chanted around Alison. In an outer circle around the stone altar, five naked human figures knelt in prayer. They were absolutely still. The only light came from four torches flickering in the canyon's fickle air. The intensity of the drums had increased in volume and tempo. Jimmy searched for a drummer and found none. A rack held five skulls grinning at the macabre scene.

Jimmy's brain was racing. Who are those other people? Accomplices? Too far for a pistol shot. Gotta get closer. He slowly withdrew his head and crept off to his right, staying behind fallen boulders and hugging the south wall of the canyon.

He slid through the Priest's campsite. A portable tape player was pounding out the drums. The insistent rhythm, cover for him. He noticed an AK-47 leaning against a rock. He kept moving, trusting his Beretta in close combat. Ten yards further and through a space between two boulders he could see the altar area.

His eyes locked with Alison's. Head upside down and unable to move, she widened her eyes in acknowledgement of Jimmy's presence. Jimmy had to clamp down hard on his impulse to rush to her. Mind spinning, he missed the sound of a kicked pebble. It registered too late.

Whirling toward the sound, he glimpsed The Priest standing in the flickering light, three feet to Jimmy's left. Naked, eyes wild, blood running down his neck, shoulders and chest. He held the sacrificial knife in his left hand and a small tube in his right. An apparition from hell, thought Jimmy.

"No!" It was a scream ripped from his throat. Jimmy was still turning and bringing the Beretta to bear when The Priest fired the poison dart at Jimmy's throat.

The dart hit, drew blood and Jimmy collapsed at the Priest's feet and lay still. The Priest lifted him under the arms, dragged him clear of the boulders and propped him against a rock. The Priest thought, Santos, you can watch Alison's sacrifice. Just like I watched my platoon die in Nam. Then it's your turn.

Jimmy's brain was shrieking. Drugged. He's drugged me. He's going to sacrifice Alison. He tried moving. Hands, feet, eyes—nothing. I can't help. I can only watch.

The Priest rejoined the group at the altar. He began to dance and chant. Jimmy stared. Jesus, he realized, the five still figures were the stuffed skins of The Priest's victims. Grotesquely dried, twisted and shrunken forms cloaked in the flickering torchlight. Earlier sacrifices forced to watch succeeding ones, their sewn-closed mouths and straw-dripping eyes testified to the horrors they had experienced.

Calm down. Calm down. No help in thinking of them. Where were you hit? What hurts? Top of his left ear. Relax. Nothing to be gained through panic. Still time before sunrise. Relax. Focus. Slowly, he forced his mind under control. He was able to soft-focus his eyes. This softened the horror. Behind this veil Jimmy began to fiercely concentrate. Make his brain speed up his metabolism, yoga breathing. Throw off the drug.

Concentrating on the danger and his rage he forced his body's hyper-production of adrenaline. He could feel his heart rate increase, his breathing deepen and speed up and sweat pour from his body. His eyes threatened to regain focus and distract his mental imaging. He couldn't close them but he could control the focus, the mental function.

No. Don't look. It won't help. He sat, heart pounding, face red and profusely sweating. Sweat was pouring down his back and under his arms, running off his wrists and ankles. He was forcing his mind into the mental state of a heavyweight boxer in the final minutes of a fifteen-round match. Eyes unfocused and red rimmed. Minutes crept by.

The drums pounded, volume steadily increasing. The Priest circling Alison like some hellish bird of prey. Time rushing toward sunrise. The intermittent whomp, whomp of the chopper. Not working. The drugs are not wearing off. Got to, he thought, got to break their hold. Got to move!

The first indication. A tiny twitch of the eye. At first, deep in concentration, Jimmy was not sure. Then he tried again. Yes! A slight sweep. The Priest, confident of his drug, was deep in his ritualistic trance, paying no attention on Jimmy. Good. His slowly lowered his eyelids. The drug was wearing off. How soon? How quickly could he move?

Jimmy's instincts, reflexes and rage had saved him. Instantly, on seeing the Priest, he had whirled to fire at him. In motion in the dim light, his body spinning, The Priest had missed Jimmy's neck. The dart flicked off the top of his ear. He got enough poison to drop him but not keep him out. His mind exercises were doing the rest. Slowly, almost imperceptibly, his voluntary motor functions were returning.

He tried to calculate the time till sunrise. Twenty-five, maybe thirty minutes. Use twenty for safety. Hadn't been unconscious, just unable to move. Real time. Fingers now working. Toes. How much longer? No way to know.

When I came in here, something seen, half-remembered. What? Why important? Yes—Beretta lost. The Priest had kicked it under the altar. What seen? Gun. Yes. Rifle in his camp. Gotta get to that rifle.

No telling the after-effects of this drug. May be weak as a kitten. Rifle. He watched the Priest. Crushing headache.

Eyes focused now on the ritual, mind turned adamantly away from Alison and her danger. The Priest made slow circuits around her body, deep in his chanting trance. A few more shuffling steps and his back would be to Jimmy.

The Priest hovered longest over her head, facing entirely away from Jimmy. Jimmy tried to raise his arm. Yes! His leg? Yes, but too slow. Two more circuits should do it. The headache, blinding. The sky beginning to lighten. A race between sunrise and his ability to move. He heard the soft whomp, whomp, whomp in the distance. The chopper. Damn Nolan and his chopper.

66

The chopper was now flying at six thousand feet. The mountains reached up to grab at it. They had arrived at the intersection Jimmy had described and seen the vehicles below. Nolan knew he was close. Now if this reluctant chopper pilot would get with the program maybe they could all go home heroes.

They could barely see the start of the trail below. They followed it and flew over the Priest's truck. He realized this was their starting point. They began an outward spiral pattern from there, agreeing not to use the spotlight until necessary. At that moment the radio began to crackle. It was LAPD base to Nolan. Static and slightly garbled, he could barely understand that it was a message from the Chief to abort and return to base. Nolan understood instantly. He was not going to be thwarted. He began surreptitiously keying his mike as base tried to transmit. The result was a complete breakup of the incoming message. The pilot looked at him with a 'what the hell is going on' expression, but said nothing.

Nolan to base, "You're breaking up. Will call in when we are out of this canyon. Out." He snapped the radio off and addressed the pilot. "I'm taking responsibility for this flight. We've got a woman and six officers up here whose lives are in danger. We're going to find them. We are going to get them out and nail the Priest. You have a problem with that?"

The pilot didn't have much choice. "You're the boss, Captain."

The SWAT team leader came over the intercom, "Captain, I think I just saw a light flicker over at three o'clock."

Nolan, "Okay, let's check it out."

As they drew nearer, the target light appeared to be a low-level source coming up from a canyon, high above the river. Bingo. Who else would be showing lights up here at 4:30 AM.

Nolan, "Okay, SWAT team saddle up. This is it. Pilot, drop us down toward those lights as soon as we clear that ridge. SWAT, I want you to rappel from the chopper onto the target." He pointed to the pale flickering light on the mountain ridge a half mile ahead.

67

Now! The Priest was turning away again. Jimmy slid from shadow to shadow, quickly but silently making his way to the rifle, Alison's danger horrible, sunrise minutes away. The Priest continued his dancing and chanting, begging the aid of Huitzilopochtli. Four huge shadows from the torches slithered over the canyon's rocky walls, seeming to writhe in agony. Jimmy pulled himself on knees and elbows through the rocks. A small dusty snake slid under a rock inches from his elbow.

In the distance Jimmy heard a faint, low rumble. God damn, did Brenner miss a note? Was that the sound of a slide? Later! Look after Alison.

The sky overhead was getting lighter. But except for the torches, it was still pitch-black down in the canyon. The sound of the helicopter was rising. It seemed to have steadied. Jimmy, his flashlight masked down tight, grabbed the AK-47 and checked it. Perfect, he thought; loaded, full magazine. He fed a round into the chamber and silently let the bolt return home.

Now for a clear shot. With a weapon this powerful, Alison must be absolutely in the clear. The AK-47 round would go cleanly through the Priest. She must be completely clear. Hurry, he thought. Any second he's gonna miss me.

The chanting continued steadily. The shadows danced on the rocks. As he maneuvered into position, the helicopter noise grew louder. Jimmy had a bead on the Priest's chest and was holding, head splitting, when the Priest saw the helicopter.

Everything seemed to move in slow motion, though it took only seconds. The Priest looked up, high over the south wall where Jimmy was hiding. He turned, ran around the altar, grabbed the torches and threw them up into the rocks. They lay scattered, flickering, smoking. One caught in the rocks and gave a bit of wavering light.

The helicopter dropped into the canyon, its multi-million candle power spotlight lighting the canyon floor like a nighttime football game. A door gunner loosed off a volley of automatic fire at the Priest. The bullets whanged off the rock floor and ricocheted around the canyon. He missed. The chopper bounced in the updrafts of the canyon.

Without hesitation Jimmy swung the AK-47 up, aimed at the spotlight and fired. The light dissolved in a spray of glass and the canyon went to black.

The chopper wheeled up and away, almost throwing the SWAT team marksman through the open door. It began to circle uselessly over the canyon. Amplified by the canyon walls, the rotor noise was deafening.

Jimmy dropped into a crouch, night-blind, disoriented and still woozy from the aftereffects of the drug and moved toward what he thought was Alison and the altar. He was holding the rifle by the carry handle on top when the rifle magazine and strap snagged on a root deep in a crack. He checked that it was well down in the crack and out of sight and left it...no time. Frantically he tried to picture the position of the altar and Alison when the chopper light had exploded. There was one torch still flickering, masked by a boulder beyond the altar. His night vision returning, he could see the altar's faint outline in front of him. The flickering torch outlined an unstable, wavy image, he scrabbled toward it, all sound covered by the drone of the chopper.

He remembered The Priest throwing the last torch as the blackness fell. The Priest should be sixty feet behind and slightly to his left. He must get between The Priest and Alison.

The Priest, stunned by the chopper, the spotlight exploding, machine gunfire and the sudden blanket of blackness, dropped to one knee and thought, sacrifice impossible, ritual not finished, sky beginning to lighten and Jimmy still mobile. Must kill him and vanish.

The chopper continued to circle with doors open and interior lights still on. Wisps of rising smoke from the dying torches rose, whirling into the rotor-beaten air. The sky grew lighter still but the canyon floor remained dark. The Priest, dodging from boulder to boulder, staying hidden, stealthily approached the altar, his black-painted body another shadow in the thin light.

Jimmy was almost at the altar and Alison when her frantic eye rolls alerted him to The Priest's approach. The Priest stood a yard away, a black shadow silhouetted by the remaining, stuttering torch, a torch staff in his right hand, knife in his left, only his eyes visible.

One-handed, The Priest swung the staff at Jimmy's head. Jimmy blocked it with his left arm and the staff smacked into his palm. He gripped it and yanked The Priest toward him into a head butt. The Priest stumbled into it and the head butt glanced off. The Priest slashed Jimmy across the ribcage as he staggered backward.

Jimmy tried a right kick to the inside of The Priest's right knee. The Priest doubled at the waist and crow hopped his legs out of the way. Jimmy, following, continued his leftward pivot and smashed The Priest in his face with his right elbow. He felt The Priest's left eye socket collapse. His eye bulged. Blood squirted.

The Priest spun to his right, stepped into a six-inch-wide crack in the rock slabs and fell back, his right ankle twisting violently. He propelled himself upright, using the staff as a cane. He spun to attack Jimmy, leading with the knife.

His head exploded into a red mist. The rifle's blast echoed around the canyon.

The sniper, Brill, fifty yards away, stepped from behind a boulder at the canyon entrance, Mag-Lite glowing. He sketched Jimmy a salute and moved to join him.

The Sun kissed the rim of the canyon.

Brill, the Shepherd and Handler cautiously entered the canyon and walked toward Jimmy and Alison at the altar. Brill glanced at The Priest to check with the light that he was down for good as Jimmy, blood all over his hands and running into his jeans, staggered over to Alison. The chopper could see that the situation was under control and wheeled away towards home.

Alison's pulse and heart rate seemed okay. He kissed her, then lifted her gently and moved her to the sleeping bag. He gave her water and wrapped her in a blanket and kissed her over and over, telling her that she was going to be okay. She was still limp as a rag doll but her eyes told him she understood she was safe. The sun moved slowly down the west walls.

68

Jimmy and Brill searched The Priest's makeshift camp and found a small first aid kit. He removed his bloody shirt. With peroxide he washed the slash across his ribs and, with Brill's help, folded the shirt into a long bandage and used the arms to tie it tightly around his body.

With his free hand, he tried his cell phone. No go, not in this deep canyon. He settled down to wait, holding Alison in his arms. She slipped off to sleep. Brill, the dog and handler followed, exhausted.

Sitting in the warming canyon, waiting, the adrenaline burning off, Jimmy fought sleep. Can't doze off now. At the sound of a footstep, he looked up. Brenner and the team were standing there. He laid Alison gently on the sleeping bag and jumped up, hugged Brenner and pounding him on the back.

"Jesus, I thought I heard a slide. I thought you'd all been swept off the trail into the river."

"Nah. Glad to see you too. Is Alison okay?"

"Yeah, I think so. It's the plant poison. She seems fine except she still can't move. Did you bring the medics and an ambulance?"

"They're about a half an hour back down the trail. Millie and Fulo are in the van."

"What the hell did I hear? I was afraid one of his booby traps had put you all in the river, that you all were buried."

"The short version: about seventy-five yards before where your first note would have been, the dog panicked a deer who tore off up the trail and triggered the slide. The note and deer disappeared into the river. Once the dust settled and we could find a safe way across the scree field, the dog picked up your scent and we kept climbing. Found your other notes and here we are."

Jimmy scanned the camp. "Thank God. C'mon, let's rig a stretcher and get Alison down to the ambulance. You can fill me in on the way."

The team used the blanket and a couple of the torches and quickly had a make-do stretcher. Brenner assigned Callahan and Susie to guard the crime scene. The dog handler and Brill volunteered to take the first carry. Minutes later, they were on their way. Jimmy and Brenner were at Alison's side, Jimmy's hand on her shoulder.

As they moved out, Jimmy gave Brenner an abbreviated version of the events in the canyon. Then, "You saw my other notes?"

"We were approaching the last trap when I read it. I sent the dog, handler and sniper on ahead of us. We'll get an LAPD chopper and come back once we've got Alison safe and fixed up, get a forensics team up here to go over the whole canyon and recover the body. Those skulls in there might help us identify some of the victims. Who fired the shot at the chopper?"

Jimmy had the grace to look slightly embarrassed. "I did. Nolan was sending a SWAT team down on ropes. The Priest was inches from Alison with a knife. Some damned fool in the chopper opened up with an automatic rifle and bullets were ricocheting over all hell and creation. I got rid of them the quickest way I could. They weren't gonna come down in the dark, especially into hostile fire."

"Oh boy, that's gonna tear it."

"Lets wait it out. Maybe no one saw who fired. Let everyone jump to the logical conclusion. We don't have to be so damned smart all the time."

On the way to the hospital, Brenner gave a full report to the Chief who called Nolan at home. He ordered him to report to his office at eight AM on Monday morning. He did. The Chief had a small stack of papers on his desk that he indicated as he spoke. "I have in front of me the pilot's log and transcriptions of the voice data recorder of your flight early Saturday."

Nolan, "I can explain, it—"

Chief interrupting, tense and face beginning to redden, "At the moment I'm inclined to give you a choice. Interrupt me once more and all options will be off the table. Now, as I was saying," his face getting redder by the second, "Your Saturday AM helicopter ride. You commandeered a helicopter, a pilot, and a SWAT team. You overstepped your authority. When I tried to order your return to base, you repeatedly keyed your mic to simulate interference. You shut down the radio and continued your flight, endangering police officers and a victim on the ground."

He held up his hand to forestall Nolan's chin rising to interrupt again. "If someone hadn't shot out your search light, aborting your mission, you'd be explaining collateral damage to me this morning. Collateral damage in the deaths of persons including a highly-respected film director, our decorated ex-LAPD officer and the police rescue team lead by a senior lieutenant. The press would have had a fucking field day.

"So, here's whats on the table. Option one, you can resign, effective today, and, in writing, swear to never say a word to anyone about your Saturday morning royal fuckup. You'll keep your pension. Or, option two, you can fight being fired, bring in your lawyer, an LAPD rep and create a ton of press coverage. With these records, I'll bury you. Your pension will be history. You decide...now."

Realizing that the Chief had him by the balls, Nolan said one word and signed the papers that afternoon.

69

In the ambulance on the way from the San Gabriels to Cedars Sinai, Jimmy held Alison's hand and called Sony's Jerry Martin, and the Medical Examiner Doc Jensen at home, waking both. After a quick situation report, he asked them to call Cedars Emergency Admitting Physician and Admin Office and do what each did best. It paid off in both cases.

Jimmy refused to leave Alison's side until the Admitting Doctor wheeled her into the examining room. When he wasn't pacing the hallway smoking and cursing under his breath, he hovered feverishly outside the door.

The Head Nurse noticed he was leaking blood through his shirt. He told her what happened. "Just a knife scratch from a fight with The Priest."

She ripped his shirt open, took one look at his blood-soaked improvised bandage and, in her sergeant major voice demanded, "Get your ass down to the ER desk, I'll call and tell them you are on the way. You need that wound looked at, cleaned up and stitched before you fall over from loss of blood. We'll be right here when they've fixed you up. No one is going anywhere." He did as he was told.

"Alison is going be fine. The call from Doc Jensen was most valuable. We went over the poison's chemistry. It's similar to some anesthetics that we use today. With just a little luck, she should be awake in an hour or two, able to leave tomorrow. I gave her a very mild sedative. She'll sleep for awhile and wake with little or no headache. The IVs you'll see are for rehydration and feeding."

Doctor Kerner was giving Jimmy a status report. Alison had been moved upstairs into a suite organized by Jerry Martin. Jimmy had just left the emergency room and dashed upstairs. They'd cleaned and closed the knife wound over his ribcage. Fifty stitches, a local anesthetic and pills for pain. The local was wearing off and he was hurting, but able to walk.

Jimmy, "Thank God. May I see her?"

Kerner, "Sure, suite 703. Best thing for her, to see you when she wakes up. Let her sleep as long as she can."

Jimmy hobbled off, as fast as he could, to the nearest elevator. Grinning.

He spent the remainder of afternoon quietly talking to Alison, convinced that she could hear him even as she faded in and out of sleep. He described, in detail, how they would soon be planning their life together, their planned trip to Monterey. He described the Georgia woods at daybreak in the fall, the smell of wood smoke through the pines, the late night hunts with old men, cigars and bourbon, riding through early morning mists so thick you couldn't see the ground from horseback. The smell of pine woods after a summer rain. Reassuring her that all was going to be okay. She drifted off to sleep.

After two hours, her eyes opened, she saw him, smiled, squeezed his hand, and said, "Hi."

ACKNOWLEDGEMENTS

Many thanks to all who helped me get from idea to fruition. Ariel Nachmann, Aryn Chapman, Eleanor Bergstein, Michael Brandman, Heywood Gould, Miles Brandman, Nicholas Meyer, Bruce Kerner, and Ruby Lavin.

All mistakes in the novel are mine.

www.ingramcontent.com/pod-product-compliance
Lightning Source LLC
Chambersburg PA
CBHW021029130626
46552CB00005B/1750